BOOK *of* REVELATIONS

A.C. BURCH

WITH ILLUSTRATIONS BY MADELINE SOREL

HOMEPORT
P R E S S

A BOOK OF REVELATIONS
Copyright © 2016 by A.C. Burch

Published by HomePort Press
PO Box 1508
Provincetown, MA 02657
www.HomePortPress.com

ISBN: 978-0-9974327-0-1
eISBN: 978-0-9974327-1-8

Cover Photograph © Deposit Photos/A.C. Burch
Art Work © 2016 by Madeline Sorel
used with permission from the Artist
Cover and Interior Design by Adrian Nicholas

"*The events in our lives happen in a sequence in time, but in their significance to ourselves they find their own order, a timetable not necessarily—perhaps not possibly—chronological. The time as we know it subjectively is often the chronology that stories and novels follow: it is the continuous thread of revelation.*"

Eudora Welty

In Memory of Bob Ferrante,
whose friendship and talent were a revelation.

AUTHOR'S NOTE

I've always found the mainstream rather dull. *A Book of Revelations* is my homage to life on the margin—a condition I considered a curse in my youth but now recognize as a priceless gift.

My sainted grandmother lived much of her life at odds with convention, though she never surrendered her dreams. As a child, I watched her substitute fantasies for facts to burnish her "golden years." Perhaps because of this, faded glamour and the mercurial power of memory have always resonated deep within me. Norma Desmond in *Sunset Boulevard* and "Little Edie" Beale of *Grey Gardens* are my favorite examples of the mind's triumph over marginalization. Such reactions to life's disappointments informed Lola Staunton's character in my debut novel, *The HomePort Journals*.

Perhaps in self-defense, I've always been drawn to outré characters who poke fun from the outer edge: Mae West, Phyllis Diller, Charles Addams, Anna Russell and her musical smackdowns, Gary Larson's beehived matrons from *The Far Side, Monty Python's Flying Circus,* The Marx Brothers' caricatures of society gorgons, so capably played by Margaret Dumont. The list is a long one.

Despite extensive training as a classical musician, I enjoy jazz and big band music as well as the occasional Broadway Show. My literary icons are equally diverse, spanning styles from Jane Austin to Henry James, Agatha Christie to Walter Mosely, Patrick Dennis to Armistead Maupin, and James Galsworthy to Bart Yates. This may be why my works are often described as straddling multiple genres.

These eclectic interests extend to the stage. A potent fear of stasis has fueled my fascination with shape-shifters, as exemplified by performers such as Ru Paul, Jimmy James, Provincetown's own Varla Jean Merman, Miss Ridgefield 1981, Dina Martina and many others. These scrappy geniuses offer perspectives far removed from Main Street. Most importantly, witnessing their courage and tenacity has encouraged me to take my own risks as a writer. I honor and thank them for that.

A.C. Burch, Provincetown 2016

Visit A.C. Burch at www.ACBurch.com or follow him on Twitter at @ACBurchAuthor

CONTENTS

PRIVATE QUARTERS

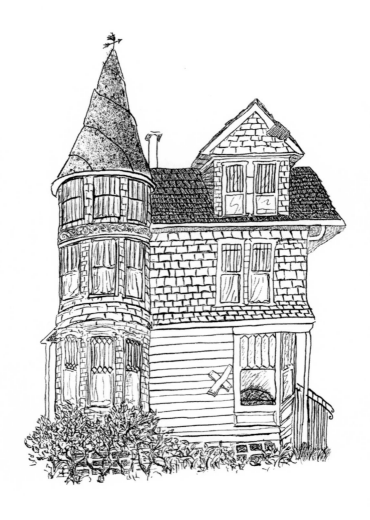

"Its circular turret was clad in multicolored bands of rolled asphalt, turning what had been an architectural tour de force into a psychedelic grain silo."

"**W**atch out for that old bastard. One kind word, and he'll bore the skin off your bones."

The whisper came from behind as I stood on a glassed-in porch gazing out at a decrepit front yard. It was the end of August, '73—a week into my sophomore year in music school. When my girlfriend's gorgon of a roommate had banished me from the apartment we three were to share, I'd skirted disaster by signing the first lease I could afford. Though this was by far the oddest house I'd ever seen, I would live here for the rest of my college days.

The "old bastard" was my new landlord, Mr. Gould, a stooped old man of seventy whose pale, wrinkled skin and halo of white hair offset features otherwise hard and grasping. His eyes constantly darted from one thing to another, and he frequently cocked his head as if he'd heard something. These quirks, plus his hackneyed expressions and rambling, teary sentiments, made him a caricature in my young eyes. But it was this apartment or sleeping in my car; he had me in a corner, and he knew it. Once I'd met his price, though, he was gracious enough to let me move in immediately.

As the old man doddered down the walk toward a late-'50s Cadillac convertible with long, pointed fins, the voice behind me grew louder.

"The hours I've wasted listening to that old fart complain: 'Too much heat! Too much hot water. The taxes. Oy vey, the taxes!' Christ!"

The imitation was perfect, but with an unnerving, caustic edge. Curiosity won out. I turned to look, expecting a wizened old biddy. At first, I saw only the faint glow of a cigarette behind a veil of sheer curtains. As my eyes adjusted, the form of a tall woman, no more than thirty-five, emerged from the dim light.

Except for the cigarette, she'd be a novice staring out from a cloister, I thought, if only for the briefest of moments.

Mr. Gould beeped his horn and waved. My shadowy companion waited until the car crept forward. Then, as I turned back to her, she clenched her right fist, lodged her left hand above her right elbow, and thrust her forearm into the air. To my amazement, she also managed an astoundingly rude noise without dislodging her dangling cigarette.

So much for religious analogies.

"You! Boy wonder! Stop gawking like you've never seen a woman before. Get in here and give me the goods."

I had no idea what she meant.

"Fill me in, sweetie—as in, who the hell *are* you? I know you're taking the upstairs apartment, so don't play dumb with me. I hear and know all in this dump. Better start off on the right foot by getting that straight."

What had I gotten myself into?

Her door swung open with a loud, torturous creak.

"Get in. Quick. Mind the cat."

I entered a narrow room whose sole source of light was the curtained window. My new neighbor was lanky, flat breasted, and slightly stooped. Her chin was pointed, her cheeks sallow, her eyes spaced far apart, and her neck elongated. She wore a white peasant blouse over tight blue jeans. A faded paisley kerchief covered her head. One hand rested on her left hip. The other slowly removed the cigarette from her mouth and pointed toward a tattered peacock chair.

"Sit."

I sat.

She sauntered to a narrow daybed that filled the far corner of the room, sat down, and restored the cigarette to her thin lips. As she arranged four orange cushions around her, two on each side, I stole a furtive glance around the tiny railroad flat.

An archway next to the bed led to a small kitchen with two plant-filled windows. Spider plants, ivy, and geraniums crowded together, cascading to the floor. What light made it through this indoor jungle illuminated a '50s gas stove whose chrome vent curved up into the wall. A porcelain sink stood on spindly legs beside it. In the center of the room, two rickety wooden chairs were placed on either side of a Formica table, on top of which was a small slate chalkboard in an oak frame, propped up by what appeared to be a dictionary.

The board displayed a date, time, and a series of hash marks.

A litter box sat by the inside wall of the tiny bathroom next to the back door. Given my unobstructed view of the entire apartment, I decided the cat must be under the bed.

"Sandy Singer," the woman said, holding out her hand palm down as if we were to dance.

I stood and took it in mine.

"Ah, the boy has manners. We'll pound 'em out of you in this hellhole."

My provincial upbringing had left me ill prepared for this strange combination of flower child and fishwife. As I maintained a self-conscious silence, she took a long drag on her cigarette, studied me further, then ground the stub into an ashtray.

"Name?"

"Matt Atwood," I answered, feeling as though my right hand should be on a Bible.

"Ah, a WASP. Rare thing these days, WASPs. Where from?"

"Assonet, Massachusetts. I'm attending the college of performing arts."

She pondered this for a moment as if I'd divulged crucial information.

"Sit down, kid."

I sat.

"So not from around here, huh? Musician or dancer?"

"Musician."

"Good. All men dancers are fags. Trust me."

I was unnerved by this pronouncement. I'd been assiduously avoiding flamboyant types in the Opera and Theatre departments, though I'd witnessed an extra pair of shoes in the men's room stalls more than once. I didn't so lack sophistication as to need such a warning, did I? What sort of a greenhorn did she think I was?

"Here's the deal," she said, unaware of the internal conflict she'd ignited. "Don't forget your living room is right above me. Don't start practicing before ten on Sunday morning, and quit by nine every night. Music students have lived here before. I'm used to them. You won't get crap from me about good music. If you stink, of course, I'll have you thrown out immediately."

I suspected she was teasing, but couldn't quite tell. No doubt I was nothing but a tiresome intrusion to be dispatched as soon as possible.

"Please let me know if I ever disturb you."

I was yielding too much ground and regretted it at once. She smiled knowingly.

"Don't worry, kid, I will . . . I will. I hear and know all around here. Keep that in mind if you know what's good for you. Drop off your number when they install your phone. That way I can tell you to pipe down if I need to."

I nodded, wondering why I agreed with everything she said the moment she said it.

"OK, sweetie, you're dismissed."

"A pleasure to meet you, ah . . . ?"

"It's Miss, but you can call me Sandy. And the pleasure was all mine, kid. Trust me."

Mr. Gould returned two days later. I was in the shower when I heard his cane tapping on the door. I threw on jeans and raced to admit him, but by then he'd already let himself in.

"So, you gettin' settled?"

Seeming unabashed, he sat on a folding chair, the sole piece of furniture in what I now considered "my" living room.

"Everything OK?"

"It's fine," I replied with only slightly veiled annoyance. "I'm bringing some furniture from home next weekend and should be set up after that."

My displeasure seemed to bounce right off him.

"Your old man gonna help?"

I couldn't understand what interest that was to Mr. Gould. Feeling it necessary to stay on good terms with him, I refrained from asking.

"No, he died when I was eight. My mother will help with the packing, but I've got friends lined up for the heavy lifting."

Not that I needed all that much help. I'd just come off of a summer in the Adirondacks hiking the mountains and sailing Lake Champlain. Compared to most guys in the music department, I was a jock.

"Not a good thing to be raised by a woman alone. Kids need a man to draw the line for them. Women let them get away with things that ruin their lives later on. Like those goddamn hippies and all their damn 'free love.' It's the fault of too much mothering; I've always said. After my wife died, it took all the strength I could muster to stop my daughter from destroying her life 'cause of it."

I sensed we were in the midst of a recurrent monolog—more recitation than conversation—and fought to suppress a sigh.

What right did he have to cast aspersions on my mother? For someone who'd had to raise two kids alone, she hadn't done that badly. Besides, what did he know about her in the first place?

As he droned on, my thoughts congealed.

"I lost my parents, two brothers, and a sister in the war. I watched them die, one by one, in front of me. That's when I vowed I'd learn to fight. I couldn't save them, but a few years ago, I fought like hell to save my daughter—and, by God, I did."

His voice grew louder as if he were justifying his actions or trying to save a soul. I thought fleetingly of Father Mapple from *Moby Dick*, then realized there was something unsettling about the way my new home so readily evoked religious references.

Mr. Gould continued as if he were speaking to someone else.

"Blood is all you have in this life, kid. No one else gives a damn—they'll try to steal whatever you have. A man has to protect his own, no matter what, sometimes even from themselves . . ."

The phone interrupted. Answering, I heard a low, somewhat-familiar, whisper.

"Don't say anything. Just listen."

It was Sandy.

"Tell the old man you have to help a friend. Leave by the back stairs. I'll have my kitchen door open. You can hide out here until he goes. He won't dare come in. No arguments. Just do it. Now."

"OK, I'll be right there."

I felt silly playing her game, but annoyed enough with Mr. Gould to welcome escape.

"I'm terribly sorry. A friend needs me right away. You'll have to excuse me."

"Good that people depend on you. The sign of a good person is when others feel they can . . ."

He made no sign of moving.

"Mr. Gould, I'm sorry. I have to lock up and leave, *right now*."

"OK, kid. OK. I'll move my keister."

He stood slowly and tottered toward the door. At the threshold, he seemed to suffer a bout of dizziness and grabbed the doorframe to steady himself. As he did, his shirtsleeve slid to his elbow, revealing blue letters and numbers tattooed on his wrist.

AU—Auschwitz.

In an instant, I understood why he was so protective of his "blood." With this revelation, I felt a sharp pang of guilt at walking out under false pretenses. Even so, Sandy was waiting.

Mr. Gould regained his balance, raised his hand in a slow, dismissive wave, and shuffled to the landing. I locked the door behind him, then raced down the rear stairs to Sandy's apartment. She beckoned to me from the kitchen table where iced tea and cookies were laid out on a white plastic doily.

"Shut the door. Quick. He can't see through the plants, and he doesn't hear, so we'll be fine."

At first, Sandy seemed to be enjoying herself. She chatted about the house and gossiped about our neighbors. Then her tone changed in an instant, and she leaned forward, eyes on fire.

"Look, kid. I really don't want that old goat around this joint. So don't encourage him, OK? He seems like a sweet, harmless, lonely old man, but he's a monster. Trust me and don't let him get too close to you."

I didn't know what to think. The old man had taken a chance on me, so I felt some obligation. If he were lonely, I could certainly understand why. On the other hand, he'd lost my respect by barging in uninvited.

"Did you know he was in Auschwitz?" I asked.

"Yeah, kid. I know. I've heard that tale a thousand times. So many times I've run out of Kleenex. Time moves on. Some things you just gotta put behind you, dontcha think?"

As it turned out, what I thought didn't matter in the least. Every time Mr. Gould pulled up in front of the building, Sandy summoned me, and I obeyed without resistance, sensing the complications that would ensue if I refused. I preferred to practice at home and counted on her continued indulgence.

Once in our bunker, we'd listen to Mr. Gould's footsteps as he explored my apartment. It felt like waiting out an air raid or hiding from storm troopers, except Sandy was a charming hostess, plying me with tea and cookies as the floorboards creaked above us.

Mr. Gould's behavior annoyed me more with each incursion. Before long, I relinquished all pity I might have felt and aligned myself solidly with Sandy. We bonded in our defense against a common enemy, and eventually our strategy paid off. The impromptu visits diminished, then stopped altogether.

A brutal, soulless renovation—no doubt perpetrated by Mr. Gould—had obliterated all traces of our building's Victorian grandeur. Its circular turret was clad in multicolored bands of rolled asphalt, turning what had been an architectural tour de force into a psychedelic grain silo. The tower's elongated, conical peak had earned our home the moniker of the "Witches' House." Children crossed the street to avoid it.

Every apartment other than Sandy's had its bedroom in the turret, whose round walls were mostly windows. There was only one section of wall large enough to accommodate a double bed, which meant my other neighbors slept directly above or below me. The circular rooms seemed to push sound upward, and the ceilings—just cheap canvas nailed to joists that barely supported rutted hardwood floors—did little to hinder its progress. I often thought the span of taut fabric acted like a giant loudspeaker, but could never prove my hypothesis. Between this and paper-thin walls, I came to know my neighbors far too well.

Alysse and Bill, or Bilious et al., as Sandy had dubbed them, slept in the bedroom above mine. Alysse was a stylish brunette with well-crafted features. Everything about her, makeup to wardrobe, seemed the result of considerable, exacting effort. The finished product was a calculating, harsh facade that intimidated most everyone who crossed her path. At the slightest provocation, Alysse decimated those she encountered. Sandy ran for cover whenever she heard the clip-clop of Alysse's heels on the stairs, and, after a couple of disastrous sparring matches, so did I.

Bill, whose Italian good looks were fading fast, was far more pleasant. His shaggy brown hair, innocent wide eyes, and unkempt mustache brought Sonny Bono to mind, though Bill's whiskers sported their first trace of gray. His equanimity was so at odds with his wife's caustic temperament it was hard to imagine how they'd survived a single date, never mind two years of marriage.

Hyman Gorstein occupied the first-floor apartment next to Sandy's and slept in the turret-room below me. He was a quiet and timid CPA type—about five foot five. His thick, round, dark-framed glasses and close-cropped hair reminded me of Poindexter from *Felix the Cat*. On the rare occasions when Hyman and I spoke, he avoided all eye contact, preferring to stare at the ground as if something far more fascinating had suddenly caught his interest.

His girlfriend was a blowsy woman of indeterminate age, heavily made up, with spectacular breasts and platinum-blonde hair. Sandy had dubbed her "Xaviera," after the author of *The Happy Hooker*. Xaviera had a penchant for cheap jewelry, halter tops, red stretch pants, and spike heels. Though I never knew her real name, I knew—all too well—her likes and dislikes, for her voice soared through the old house with all the verve of a Wagnerian soprano.

At nine sharp every Sunday morning, Hyman mounted Xaviera for an impressive hour of lovemaking. She was either clueless or astoundingly indifferent to the acoustical vagaries of the old place, for, with each of her frequent climaxes, she screamed "Hyman, hold me" at the top of her lungs. Her weekly serenade caused me intense speculation: there had to be much more to Hyman Gorstein than met the eye.

Sometimes, as Xaviera's vocal pyrotechnics resounded through the turret, Alysse and Bill joined the fray. From above, the squeak of their bedsprings and the thump, thump of their headboard played a primal ostinato to the raucous aria from below.

My girlfriend, Claire, was a staunch Catholic who routinely reminded me she was giving herself "in anticipation of marriage." She staked her claim by staying over most nights, lest I forget. Far from yielding, as Bill and Alysse sometimes did, to the Sabbath's rampant eroticism, Claire was mortified. At the sound of Xaviera's opening motif, Claire would leap out of bed, race to the far end of the apartment, and, clad in her modest flannel nightgown, practice her French horn. While its mournful tones shielded her ears from the earthy rites pervading the house, they did little to mask sound in the turret where I lay, a petulant island of frustration amidst a writhing sea of passion.

I don't think it ever occurred to Claire that our intimate moments—my soul-searing moan at climax, and her more genteel, though heartening, "Yes, yes, YES!!!"—were overheard as well. I, on the other hand, was convinced that Sandy paid close attention. Already feeling outgunned and outmanned by Hyman's herculean performance, I tried mightily to dismiss the thought.

One particularly bawdy Sunday, I kept a running tally of Xaviera's outbursts, only to discover the next day that my count matched the hash marks on Sandy's slate. It was easy enough to confirm: the chalkboard—complete with date, duration, and the occasional exclamation point—sat upright on her kitchen table until the next marathon. To the uninitiated, it appeared she'd been tracking laps at a swim meet, but once I was in on the secret, the tally became a constant reminder that all with Claire was not quite what it might be.

"Cocktail?"

Sandy's question was often more plea than invitation. Once she learned of Claire's after-school job, I came home like a '50s breadwinner to a premixed drink and inquiries about "my day."

Although she was by far the strangest, most demanding person I'd ever met, Sandy's quirks held a certain charm for me. What's more, she served up salacious revelations about our neighbors with candor that made me feel worldly beyond my years. While seeming to have little to no life of her own, she was so fully invested in the lives of those around her I soon preferred her nightly reports to the evening news.

As our friendship deepened, the topic of Hyman's Sunday morning ritual grew inevitable. I awaited this discussion with a strange mix of dread and delight, for Sandy's wit was well honed. The moment arrived during a protracted

Sunday session when Xaviera was in particularly fine voice. Twenty-five minutes into the endurance contest, as Claire practiced pedal tones and I lay on our bed contemplating the inequities of life, Sandy summoned me.

The noise in her apartment was so loud that Hyman and Xaviera seemed to be in the room with us. In the background, Claire's French horn sounded as if from a distant mountaintop—a dolorous lament for our wanton household. Sandy sat cross-legged on the bed, the ever-present cigarette in her right hand. She looked up at me with a wry half-grin.

"You knew we had to talk about this sometime. Right, kid? We can't dodge the subject any longer. Can we?"

Just then, Xaviera let loose.

"Hold me, Hyman, hold meeee . . ."

"No. Hold *me*, Hyman. Hold *me*. It's *my* turn," Sandy yelled through the wall. "You keep forgetting *my* turn."

I recoiled, expecting obscenities, or at least pounding fists. There was nothing but more grunts and moans. Sandy seemed to revel in my astonishment.

"Don't worry, kid. They're too into it to hear. I do it all the time, to no avail. But I gotta tell you, this situation *is* getting to me. I've left the little twerp notes and tried to talk with him, but nothing does any goddamn good. It's like living in the projection booth of a porn theater.

"The way that slut carries on! It's damned unfair! Here I sit, alone, week after week . . . I can't think of *anything* but sex. After all, I haven't gotten *any* in six years. And there *she* is like clockwork every Sunday, yowling like a finalist in some Bavarian yodeling contest."

I'd never seen Sandy so energized. She shifted on the bed as if about to race out of the apartment. The wild gleam in her eye unnerved me.

"Have you ever tried to do the *Times* crossword under conditions like this?"

She pointed to the wall with a broad sweep of her arm, sending cigarette ash scattering along its arc.

"Last week they asked for a six-letter word describing a lyric vocal quality with a strong dramatic element."

"Yes. Spinto. A type of soprano."

I'd learned the term just days before and was thrilled to be using it in adult conversation.

"You know what I wrote?"

"No, what?"

"Orgasm. Can you believe it? That's how distracted I am. Our slumlord won't do a damn thing—the bastard—not even fix these papier-mâché walls so I can have some peace and quiet. I've complained to him a hundred times, and he just says I'm making things up."

I tried levity to calm Sandy down.

"But you have fun with your chalkboard."

"Oh, so you're onto that, are you, kid?"

Her eyes began to shine in a different, more frightening, way. I felt my color rise.

"Wanna know how you measure up against the competition?"

She studied my face for a moment, then cackled.

"Told you when you moved in, kid. I hear all. Fair warning and all that. No fault but your own. But I gotta tell ya, your girlfriend needs help if she's gonna give Xaviera a run for her money. A more focused voice, with greater carrying power, is what's called for. Claire ought to know that; she goes to music school, doesn't she? That French horn act just ain't gonna cut it if she wants to play in the big leagues. Or perhaps she lacks sufficient motivation?"

Just then, Claire began the opening solo from Dukas' *Villanelle*. I listened in abject mortification, wondering if she had any idea our most intimate performances were being judged. As if to manifest my discomfort, Xaviera let forth a guttural, elongated moan that seemed to invoke every orgasm in the annals of humanity. With no further need to hide her research, Sandy walked to the kitchen, picked up the chalkboard, and carefully drew a diagonal line through the third set of marks. She drew another hash mark and four exclamation points before proudly displaying the results. The tally had reached sixteen—apparently a new record.

Her phone rang. I seized the opportunity to slink away.

Over the months and drinks that followed, Sandy spoke of her privileged childhood at "The Shore." She never named the town, though she talked at length about a succession of exclusive private schools. She also revealed a problem with drugs and alcohol that had precipitated a six-month commitment to a mental institution.

Her father had subsidized the rent since her release nearly twelve years before. She was adamant she'd licked the "situation" by limiting herself to "social drinking." I doubted this. If I were more than fifteen minutes late for our cocktail hour, she seemed on the verge of an anxiety attack.

Sandy worked three half-days as a biller at a nearby psychiatric clinic to provide money for incidentals and, I surmised, significant quantities of liquor. When not tracking down incorrectly coded medical procedures, she sat at home reading and doting on her cat, a regal Abyssinian, who still hid from me most of the time.

Sandy's routines both intrigued and disturbed me; some tested the bounds of our friendship. From my youthful vantage point, her quirks were fraught with the foibles of advanced age, and I rationalized most of them. Her eavesdropping during my most intimate moments remained a source of consternation.

There was little to do other than be more discreet, but I couldn't always achieve it. Once, when Claire was away on a protracted tour, I relieved my tension with a boisterous solo performance. The moment the deed was done, I realized Sandy would have heard and would be sure to comment. Mortified, I avoided her for two days, skulking down the back stairs and coming home late at night. To her credit, when we finally ran into each other, she didn't say a word.

To some degree, the better parts of our friendship tempered my frustration. As I often reminded myself, Sandy *had* been up front about her reconnaissance. Even so, I remained cautious, sensing her rigidity and domineering nature protected a fragile spirit with but a tenuous grip on reality.

There were clues: the few pieces of bric-a-brac in her apartment had specific, inviolate placements. There was hell to pay if I touched one. Most telling, her chores were executed the same way at precisely the same time each week. Each task had its own peculiar ritual. Her method of doing dishes fascinated me. She soaked them—plates, glasses, utensils, and all—in a dishpan filled with Tide, swearing this got them cleaner with far less effort than any other method. To me, the process left a soapy aftertaste that rendered her cheap liquor nearly undrinkable.

More than a year passed in skewed domesticity, soapy drinks, and savory gossip. One lazy Saturday in October, I was about to leave for the library when the phone rang.

"Can ya come down now, sweetie?"

It took me a moment to recognize Sandy's voice, which was thick and sloppy with drink.

"I was just heading out."

"I gotta tell ya sumthin'. S'important."

I grabbed my books and hurried downstairs. Sandy was waiting at the door and quickly pulled me into her apartment.

"OK kid, I gotta talk to somebody, or I'll go mad," she whispered.

I sat in my usual spot, then sipped the drink she'd already poured for me.

"You know the new girl at work, Janet, I've been telling ya about?"

I nodded.

"Well, she got to talking yesterday about her husband and her adopted daughter, Cheri. I asked when she was adopted, just to show interest. Janet said June of '61. That struck a chord, so I asked where the baby had been born. The answer was here, in New Haven. Then I asked if she'd gotten her through an agency. Janet said no, it was a private adoption. A doctor had a patient—an unwed mother— who'd had a breakdown. Then I asked if the doctor's name was the same as a flower."

There was a long pause as Sandy drained her glass. When she spoke, it was in a distant voice as if describing an accident on TV.

"Janet said yes—Dr. Rose, though she seemed to get nervous. I spent a lot of time reassuring her I had a damned good reason for asking. After a while I could see her curiosity was getting the better of her, so I asked if the girl's birthday was June 1, and Janet said yes. Things were tense for a moment, as if she thought I'd been snooping into her private life. She just sat there staring at me as if I were a witch or something. I got scared she'd clam up, so I just blurted out the kid was probably mine."

"Is it true? Is it your kid?"

"Yup. In my wilder days, I screwed around a hell of a lot and got knocked up. Never could figure out who the father was. It was a crapshoot; there were just too many contenders. In any case, the baby was born June 1, 1961. My father didn't know I was pregnant until just before she was born. When he found out, he had his young physician friend, Dr. Rose, put her up for adoption. Then my dear father had me committed. S'posedly it was to dry out, but I always knew it was to keep my baby from me."

Sandy refilled her glass and mine, though it was still half full. Feeling pangs of sympathy for her and rage at her father, I gave up on the library.

"Holy shit."

Sandy rearranged the two conch shells she kept on the coffee table so they were equidistant from each other. This took several tries until she was satisfied.

"Exactly, kid . . . And here's the kicker . . . I asked if I could meet Cheri. Janet said she'd think about it and get back to me. I begged her not to keep me waiting, and she told me to back off, or I'd never see Cheri even once. I'm going nuts, just waiting for an answer."

"Wow."

The word had hardly left my mouth before Sandy snapped at me.

"Yeah, kid, 'wow.' That sums it up. I spend twelve years of my pathetic life wanting to see my baby, and when I have the chance, you say 'wow.' Yeah, that covers it nicely."

"Sandy, that's not fair. You've just hit me with . . ."

"I know. I know. I'm sorry. It's just I *have* to see her. Even just once, to know she's OK. That there aren't problems from the stuff I was doing back then. You unnerstand? I just have to know for sure."

Nearly a week later, I learned Janet had sanctioned a single meeting for the following Saturday. Between a hairdressing appointment, a new outfit, a facial, and a class in makeup application at a downtown department store, Sandy's transformation crowded the week with a flurry of nervous anticipation. Even her old Volkswagen shined like new. I saw to that myself.

The big day finally arrived. Much to Claire's chagrin, I spent hours helping Sandy choose what to wear. When at last I escorted Sandy to her car, she seemed the epitome of the cosmopolitan woman. Sensing her anxiety, I lightly kissed her cheek and wished her luck. As she drove away, her right blinker flashing as she turned left, I felt like a parent sending an only child off to college.

While she was gone, I paced and fretted. At the sound of her car in the driveway, I raced downstairs. The visit, though brief, had been a success. Cheri was all Sandy had hoped for: bright, articulate, and beautiful. Sandy had held up her part of the bargain, posing as "a friend from work." As she told things, she'd managed to impress Janet with her sincerity and honorable intentions.

"I'd have killed for a cigarette, but I just sat there all smiles and ladylike. Cheri showed me her books for a while. Then we did some watercolors together. I tried to tell her you don't always have to stay within the lines; that sometimes wonderful things happen when you stray outside them, but Janet put an end to that discussion, and fast."

I smiled to myself, imagining Janet's consternation. From what little I knew of her, she stayed well within the lines at all times. She'd agreed to keep Sandy informed of significant events in her daughter's life, but had nixed any further meetings for the time being. Pouring her third Scotch, Sandy told me she'd finally acquiesced, "for the good of the child."

Things took an odd turn after that. Whenever children passed the Witches' House on their way to or from school, Sandy stood watch on the porch. Her gaze was so intense they often ran off in alarm, adding credence to the already tarnished reputation of the ramshackle old place. When I suggested she spare herself such indignities, she ignored me as if I hadn't said a word.

At other times, she simpered and giggled like a schoolgirl. Whenever these moods hit, she stood in her doorway chain-smoking, as if awaiting a gentleman caller. She continued to hide from Alysse but often waylaid Bill, who lingered, laughing, joking, and seeming to relish the attention, until his wife's stentorian voice summoned him for a second, or, often, a third time.

As Sandy's routine changed, so did the subtle rhythms of our household. Cocktail hour became protracted and unsettling, as if she had something important to say to me, but could never find the courage. She rambled on, talked in generalities, begged me to stay longer, and often drank until she passed out.

Placing a comforter over her, I'd tiptoe upstairs and ready myself for battle. Claire took violent exception to these extended visits, despite protests that I was helping Sandy through a difficult period. Sandy needed me, I argued, insisting Claire's suspicions were unfounded and absurd. We fought night after night, retiring to bed with newfound tensions that felt ominous and incendiary. As other, long-denied, possibilities roiled in the recesses of my mind, I began to distance myself from her. Somehow sensing this, she repeatedly tore into me, enumerating an ever-expanding list of sacrifices she'd made on my behalf. Bill and Alysse's arguments seemed more frequent as well, while Hyman, at the first sound of Sandy's voice, would scuttle away without a word. She was suddenly, unpredictably, everywhere at once.

In mid-February, a blizzard brought the city to a halt. Trapped in the house for the evening and eager to avoid another round of Claire's recriminations, I knocked on Sandy's door. She opened it a crack, recognized me, and pulled me inside.

"Does it smell in here?"

She sounded like a child conspiring to hide something from her parents. Her eyes were wide and bright. She squirmed in unconstrained glee.

"Huh?"

"Does it smell in here?"

"Just of too much air freshener. Why?"

"Well," she said, flopping on her bed, "Bill just left. We had sex."

There was an awkward silence while I processed her announcement.

"Alysse is stuck in Boston. Bill didn't have to work, so he came to visit. We had a couple of drinks, and one thing led to another . . ."

I wasn't sure what to say. Congratulations came to mind, though I rapidly dismissed the thought. Then Sandy changed the subject with a breezy nonchalance that did little to mask her elation or quell my discomfort.

Things seemed to settle down after that. Bill and Alysse fought less. Sandy dropped from sight, tamping down Claire's suspicions of infidelity. The house felt dismal and empty. Only Xaviera's Sunday jam sessions continued unabated.

Two months after the storm, I heard Mr. Gould and Sandy arguing in her apartment. Claire was practicing, so I couldn't discern much of what they said, though the rage in their voices troubled me. Sandy's was shriller than I'd ever heard it, while Mr. Gould roared and pounded the floor with his cane. Whatever the disagreement, it was major, and its outcome unlikely to bode well for Sandy. I began to think how the building—and my life—would change if she were evicted.

Suddenly all went quiet, until a siren's wail brought me to the window. Looking down, I saw an ambulance, lights flashing, park in front of the house. Within moments, a stretcher rolled down the front walk. Mr. Gould lay on it. His lifeless eyes stared upward as Sandy walked beside him, holding his cane and clutching his hand. To my astonishment, when the ambulance pulled away, she ran to her Volkswagen and drove off in pursuit.

That night, I banged on her door. Though I heard movement and what sounded like muffled sobs, she didn't answer.

Several weeks later, as I was loping up the front steps, Sandy intercepted me.

"Matt, I've got to talk to you. It's urgent."

Her usually pristine apartment was a wreck: the plants were dead, the sink full of dishes; there was cat hair everywhere, and the litter box stank. The cat crept toward me and rubbed my leg. Its fur was matted. It looked thin and frantic.

"I don't know how else but to come right out with it," Sandy said, seeming oblivious to the chaos around her. She fumbled with a pack of cigarettes, then a match, finally lighting it after several attempts. "I'm in trouble. I need five hundred dollars right away. It's a loan. I'll be able to pay it back in a few weeks."

"What's wrong?"

"You remember the day of the blizzard?"

"Yes."

"Well, I'm pregnant. And before you say anything, yes, it's my own damn fault."

I stood mute.

"After I met Cheri, something came over me. I'm not proud of what I did, but I wanted a child of my own more than anything in the world, and I set out to get one."

My astonishment must have shown. She leaned toward me and started to whisper as if sharing a deep, dark secret. "At first, I went out nights to get laid, but I guess I sort of chickened out. None of the guys that spoke to me seemed as though they'd treat me right. After all, I haven't been out in years, and it does take me a while to get used to things. They just didn't seem as if they'd understand.

"Then I thought maybe I'd feel more comfortable at home, so I tried to get in Hyman's pants. I figured he owed me for all I've had to put up with. I told him it wasn't that big a deal since I was practically a participant already. God knows his slut of a girlfriend hasn't the morals to give a damn, but he ran off like a scared rabbit. Bill turned out to be easier. We only did it once, but it was enough."

I suddenly felt as though *I'd* had enough. Enough of Sandy, enough of being an adult—enough of everything. She stood wringing her hands, waiting for my reply, but I couldn't get past what I'd just heard.

Was this what she'd wanted to ask me? To father a child? My stomach churned and my knees weakened. I felt her eyes on me, pathetic and pleading. I couldn't bring myself to look at her.

"So what's the money for?"

"I've got to get an abortion this time."

"Why?"

"The situation has changed dramatically."

"What do you mean?"

"How to say this . . . I'm not who you think I am," she said, her lower lip quivering.

"Go on."

"Well, when I got out of the hospital, my father set me up in this apartment."

"You told me that."

"But not all of it. I let you think he was some wealthy man from the shore."

"Isn't he?"

"Not exactly. We did have a summer place in Branford, but there's more to it. Actually, he lives here in town . . . He owns apartment buildings . . . and drives an old Cadillac?"

I was still hung up on her designs on the men of the house. Her clues went right over my head.

"And walks with a cane?" Sandy said, leaning close. "And, 'Oy vey, the taxes'?"

"Mr. Gould? Your father is Mr. Gould?"

"Yes."

"But your name is Singer."

"I changed it as soon as I was old enough. It's the only independent thing I've ever done in my whole goddamn life."

"You've got to be kidding! Why the hell didn't you ever tell me?"

"Look, kid, spare me the theatrics, *please*. I didn't tell you because I didn't want you both ganging up on me. I wanted you to be *my* friend, not his. I didn't want you to go sour on me because of all the nasty things I knew he'd tell you."

Sandy's eyes softened. For a moment, she seemed a frightened, lonely child. Then she rallied.

"I don't want to go into all of it right now. I need money, not a lecture. I'm desperate. It's almost too late. Will you loan it to me, or not? You're my last hope. I've tried everyone else."

As I pondered the enormity of her request, she pressed on, her voice growing louder and more urgent.

"I've been chasing that bastard Bill for his share. He wouldn't pay until I threatened to tell Alysse, then he finally agreed. But there's a catch. They're moving to Cleveland. He says it will be next month at the earliest before he has any money. I can't wait that long."

Her eyes filled with tears. She turned her head to the wall for a moment and wiped them away.

"Forgive me," I said, "but I still don't understand. Why have an abortion when you want a child so badly?"

Sandy's face contorted in rage as she turned to face me.

"My goddamn father. I told him a few weeks ago because I knew I'd need a bigger allowance. We had a terrible argument. He had a stroke right where you're sitting."

"So that's what happened? I saw the ambulance."

"Yes. He began to speak last week. All he'll talk about is how I'm not fit to be a mother. I'm afraid if he works himself up again it'll kill him, so today I told him I'd had a miscarriage. I couldn't think what else to say.

"I've been a worry to him all my life. It's bad enough I'm responsible for his stroke; I can't be the cause of his death . . . It'd be his final guilt trip. I'd never get over it, and he knows it. That's why he won't let up. I have to make my goddamned lie the truth, even if it means giving up the only thing I've ever wanted in my entire pathetic life. I can barely live with the thought, but I've finally convinced myself it's better than being saddled with guilt for the rest of my days. Or at least, I think it is."

Sandy's right hand twitched involuntarily. After a moment, she folded her arms across her chest. She seemed to shrink into herself, aging in front of me as she awaited my answer.

"OK, Sandy, I'll lend you the money."

I had almost enough saved for a new trumpet. It could wait. I felt out of my depth—sickened—yet in total agreement with Mr. Gould. No child would stand a chance with Sandy for a mother, and she'd never allow another adoption.

"God bless you, Matt. I've been freaking out, trying to figure a way out of this mess."

Her face was red and streaked with mascara. Her features shifted back and forth between regret and stoic determination. She repeatedly rubbed her right thumb and forefinger together as if they were no longer under her control. Her smile, when it finally came, seemed grotesque.

"Guess it wouldn't make a difference if we had a drink to seal the deal, would it? I've been on the wagon these last couple of months."

The apartment seemed to close in on me.

"No thanks, Sandy. I've got to run. I promised Claire I'd make dinner. I'll bring the check down later."

I made a mental note to bring food for the cat.

Mr. Gould died two days after the abortion. Sandy asked me to come with her to the funeral, which at her request was private. We were the sole mourners at the graveside service. Sandy said Kaddish in a voice without inflection. As she received condolences from the rabbi and mortuary staff, she stared sullenly at her feet. Slowly I came to understand the prayers were not for her father, but for her aborted child.

Sandy followed custom to the letter, sitting for hours on her apartment floor by the weak light of a shiva candle. The curtains were closed, the mirror covered. She didn't cook or wear shoes. I was her only visitor, coming once a day with food for her and the cat. For my efforts, I received a cursory thank you on my way out.

Her mourning complete, Sandy stoically resumed what little remained of her shattered routines. She seldom answered her door. If she did, she spoke in disinterested monosyllables without any of her usual sarcasm or drama.

Months passed. Concerned about Sandy's circumstances and anxious to recoup my loan, I finally researched Mr. Gould's will. Despite their years of estrangement, he'd left money in trust for his only child: a yearly allotment not to exceed twelve thousand dollars, adjusted for inflation. She had lifetime use of her apartment and could request funds for its upkeep on an annual basis, but only to protect or enhance the investment. Mr. Gould's properties were also held in trust. Dr. Rose was executor and sole trustee, his approval required for any extraordinary expenses Sandy might incur.

Most significantly, there was a sizeable bequest for the granddaughter Mr. Gould had, by his own deposition, never seen. Cheri would inherit all his properties, along with nearly two million dollars plus interest, on her twenty-fifth birthday. There was also a fund set aside for her education. If Sandy had any contact with the child before then, her own allotment would cease and her funds would go to a local drug rehabilitation center. Dr. Rose was instructed to inform Janet of the bequest and ensure Sandy did not violate its terms. Every base was covered: upon Sandy's death, the residue of her trust would go to the daughter she was forbidden to see. Mr. Gould had protected his "blood" unto the next generation.

Whether in atonement or inviolate routine, Sandy remained entombed in her minuscule flat. Eventually, I wrote her about the loan. She replied, by a note slipped under my door late one night, that she was out of work and had a "cash flow problem" until some final details of her father's estate were settled. Until then, she was receiving the same allowance and was unable to repay me. She promised to pay me the moment things were settled.

Bill had never paid his share, and now he was relocating again—this time alone. Sandy had finally contacted Alysse, who steadfastly denied Sandy's claims while concurrently suing Bill for divorce. Eventually, Alysse's attorney threatened a lawsuit, which put an end to Sandy's efforts.

A few weeks later, I received a terse statement from a new management company informing me I had a credit against rent for the full amount of the loan, plus interest. From then on, Sandy and I exchanged pleasantries if we met on the porch, but she was always busy when I stopped by for a visit.

I missed our conversations and longed to discuss my deteriorating relationship with Claire. As my graduation neared, her marital expectations were mounting exponentially. Her family and our friends seemed to accept our engagement as a foregone conclusion. Everyone seemed certain but me. I yearned for Sandy's perspective and what I hoped would be her unequivocal support for what was becoming an increasingly inevitable break-up.

Though unemployed, with only a cat to care for, Sandy was never available. Even so, I could see telltale signs of financial stability: weekly grocery and liquor deliveries, as well as a sullen Puerto Rican woman who came twice a week to clean and, no doubt, wash the dishes. Reluctantly, I stopped trying to penetrate the shroud Sandy had wrapped around her life. We spoke less and less, until one day we passed each other on the porch without a word.

Renovations on Alysse and Bill's vacant apartment were nearly complete when an officious-sounding woman phoned on behalf of a Miss Gould. It took me a moment to realize she meant Sandy. In clipped tones, the woman informed me that repairs had been scheduled for my apartment and Hyman's as well.

I had the option of moving upstairs to Alysse and Bill's former digs by the end of the month. My rent would stay the same. I was being offered the newly refurbished space at less than the market rate. Per Miss Gould, I had first dibs. If I refused, Hyman would be offered the apartment, and I'd be out on the street. I had three days to decide and two weeks to move.

I chose the upstairs apartment, taking Claire, her marital expectations, flannel nightgown, and French horn, with me. Hyman moved out two weeks later, taking Xaviera with him—by far the better deal, as things turned out.

Work crews descended on both vacant flats, ripping out the canvas ceilings and inadequate partitions and replacing them with insulation and double sheets of plasterboard. It seemed Sandy had displaced us so her quarters could be soundproofed from the outside in, thus avoiding all but minimal disruptions to her hallowed routines. For ten days, the neighborhood echoed with sounds of radios, saws, and hammers. Then one day the work was finished, and the strange old house went quiet.

Too quiet.

Claire and I never settled into the new place. Inhumed frustrations on both our parts erupted from the moment we unlocked the door. As each day passed, Claire became more demanding—more like Alysse—and I bristled with increased resentment. On the day Claire moved out, I came home late, and drunk, to a lonely, dark apartment. A neatly wrapped package lay at my door. Thinking it a peace offering, I rapidly tore into the festive paper, expecting some attempt at reconciliation, or, better yet, a token of forgiveness.

Inside was Sandy's chalkboard. She'd wiped it clean. There was no note, but her message was clear enough: she'd intentionally withdrawn from the world, forsaking her listening post along with our friendship. I knew intuitively this was Sandy's way of telling me she knew of Claire's leaving and that I was on my own.

I wish I could say I felt sad. No doubt on some level, I did. In my own way, I'd come to care for Sandy, though what I remember most from that moment is an overwhelming sense of relief that bordered on euphoria. With her self-imposed entombment and Claire's unequivocal departure, I was free of scrutiny. Never again would I have to acquiesce to their all-too-similar expectations.

I dropped the slate. It shattered into several sharp fragments, all of which detached themselves from the confines of the oak frame. Surveying the shards, I felt smug satisfaction and an unanticipated surge of determination. Flush with defiance, abetted by drink, I hurried to a local bar—a place I'd never dared enter. Within the hour, I'd charmed an attractive man into spending the night.

CURTAIN CALL

"*Today was one of the 'good days,' when all the
components coalesced into a genuinely engaging appearance,
as opposed to an 'off day'—usually after a night of drinking—
when her features morphed into something oddly askew,
drawing second glances for all the wrong reasons.*"

*I*n the privacy of the limousine, Toni Greystone finally allows her taut smile to deflate to a less-than-flattering scowl. She'd banked everything on this effort, and it turned out to be an unmitigated fiasco.

With long-practiced nonchalance, she pulls a compact from her purse and surveys the image it reflects. Her features, while no longer those of a woman of twenty-five, are still attractive, thanks to a masterful use of cosmetics. Tonight's disaster notwithstanding, she's hard pressed to find a flaw. Her expensively styled black wig has kept its secret. Deft application of dark red lipstick has recast a thin upper lip that, unattended, might convey pettiness. Mascara, eyeliner, and eyelashes are all still meticulously in place. Today was one of the "good days," when all the components coalesced into a genuinely engaging appearance, as opposed to an "off day"—usually after a night of drinking—when her features morphed into something oddly askew, drawing second glances for all the wrong reasons.

No, it's not my looks. Something else must have queered the deal. A gesture, choice of words—I'll never know.

"Driver, back to South Beach."

She speaks imperiously, as if a ride in a chauffeured limousine is a daily occurrence. Filling a tall glass with gin, she rummages in her purse, retrieves a small white pill, and downs it with a hasty swig. As the car negotiates the winding driveway, she raises the privacy screen, sits back, and reflects on all that went so very wrong.

Really, it all began well enough. The stretch limo certainly sailed past the gatehouse without drawing unwanted attention. Attaching herself to the gaggle of geriatrics deposited by an ancient Bentley was a stroke of genius. The old fools didn't notice her, and the security staff assumed she was with them.

Funny thing. So much security, yet each employee seemed to expect someone else to make the call. What's the sense of that?

In any case, their disorganization worked to her advantage; she got in.

It felt strange to be back. She'd visited several times before when Hélène, Carter Sandstrom's wife, was in Europe. Despite the boisterous demimonde he always invited as cover for their trysts, Toni never felt comfortable in the place. The live-in staff was cordial to a fault, but she found the house too vast—and too Palm Beach.

Tonight it indeed seemed daunting, ablaze as it was with lights and activity. The regiment of waiters, the array of circular tables, and the ten-piece orchestra on the terrace gave it the aura of a five-star hotel. The party was to celebrate the naming of a cancer ward for the recently deceased, extraordinarily wealthy, Hélène. It was her last bash, in a way, and she'd planned it to the last detail, save one: Toni.

Poor Hélène—poor, rich, clueless Hélène. It was fitting I made an appearance, not that I'd have been invited, of course, but fitting nonetheless. I kept her marriage intact—the heartless bitch—building Carter back up after all her nasty accusations.

I doubt he'd have gotten through it without me. Such is the lot of the "other woman," I guess.

In the limousine, Toni raises her glass.

"Well, Hélène, here's to you. Happy trails, honey. Whichever way you're headed."

As the limo leaves the island, Toni pours another gin and recalls the look on Carter's face.

Good old unflappable Carter Sandstrom. When she descended the grand staircase into the ballroom, his shock registered for just an instant, but long enough for her to see he was dumbfounded. She waved her gloved hand delicately—each finger floating back and forth as if she were riding in a royal carriage—then clutched the fur boa to her neck for added effect as she surveyed the scene. She'd once seen Susan Hayward do that in a movie.

Carter recovered quickly, raised an index finger as if to prevent her from moving, and tried to part the throng. Halfway across the long, ornate ballroom, his progress was blocked by an aggressive, bejeweled dowager. Seeing the woman's S-shaped contour stuffed into a straining and ominously strapless gown, Toni thought of Margaret Dumont, smiled to herself, and turned away.

Toni hadn't done too badly in the fashion department. Her long and low-cut black silk number drew stares from many of the men and several of the women.

Surely it wasn't because they thought it in poor taste. It *was* black, after all: elegant for evening, yet still respectful of the dear departed. Perhaps the sequins were a bit too South Beach for this crowd, but they'd just have to get over themselves.

She used Carter's predicament to score a martini and escape into the crush. Circulating turned out to be far less difficult than she'd anticipated. Few of the guests knew each other, making it easy to mingle. Most of them were nipped, tucked, and twisted into an artificial youthfulness that made her feel pubescent by comparison. They were no more legitimate; they just had tons more money.

Carter and Hélène were the topic of every group she joined. Toni's opening gambit was always the same: Were you a friend of Hélène or of Carter? How did you know them? Wasn't it a shame? Followed by the finale: an emphatic something must be done about this dreadful disease. Then on to the next bunch.

Toni kept Carter at bay for nearly an hour, circulating away from wherever he, the beleaguered host, happened to be engaged. The size of the room and the crush of social climbers, a key part of her plan, gave her a distinct advantage. She needed time to show him she could—and would—behave well, before having the conversation they both knew was inevitable.

Carter looked so handsome. And far less gaunt than when she'd last seen him. Was it truly eight weeks ago when he'd last escaped to South Beach? Hélène had been in the final days of it by then. He'd needed comfort and release from the nightmare of the hospital. Toni had done her best.

Carter stood out tonight, even in such a high-toned crowd. His impeccably groomed mustache was as elegant as ever. His height, dark tan, and the midnight black of his tuxedo made his white hair a beacon. Each time she met his gaze, she saw fire in those deep blue eyes. She hadn't anticipated her presence would spark quite this depth of annoyance. A second martini did little to calm her nerves, but a conversation with the dapper gentleman at the terrace bar was a welcome distraction.

"They don't make many women like you these days," the old duffer said, shifting on his bar stool and tossing his line like a pro.

He was short—almost as round as he was tall—with a bloated, red face that betrayed years of hard drinking. His eyes sparkled from behind round black glasses with remarkable vitality, giving him the appearance of an inebriated owl.

Toni made her voice a bit breathy and leaned close, thinking she might as well give him a treat.

"I've heard that line before."

"No one has a sense of style anymore. The slits in that dress! Nonstop from Tierra del Fuego to Panama! You should have a permit to wear that thing. It could give some poor bastard a coronary."

"Why thank you, sir. So very kind of you to notice."

She brought her hand to her throat. She was enjoying this.

"I'm not the only one . . . Half the men in this joint have their eyes bugging out of their heads, and all the women are green with envy."

"Why, surely you exaggerate! Or have intentions that are less than honorable."

She raised her glass, batted her eyelashes, and took a large, luscious sip while staring him straight in the eye. The old goat roared in delight.

"At my age, having less-than-honorable intentions is one of the few pleasures left me."

"Don't sell yourself short. You know what they say: where there's a will there's a way."

She smiled seductively, waiting a beat for her double entendre to hit home. As the old duffer shook with laughter, she felt a strong hand on her shoulder.

Carter.

His tone was cordial, but underneath was a steely edge.

"Sorry to intrude, Washburton, but there's something important this young woman and I must discuss. In private."

Passing clusters of guests, Toni tried to look blasé, as if Carter were taking her to see a newly acquired painting. Once in the plush elegance of the library, he slammed the door and pushed her onto the chesterfield sofa. The solid door muffled the sounds of the party, creating a sudden, taut stillness. Toni began to worry she'd underestimated the situation.

After an interminable pause, Carter finally spoke.

"Who the hell do you think you are, coming here like this?"

She'd never seen him this way. His face was contorted in rage. She remained silent, eyes downcast.

"You're making a fool of me, exposing me to scandal, to say nothing of showing disrespect for my wife's memory. What are you trying to do, ruin me?"

Toni took a deep breath, waited a moment to steady herself, and spoke in the most reasonable tone she could muster.

"Carter, come on, now. I'm not here for any of those reasons, and you know it. You weren't yourself when you sent that eviction notice. You wouldn't take my calls. This was the only way to see you. As for Hélène, I've respected your wife for the last five years; I'm not about to create a scandal now she's dead."

He calmed down a bit, but continued to pace the rich oriental carpet. She tried again.

"Carter, please listen to me. I'm here because I love you. You can live your own life now. We can be together, not just sneaking around behind people's backs. I certainly want that, and I think you do, too."

Her declaration seemed to catch him unawares. He stepped back and stared at the Magritte hanging over the fireplace, then seemed to retreat into himself. Finally, he spoke in a flat, detached monotone.

"You could never pull it off . . . You'd never fit in. These are sophisticated people. You could never make it work."

"That's why I came, to prove to you I could. I don't know why you want to bother with these people, even if they are as sophisticated as you say, which I strongly doubt. They're your wife's friends. It wasn't too long ago you called them a bunch of snobs and didn't want a thing to do with them. We can live anywhere we want now, but if you want to stay here, I promise I'll make it work."

She took a long sip, finishing her drink while assessing the impact of her words. Carter turned away as if to avoid her gaze. When he finally spoke, it seemed his mind was made up.

"I've worked my whole life to put my past behind me and be accepted by 'these people.' I'm not about to give it all up now. We've been over and over this. I don't want to discuss it anymore."

"Then let me prove I can make it work, Carter, at least for tonight. You can't stay in here with me much longer, or you *will* have a scandal on your hands."

"Promise me you'll leave right away."

"People will talk if I leave after being in here alone with you. Wouldn't it be better if I left after the remarks? Don't you have a speech to make? No one can leave before then without calling attention to themselves."

Phipps, the butler, knocked softly, then slowly opened the door.

"Excuse me, Ms. Greystone," he said, nodding deferentially toward her, "but the master of ceremonies is suggesting it's time for Mr. Sandstrom to return to the head table. The speeches are about to begin."

Carter looked even more annoyed.

"Yes. Yes. I'll be right there."

The butler quietly shut the door as Carter's face clouded. When he spoke, his tone was curt.

"Stay here for a few minutes and then you're on your own out there. For God's sake, don't do anything stupid. Get out of here as quickly as you can without making a scene. We'll talk again, soon . . . I promise."

All at once, his features softened. He placed his hand on her cheek and stared into her eyes. She looked up at him with all the sincerity she could muster. After a moment, he dropped his hand to her shoulder, patting it pensively. Then he was gone.

Sounds of the chattering throng spilled through the open door as Toni sat quietly, turning the empty glass in her hand, reflecting on how things had come to this point.

The last five years had been a series of thrilling highs and frightening lows. When Carter had initially suggested the arrangement, it meant freedom from worry for the very first time. She'd been willing to go along simply for that. Even so, she paid her own freight as best she could. The money from her performances went for everyday items. He didn't pay for anything but condo expenses and the lease on the car.

It was great at first: the ocean view, the travel while Hélène was in Europe, the absence of want. Initially, they spent a lot of time together, but later on, as Hélène's condition deteriorated, the weeks stretched out in endless waiting. On Saturdays, Toni would do her show, then go home to pray for a brief phone call or an increasingly rare visit. Pills and liquor didn't entirely vanquish her growing loneliness, but they helped.

The lawyer's letter instructing her to vacate had come as a complete surprise. It was so formal and so cold. What's more, it arrived only a week after Hélène's death, just as Toni was pondering the right way to reconnect with Carter.

There was no reason to turn her out she could think of, other than the fact he no longer needed her discretion. The suggestion that she might buy the apartment at seventy percent of market price was ludicrous. The place had skyrocketed in value over the last three years. He must have known she didn't have that kind of money. What irked her most was the realization Carter meant so much more to her than the security his money bought. At first, this thought had surprised her. Then it prompted her to action.

After a few minutes, Toni left the library and returned to the terrace. By then everyone had respectfully turned their chairs toward the head table in anticipation of the speeches. It was easy to stand inconspicuously on the sidelines and watch from there.

After a while, it was Carter's turn to speak. He did so in a full, rich voice that showcased his wit, charm, and indisputable attractiveness. He spoke fondly of his dead wife, recounted her many charitable works, and interjected enough anecdotes to convey theirs had been a happy, fulfilling marriage. He spoke of her love of Europe and his regret that he could not always accompany her due to the pressures of business. Toni thought she saw Phipps look her way with a knowing smile, but she stared straight ahead, feigning interest in Carter's loving tribute.

The speech ended to tumultuous applause. Then the orchestra played some appropriate transitional music, reminding her of the Academy Awards. Toni was the first to signal the bartender.

"Tonic water and lime, please."

She searched for a dark corner. It was time to be very, very discreet.

"Young lady . . ."

It was the old man, Washburton, again, still seated at the bar.

"Why not sit here and keep me company for a while? There's no one out there who will appreciate you as I do."

"You know, you're probably right." She sighed and sat on the stool next to him.

It was as good a place as any to wait out the minutes until her departure. She went through the motions of listening as she rehashed the conversation with Carter in her mind, trying to decipher his conflicting signals and anticipate his next move.

After a few minutes, she became aware the old buzzard was growing bellicose. He'd obviously had much more to drink while she was in the library. His words were thick, his voice strident. Suddenly, his hand was on her knee. She gently moved it aside. He clamped down on her right hand with a firm grip. As she struggled to escape, he leaned toward her and hissed in her ear.

"It's always the same; the bits on the side like you think they can move in whenever there's a vacancy. They never see they've been bought and paid for just like any other acquisition. Time to move on to greener pastures, dearie. I've got a few bucks stashed away."

"I beg your pardon?"

She felt her color rising.

"Now, now, sweetie. No disrespect meant. No disrespect . . . We've all got our place in the world. Just so happens, yours is on your back with your legs up."

He laughed loudly at his own joke, raising the collective eyebrows of a clutch of matrons at a nearby table.

"I am a close friend of the Sandstroms. How *dare* you speak to me like this!"

Toni stood to leave. The old man pulled her back onto the barstool with surprising force.

After that, things seemed to unfold as if in slow motion; more guests turned to watch. She saw Carter, still seated at the head table, break off his conversation and stare in her direction, his features contorted in fury. Then, as if on cue, the orchestra stopped playing, and the musicians took their break.

"And I'm the family accountant, dearie. That makes me even closer. I win."

Washburton's voice continued to crescendo, filling the void left by the musicians and halting all nearby conversation.

"Let me see; it's 1800 Collins Ave in South Beach, isn't it? Apartment 15-J? Condo fees are $410 a month, parking included; the lease on the Mercedes is $520. Miscellaneous expenses bring your upkeep to $1200 a month, not including capital investment, which fortunately is appreciating again. So divide twelve hundred by thirty—which is close enough for this exercise—and you rent for $40 a day. Divide that by twenty-four, and you go for $1.67 an hour. What a deal! Even without the real estate! Good old Carter never could resist getting something on the cheap."

The old man slapped his knee. For an instant, there was a stunned silence. Then some of the guests leaned over to speak to those at other tables. Toni imagined their shocked comments diffusing across the ballroom like dye in water.

She finally broke free of the old letch and walked toward the head table, looking neither right nor left. Carter glared at her, sending a clear warning to stand down. She continued to strut across the ballroom, head up, back erect, moving at a languorous pace bound to draw further attention and meeting his increasingly hostile gaze without once looking away.

At last, she stood in front of him.

"Carter," she said in a loud, clear voice, stretching the syllables of his name in a regal drawl, "I regret I have another engagement that *compels* me to leave so early. I do apologize. I'd like to thank you for your kind invitation and say how very pleased dear Hélène would have been with your tribute. She was the most fortunate of women to have such a loving husband."

Toni held out her hand, noticing how well her cocktail ring reflected the candlelight. Carter stood, his eyes raging.

He took her hand, squeezed hard, and in an intense whisper said, "Get out of the place by the end of the week or I'll throw you out—or worse."

She smiled graciously and nodded her head as if they had exchanged pleasantries.

As she descended the terrace steps, the ocean breeze caught the slits in her dress and pushed them back, fully revealing her long, shapely legs. At the bottom of the stairs, one of the musicians whistled; another let out a loud catcall. As the two men high-fived each other, the ballroom erupted in excited whispers.

Jolted from her reverie by the sight of a cruise ship, Toni realizes they are crossing the MacArthur Causeway. She's been so engrossed in her thoughts, the hour-long trip to South Beach has seemed mere minutes. When the limousine draws up to her building, she tips the driver, signs the charge slip, and flounces to the front door. As the car speeds off into the night, the near-empty decanter leaks a drop of gin onto the back seat.

Into the lobby, blow a kiss to the concierge, up the elevator, down the hall, fumble with the keys, open the door. Shut the door, play Billie Holliday on the stereo, another drink, another pill . . .

Home, sweet home.

"For how long?" Toni wonders aloud, scanning the familiar surroundings. "It will be tough to leave all this."

She traverses the room, zeroes in on a photograph taken on one of her many jaunts with Carter, and studies the happiness in his eyes. She turns from the photo to survey herself in the mirror over the fireplace.

"I mustn't let things get to me," she says to her reflection. "It's just a temporary setback. He'll come round. What we have is unique. He'll see that, when he tires of those pompous asses in Palm Beach. That crowd he's so concerned about can never give him what I can."

By now, she's lost track of how many pills she's taken. Her mood is one of chemically abetted rebelliousness touched, as always, with an ample dose of theatrics. No self-pity—not her—never that.

"The show must go on," she says to the mirror, yielding to an ever-increasing haze that numbs her pain while stoking her fighting spirit.

She thinks of Barbra singing "My Man," and Judy's "The Man That Got Away." Both songs invoke the timeless alchemy of the injured woman, a torch song, and a circle of light on a scarred wooden floor. Toni will find the courage to go on where she's always found it—onstage.

She throws open the sliders to the balcony and steps out into the cool night air. The full moon shines above like a spotlight. The blinking neon of the streetscape below evokes the lights of Broadway. Billie's sultry voice harkens back to the Blue Note, with its shabby sophistication and solitary follow-spot.

Toni clambers onto the wide cement ledge. A dim glow from the apartment above illuminates the concrete span against the blackness beyond. It's just like looking out into a darkened house. She steps sideways, her stilettos echoing on the rough surface. A voice from deep within urges caution but is overruled by the swirl of emotions and chemicals coursing through her brain.

Billie, her voice crimped and brimming with pain, eases into Duke Ellington's classic: *In . . . my . . . solitude . . .*

Toni sashays the length of the ledge and back, her husky voice caressing the lyrics, projecting them into the darkness with newfound resolve. Her black dress shimmers, its sequins reflecting neon and moonlight. The breeze lifts the fabric from her legs.

Not quite like Marilyn, but provocative nonetheless. The moist night air envelops her.

She undulates in time with the music, her right hand caressing an imaginary microphone; then she paces the stage like Judy, every ounce of yearning made manifest in song. Leaning forward, Toni stretches the lyrics, ready to sell the finish for all she's worth.

The telephone rings several times, stops, then starts again. Toni doesn't hear. She's back on stage—the only place she belongs . . . the only place that's truly safe . . . cradling a loving—if imaginary—audience in her outstretched hands. Love, loneliness, life . . . She'll leave these things to fate . . .

Billie brings the song home alone.

Monday's *Miami Herald* contains a small article on page twenty-seven:

Local Performer Dead in Apparent Suicide

In the early hours of Sunday morning, beloved female impersonator Anthony Grey, known professionally as Toni Greystone, is believed to have jumped to his death—in full drag—from the balcony of a Collins Avenue condominium.

A talented entertainer and much-loved South Beach celebrity, Mr. Grey was well known for his caustic impersonations of famous vocalists, society luminaries, and trophy wives.

The owner of the condominium, Palm Beach socialite Carter Sandstrom, was unavailable for comment.

GÖTTERDÄMMERUNG

*"The 'Liebestod' from Tristan is, to me, Wagner's
consummate tribute to love."*

*I*t was late January of '38, and I'd been a substitute at Radio City for the better part of a week. At that time, I took any gig I could; money was scarce and work that paid well even more so.

One of the acts was the *pas de deux* from Tchaikovsky's *Swan Lake*. I played the violin solo onstage from memory twice a day, and toward the end of the week, I had it nailed. Not that I thought anyone was listening. I was certain the audience dozed through the longhair stuff while waiting for the Rockettes to kick up their heels. Despite playing second fiddle to a chorus line, I played my best.

After my last performance, the stage manager escorted me to a VIP lounge, pointed at the door, and left. I knocked. A gruff voice told me to enter. Once inside, I was stunned to see the maestro sitting in a leather chair next to a chrome table, a snifter of brandy in his hand. He was a god in my world—I'd seen him only from afar at Philharmonic or Met performances. I never suspected he'd come to Radio City, to say nothing of summoning me after a show.

Bright light streamed from a floor lamp behind his chair. As my eyes adjusted, I studied the famous long white hair and imperious mustache. He was seventy then, elegantly dressed in a blue blazer with a black silk cravat. His dark eyes were clear, penetrating—almost demonic. Immense power surged from them. On his right hand, he wore a large gold ring.

The door shut behind me with a disconcerting thud. I stood mute with my fiddle and bow in my right hand. He placed the snifter on the table and sat quietly for a moment, sizing me up—or so it seemed. Then, at last, he spoke in a deep, heavily-accented voice.

"So, you are loving playing this joint?"

I wasn't sure if it was a question or a snide remark.

"I love playing great music, Maestro, whenever the opportunity presents itself. A composer should be honored wherever his music is performed."

"That is a good answer for someone so young. I am sure Pyotr Ilyich, he is grateful—for the thought *and* for the music you made tonight."

The maestro smiled gently.

"Tomorrow, you come play for me. My assistant, she makes the arrangements."

I stood there, rooted to the floor, not fully fathoming what I had heard. He smiled again as if he understood. Was this the fabled dragon who routinely scorched musicians with his fiery temper?

"You know the Mendelssohn, yes?"

I nodded. Every violinist worth his salt knows the Concerto in E Minor—a tour de force that separates the good from the great.

"Third movement, Allegro molto vivace. From memory, tomorrow. I will accompany you. Perhaps you should practice some tonight, no?"

He reached for his brandy, brought it to his lips, and dismissed me with a wave. I bolted from the room and ran right into a beautiful young girl who stood just outside the door. As we collided, I pulled my fiddle and bow close, then reached out with my free hand to stop her fall.

"Mr. Tischler, we need to set up your appointment."

My arm was still tightly wrapped around her waist. She was breathtakingly lovely, with long black hair, intense dark eyes, and sensuous lips within inches of mine. It took all the strength I could muster not to kiss them. The look in her eyes was part surprise, part recognition—as if she had somehow foreseen our odd encounter. She smelled of lilacs.

I let go of her after a moment. She was all business; what made me think this could be the time and place for romance?

"I beg your pardon?"

"An appointment with the maestro. Tomorrow morning at Carnegie Hall. You will present yourself at the business office at 8:50. I will meet and escort you to the stage. He will audition you then."

Her English was flawless, with the slightest trace of Tuscany. I wasn't sure who was more intimidating: the god in the room behind me, or the goddess standing in front of me.

"Yes—of course. The appointment—certainly. Yes, I'll be there."

Always so good with words, I was.

I practiced the Mendelssohn for hours that night. There was no point in isolating the third movement; it was the culmination of the entire work. I played all three movements in sequence, over and over again. Neighbors banged on the pipes and pounded on the floor. Still, I practiced.

Around three in the morning, I tried to rest, but it was useless; the Mendelssohn kept running through my head. There was no sleep to be had that night, but I had the concerto—all of it—under my fingers by morning.

I was in sight of Carnegie Hall when a lens popped out of my glasses and shattered on the pavement. Staring down at fragments I could barely see, I nearly gave up and went home. But I knew a chance like this would never come again, so I groped my way to the business office.

There she was, the goddess, waiting in the hall for me.

"Miss . . ."

I stopped—I had never asked her name.

"Call me Luciana. Everyone does."

She looked celestial in the haze of my blurred vision. I smelled lilacs again.

"Luciana, my glasses broke as I was coming here. I can barely see."

A half-smile illuminated her face.

"Is good you are playing from memory today, no?"

Was she mocking me with the sudden appearance of a full-blown Italian accent? I couldn't tell, but she certainly didn't seem to care about my predicament.

I followed her in silence, down a winding stair to the wings.

"Wait here until you are called. Do not speak unless he asks you a question."

She turned and made her way through the curtains. The *click clack* of her heels echoed down the stairs, then slowly faded as she vanished into the unlit hall.

After what seemed an eternity, my name was called, and I stepped into the glare of a single spotlight. A bald man sat at a grand piano. I was confused—the maestro had said *he* would accompany me.

"Mendelssohn, Mr. Tischler. First movement, Allegro molto appassionato."

The maestro's inimitable voice sounded from the darkened cavern of the orchestra seats. For a second, I was taken aback. He'd told me to prepare the third movement. Then I realized he was trying to unnerve me with both the pianist and the choice of movement. I was on solid ground. I always practiced the complete work, never just the difficult parts. You have to get in and out of the rough spots, after all. It's as much about entering and exiting them as anything else.

We began. The pianist was good, cautious—but good. After a while, the maestro's voice called out from the depths of the hall.

"Stop. Second movement, Andante, if you please."

I felt both exhausted and disoriented, given my lack of sleep and diminished vision. Still, I played the luscious Andante with all my heart.

The maestro interrupted us again after a few minutes.

"Stop. Wait. I come now."

As I tensed, wondering what had gone wrong, he sprinted to the stage, making a lie of his age. The bald man shifted to the edge of the bench and made ready to turn pages.

The maestro sat down at the piano, just a few feet from me.

"Third movement, Allegro molto vivace, from the exposition . . .

"One, two, one!"

His tempo was faster than I'd ever practiced. I jumped in, barely having time to think. His accompaniment was magnificent, bringing the music to life in ways I had never considered. Yet, within seconds, we played as if of one mind.

His interpretation was so masterful and true I felt liberated, even forgetting with whom I was playing. Chills pulsed through my body, and tears gathered at the corners of my eyes. By the time we were finished, I was emotionally and physically exhausted. Even so, the moment ended much too soon.

The hall was silent—far too silent. In my anxiety, I plucked the broken hairs from my bow and looked around for Luciana. I couldn't see her anywhere. The maestro shifted on the bench.

"Is not bad, Mr. Tischler—not bad at all—for a music hall fiddler who is . . . how you say? . . . still wet behind the ears."

He chuckled softly. I smiled, not knowing what else to do. I was twenty-three, then. I certainly wasn't going to contradict him.

"And now, the sight reading. Stravinsky, *L'Histoire du Soldat,* measure 132—if you please."

He sat back, arms folded, eyes on me, as Luciana came from backstage with a music stand and several pieces of music. I looked at her in horror. I couldn't possibly sight-read without my glasses.

It was as if she didn't see me.

Suddenly, the maestro spoke.

"You are, perhaps, in need of these?"

He reached into his pocket and pulled out a pair of magnifying glasses identical to those he was wearing. I tried them on. To my astonishment, I could read the music. He smiled.

"This, most good conductors, they learn early in the career. The audience, they care not if the glasses they break or the clothes they have the rips or stains. You are there to perform great music. *That* they expect. All other problems are not theirs to have the worry of. Always, always, two of everything—you never know."

He seemed to enjoy my discomfort. When he'd turned back to the piano, I mouthed my thanks to Luciana. She winked, or so it seemed. With the magnifying glasses on, I couldn't see her well enough to be sure.

The maestro accompanied me for much of what I read, reworking passages and interpretations, yelling instructions, singing along. I felt exhilarated and terrified at the same time, knowing my life would never be the same: If I got the gig, it would be heaven. If not, I'd never recover.

So compelling was our music together, an hour passed in an instant. Finally, as the maestro reached for yet another score, Luciana whispered something in his ear. He smiled at her lovingly, then turned to me.

"Young man, I leave now for the studio rehearsal. Tomorrow you join us to prepare for Buenos Aires at the first of the month. My granddaughter will escort you to the office to sign the necessary papers."

I nodded. No words would come. He held out his hand for his glasses. Luciana smiled at me and pointed the way.

Only then did I fully realize I had been hired by the greatest conductor of the century.

Buenos Aires was just the beginning. We traveled the world and performed with all the greats. It was not always easy: the maestro could be a stickler for detail, and incredibly demanding. There are many stories I could tell of his tantrums.

Two years later, Luciana accepted my hand in marriage. I'd auditioned for more than I realized, that fateful day when my glasses broke on the way to Carnegie Hall.

Five more seasons passed, and I became concertmaster. The maestro refused to hear my audition lest he create ill will amongst his musicians. Despite our connection, a committee of orchestra members chose me with only one dissenting vote. I made my debut with the Mendelssohn.

In '46, I returned to Radio City, but this time as a featured soloist with the greatest orchestra in the world. I awaited my stage call in the very lounge to which I had once been summoned.

One incident during our years together stands out above all others, when I learned how great musicians deal with the inevitability of mistakes, and the truly great put fear to good use.

It happened opening night at the old Met, in '49. The opera was *La Forza del Destino—The Force of Destiny.* The overture begins with a motif of three famous quarter notes that signify Fate. Someone in the brass section, one of the "brass jocks," as we called them, nicked the third note. It was embarrassing, being the first three notes, opening night, and all, but I didn't give it much more thought than that.

The rest of the performance was uneventful. Shortly after the opera ended, the maestro came to our dressing room. He stood silently in the doorway until, sensing his commanding presence, we stopped talking and turned to face him.

"Is fine for you," he said at last, his face scarlet, his voice overflowing with fury. "You go home to your wives and your families, happy. But today," he paused and stared at us, eyes aflame, "today, because of what happened out there, part of me *died*."

Then he turned and walked away, leaving us standing there heads down, like errant schoolboys.

Later that night, over cognac, I asked the maestro why he'd taken all of us to task for one man's mistake. His cigarette smoldered in its holder as I waited for his reply. When it came, it was an answer I shall never forget.

"There are so many notes in the performance—the mistake, sometimes, it cannot be avoided. This I do accept, even though it causes me the pain. There is more to this, however.

"If the artist, he does not try for perfection with all his heart, then the music he makes is not his very best. His true best comes only when he performs beyond what he believes possible. A musician must continually be surprised by what he does and not limit himself. Beyond all things, he must never grow complacent. If being afraid pushes him beyond his limits, then I will use his fear. On that . . . how you say? . . . you can count.

"You may not know it was Davison who missed the third note this evening. He came to me immediately after the performance and made the most humble of apologies. Of course, I already knew he did it; I know my musicians better than they know themselves. I told him to wait and went to speak to the others. You heard what I said to them, but to Davison, I said not the single word of anger. There was not the need. To him, I am sending the big bottle of grappa. He was honest and played magnificently after his mistake. This is as it should be.

"Do not say anything of this. Let the others think what they will. They will be a bit more afraid from now on, and this . . . it is not a bad thing."

The musicians there that night never did forget. Over time, *La Forza* became our watchword for caution in the face of imminent disaster. It was partly a joke, and partly a reminder of a moment that had shamed us all. As the years passed, every new player heard the tale as a rite of passage. The story was told even after Davison retired in '52 never having learned his rare mistake was the stuff of legend.

In April of '54, I was once again at Carnegie Hall, at what turned out to be the most controversial concert of the maestro's career.

Before telling what actually happened that night, I must first apologize. I've never been good with words; they're not my medium. Using mere language to describe any performance—to say nothing of the opulence of Wagner's music—diminishes it. The greatest of writers could capture only a portion of what is expressed in a single measure. For someone like me to try is folly doomed from the start.

The glorious sounds of a great orchestra are achieved through finely honed precision. We work tirelessly to maintain control—to execute flawlessly—so as to liberate the music from the page. And, every once in a while, the notes, timbres, dynamics, and articulations align in perfect concert with the composer's intent. When they do, it's a revelation; but, like anything so intensely personal, an experience nearly impossible to convey. I tell you now, my meager words will not suffice. They will not begin to do justice to the performance that day. They will be as inadequate as the now-ancient phonograph recording—just a distant echo of a moment in time. Having said these things, I shall do my best to describe how it was that fateful day.

The all-Wagner program began with the "Vorspiel" from *Die Walküre,* continued with scenes from that opera, and closed the first half with an orchestral rendition of the famous "Ride of the Valkyries." After intermission, the program was comprised of excerpts from other Wagner operas: mostly preludes and overtures. We were to end with the "Prelude" from the third act of *Lohengrin.* The radio executives had demanded a "potboiler" to close out the national broadcast.

The trouble began just before the *Lohengrin,* during the "Prelude" and "Liebestod"—"Love Death"—from *Tristan und Isolde.* The maestro got through the "Prelude" well enough. With his mane of white hair and bright, powerful eyes, he looked like an ancient deity up on the podium, commanding the forces of the Universe. We in the orchestra were on edge as always, like marionettes responding to the tug of his baton: fearful, yet exhilarated, as once again he revealed the essence of the score.

Suddenly, during the "Liebestod," life seemed to drain from him. One second he was conducting a gradual *crescendo,* coaxing forth broad waves of sound that crested over the *tremolo* in the strings. The next, during the *decrescendo* that followed, a veil dropped over his eyes.

It was during the section, early on, in which the violas and violins pass the countermelody between them. Eighth note, then triplet: tah-da-da-da, tah-da-da-da—a whisper between them. It happened right there. The light left his eyes, his face drooped, and he seemed lost. After a few seconds, he began to move his arms aimlessly, as tears streamed down his face. I saw them first, but only a split second before the others.

The maestro invariably conducted from memory. The closed score was on the podium solely as a tribute to the composer; it was of no use in performance. With the failure of the maestro's direction, the orchestra was a rudderless ship in heavy seas. One by one, the musicians looked to me. I shall never forget how lost and afraid they seemed as he stood in front of us ashen-faced and disoriented. Without giving a second thought, I began to mark time with my violin. My movements were nearly imperceptible: up down, up down, one, two, one, two . . . To my surprise, the maestro began to follow my beat. This titan of a man, whose interpretations were sacred, who had dominated his handpicked orchestra for so long—*he followed me*!

I continued my subtle motions to articulate the repeating triplets and broad *crescendi*. Then I marked the gradual, rolling *accelerando*; its lush sound intensifying, illuminating—sanctifying—the mysteries of the heart. Through it all, he stood there awash in some of the most glorious music ever written, moving his arms just enough to deceive the audience.

The "Liebestod" from *Tristan* is, to me, Wagner's consummate tribute to love. At the point in the drama in which it occurs, Isolde has fallen rapturously in love with Tristan, who dies in her arms. When his spirit appears and beckons her to join him, she falls dead from grief and longing.

In the midst of all that beauty and passion, the maestro stood before us like a frail old man waiting for a bus. I was barely able to sustain my focus, so concerned was I that he might topple from the podium, but I marked time, doing what little I could. Somehow, we found our way to the end. I raised my bow with a subtle flourish, then held it in midair.

The orchestra stopped as one.

The maestro did not stay to acknowledge the applause, but immediately left the stage with a tenuous, halting step. Within a minute, word came from backstage, passed on by each desk of violins.

"Go to the green room. Luciana wants you. The old man's in a bad way."

The murmurs began when I stood. Up to this point, the audience had not noticed anything amiss. When I left my seat, they knew something was wrong. This is where the stories of that day have their origins, in the speculation of the audience.

Once offstage, I raced to the green room. Luciana opened the door. Her eyes were awash in tears. I quickly pulled her to me, thinking back to our first, unexpected, yet somehow pre-ordained embrace. She disengaged hastily, then turned to speak to her beloved grandfather.

"Nonno?"

How strange to hear him called that away from home.

"Edward is here. Nonno?"

She spoke as if finding difficulty in getting his attention. He sat in an overstuffed wing chair, a glass of water in his hand. His features partly in shadow, he looked feeble and distant, his eyes still moist, his face mottled and red. He spoke haltingly in a voice I could hardly hear.

"Ah, Tischler! You were there. You saw. The muse, she has abandoned me."

I understood. I *had* seen it. It was less than two hours since he had conducted *Walküre* and summoned the shade of Wagner himself. Whatever divine source had nurtured the maestro's genius, it was no longer available to him. I suspected a slight stroke, but what did I know of medicine? Yet I understood intuitively: the mystic link between conductor, composer, and orchestra had been severed. I nodded slowly. What words could I possibly find?

"Nonno, you are not well," Luciana said. "We must go home . . . Now. I'll send for the car."

She looked to me for support. My ambivalence must have shown, for the maestro settled things by clutching my hand.

"No. I must go back. They wait for me out there. I have never let them down. I must finish my final performance."

I could barely hear him. He searched the room, as if for something he'd lost, then beckoned me to sit beside him. As I did, there was a knock on the door. It was Snell, the stage manager. He whispered through the closed door, his voice betraying his anxiety.

"Maestro, everyone is waiting! We've used nearly all the extra time we have. We *must* start the *Lohengrin* in four minutes to keep to the radio schedule!"

"Tischler." The old man looked at me, his eyes wide in appeal. "You will do this for me? Yes?"

I knew before he finished speaking. He was asking me to lead the orchestra for him as I had for the "Liebestod"!

This was very different from what we had just done and far more difficult. I had done little but bring the "Liebestod" to its conclusion. A couple of *accellerandi*, a *ritarardando* or two, perhaps . . . the *pianisissimo* at the end, then a cutoff. What was that? Nothing! Besides, there was time between the notes to think.

The *Lohengrin* was the third act Prelude, marked *allegro vivace*. The piece moves like the wind and opens with a thunderclap—a triplet marked *fortissimo*. It's a challenge for any good conductor to get full power and clarity on the first notes, to say nothing of a lowly violinist who hasn't conducted since music school.

My mind reeled. I couldn't provide a solid downbeat from my seat without giving things away. Even if we managed to start together, how would I mark the proper tempo for the recapitulation? The theme's final statement, which the maestro always conducted *presto con fuoco,* displaces the *ritenuto* in a single downbeat. I could never transition more than one hundred musicians to that frenetic tempo without the audience realizing I'd usurped his place.

He seemed to read my thoughts. His eyes pleaded with me. Despite numbing fear that brought chills and near-nausea, I simply could not refuse him, this giant of a man, whom I'd come to know and love so well. I placed my hand on his shoulder, trying my best to appear jovial and unconcerned.

"Maestro, when you get back out there, I'm sure you will have no need of me, but rest assured I will be at your side as I have been for all these years."

I turned to look at my wife, who stood sullenly in the corner. Her stony glance was an accusation of murder. I crossed the room, kissed her frigid cheek, shrugged helplessly, and left.

Snell was waiting outside, a pained expression on his face.

"You must get word out quickly," I whispered, "I think the old man's had a stroke. I'm afraid he can no longer conduct from memory. Tell everyone they must watch me, and to remember *La Forza.*"

Snell hurried to the far corner of the stage. He stopped at its edge and spoke through the curtain: first to the percussion, then moving on to the brass, then finally the double basses.

I watched as word spread from back to front, then walked backstage behind the first violins. I parted the curtain and entered from stage right. It was not respectful to take the maestro's path through the orchestra. Besides, it was tempting Fate.

Once at my seat, I signaled the orchestra to tune, which provided even more time for word to be conveyed. Then I sat and made ready as if nothing were wrong. From the darkness beyond the stage, the whispering audience brought to mind the hiss of a giant serpent.

Awaiting the maestro's entrance, I recalled the furor that had erupted when the program was first announced. War memories were fresh, and Hitler's appropriation of Wagner's music—to say nothing of the composer's descendants—was widely known. For someone like me, it was appalling to think the maestro would sanction such a performance, knowing full well the outrage it would provoke.

He was taking a tremendous risk. More confident in myself after all my years with him, I'd broached the subject during one of our after-dinner chats.

"This, I must say, I have been expecting," the maestro said while refilling my glass. "You would not be the man you have become without raising such things, and I applaud you for it. There is much I wish to say to you about this decision.

"Please to remember, I was a lad of seventeen when Wagner, he died in Venice. Already, I perform his music in the opera pit, and in eight short years, I conduct it. Musicians' stories, they pass from one to another for decades, but this you must understand: I heard what I now tell you from those who knew him—from the first generation.

"This hero of . . . how you say it? The master race? He compose in the room lined with the satin, dressed in the woman's underclothing. I know, too, of the mad prince who would have abandoned his kingdom to offer himself as a lover."

I stared open mouthed. I thought I knew all the maestro's stories by now. He nodded his head slowly as if to confirm all he had just said.

"Hitler and Mussolini—the godless bastards—they drive me from my homeland. Even as they do this, I think of one as the draft-dodger and the other the lousy painter with the buffoon's mustache. By thinking this, I endure. Not just endure, but triumph in the end. My performances sell the millions of war bonds that help put them in their graves.

"I, too, felt the pain so many feel, even as, in the end, I triumph over my enemies. I also know the peace: how important it is to allow life to go on. To make the peace for myself—and so many others—Wagner the man must be seen separate from Wagner the composer. This, it must be understood soon or his beautiful music, it will wither away and die. As I am the victim, I must show the way. But my time, it is so short."

"How can a man be separate from his music?"

My confusion must have shown, for the Maestro smiled, picked up the bottle of port, and held it to the light where it glowed a disconcerting ruby red.

"This bottle in my hand? What does it do? It holds the wine, does it not? Would you judge the wine inside by the look of this bottle? Of course not. You would be called the fool. Sunlight, rain, fertile soil, the farmer's daily toils; these things, *they* work together to produce the noble vintage. The bottle, it plays no part in these mysteries. None! It houses the fermenting grape until the time for the drinking is right. Nothing more. It is but the vessel that cradles the essence of the grape, existing but to be filled, emptied, and abandoned.

"Wagner, he, too, was nothing but the vessel. In death, he becomes the . . . how you say, the patsy . . . for Hitler's madness. Wagner the man with his evil words . . . I call him the *finocchio* and leave him to his lingerie. But Wagner the composer . . . ah! What blessings flowed when he unsheathed his pen! Such music! A gift from the gods. This I understand well, for whenever I perform the great music, I too am nothing but the vessel for the muse . . .

"And so my answer to you is this: to make the peace—and the best music—never fear to damn the mortal, but always, always remember to embrace the divine . . . *wherever* you find it."

The sound of applause shook me from my reverie. I looked up to see the maestro tottering toward me. Ranks of violins and celli tapped their bows in the universal sign of respect and encouragement as he passed. It was as if their admiration and affection carried him down the aisle. In the wings, I could see Luciana watching, pale and tremulous. Our eyes locked for the briefest of moments, then her gaze shifted back to the maestro's progress. Her prior consternation had been tempered by the slightest trace of hope—or so it seemed from where I sat.

When the maestro reached the podium, he clutched the rail, bowed to the audience, turned his back to them, and stood perfectly still. I tensed, fearing I might have to leap up and break his fall. However, with what appeared a major effort, he pulled himself up the three small steps.

The hall grew silent.

Most of the musicians were already watching me. The maestro seemed aloof and preoccupied. His baton rested on the music stand. For a minute or so, he made no effort to pick it up.

Finally, I leaned forward and whispered, "Maestro, we *must* begin the *Lohengrin*."

He shook his head as if to clear his mind, then finally raised his baton.

We raised our instruments. I held my bow high off the strings and surveyed the orchestra one last time. All the musicians were poised and ready. Every eye was upon me.

The maestro nodded.

I took a deep, loud breath and lowered my bow while moving my fiddle slightly downward. The maestro followed as he had before. He kept the baton well out of sight of the audience, but he was dreadfully off tempo.

After what seemed an age, the first triplet fired like a gunshot, in perfect ensemble.

We had begun well. The strings took up the theme, followed by the triumphant entrance of the trombones and French horns. Their playing was masterful and insistent, leading the way with a flowing, forceful sound that imparted courage to the rest of us. The strings drove the supporting triplets with feverish intensity—sustaining, coaxing, spurring the brass to even greater heights.

We were underway and safe—for the moment at least. My colleagues were working hard for him, as I knew they would, with a verve that defied the audience to discern our predicament. Even so, failure was still very much a possibility. How we had laughed to hear how the BSO had fallen apart while playing "The Star-Spangled Banner" in Hartford. They'd entered in shambles with that simplest of drinking tunes, because of Koussevitzky's imprecise downbeat. Perhaps now, it was our turn.

The maestro's face was a pale, disconcerting gray as he stared straight ahead, moving his arms without affinity for the music. It was up to me. I indicated the *ritardando* into the *rubato* section. The orchestra followed me to a man, the tempo slowing exactly as I'd wished. There was no doubt I had my colleagues' complete attention. That was the easy part. We were playing very well, and the elegant theme within the woodwinds was like chamber music; it could sustain itself. But how to cue the recapitulation?

My thoughts were consumed by this single question, yet no answer came.

The maestro stared down at me, his forehead furrowed as if he were reading my mind. I sensed he still remembered the challenges of this transition, even if no longer recalling the actual notes that comprised it. I smiled back, struggling to appear calm and reassuring. Then the unthinkable happened. He placed his baton on the stand, stood still, and lowered his hands to his side. It was clear to everyone, musician and audience alike, that he'd stopped conducting.

A great conductor sees himself as first amongst equals, and the immortal gesture of lowering the baton is the ultimate compliment he can pay his orchestra. It declares to the audience that *these musicians are performing so well, they have no need of me.*

The maestro had never done this before. I felt a chill pass through me—the same feeling as so many years before, when I first auditioned for him. We'd experienced so much together: so many tantrums and glorious moments, I knew the gesture was his way of saying what mere words could never convey—his unshakeable faith that we would see him through.

With that affirmation, the orchestra reared and soared, like a mythic winged creature, to new heights of sonority. They followed my direction as if we were one instead of one hundred and ten. I grew bolder and so did they, anticipating when I stretched a note or pushed ahead of the beat. Despite the numbers, our playing was as intimate as that of a string quartet. Through it all, the maestro stood before us awash in sound, arms at his side, impassive except for the tears drenching his shirtfront. I quickly surveyed the orchestra. To a man, my colleagues were also struggling to contain profound emotion.

It was now only a few measures before the dreaded *ritenuto* and recapitulation, and I had still not figured out how to cue the final tempo. The more options I considered, the more insecure I became.

Again the maestro looked down at me. This time, there was no masking my fear—I was about to fail him and my colleagues. In an instant, he picked up his baton and began to conduct, just moments before the troublesome measures arrived.

His direction was solid. I stopped marking time to follow his lead. The others did likewise, and all was as it had been. He was back: probing our spirits, urging us onward, inspiring and uplifting us with his revitalized will.

When it arrived, the *ritenuto* was more considered and elegant than I ever could have conceived. Then he indicated a subtle *caesura*, unanticipated and unrehearsed.

For almost a beat, total silence held sway.

The audience was absolutely still, in rapt attention—no noise, no movement, no coughing—entirely with us. You can always tell when the muse visits them: the key lies in the totality of their silence—even their breathing stops.

Then the maestro gave a mighty upbeat. His baton cut the air like a sword, setting a stunning tempo for the recapitulation—*prestissimo con molto fuoco*. His arms carved the air in broad swaths, like a sorcerer conjuring the fires of hell.

The sonorous basses laid a foundation of bedrock. The strings burned with intensity. The low brass reverberated throughout the hall. We had *never* played like this. Our massive sound grew and grew until it seemed our music would burst through the roof and ignite the very heavens.

I looked to the wings. Luciana stood still, head bowed, eyes lowered, hands clasped. As the celestial sounds swirled around us, there was little doubt as to the answer my dear wife's prayers had received. Our music was transcendent.

The orchestra sounded the final, glorious notes with sonority the likes of which I've never heard before or since. The reverberations gradually diminished to a splendid, inviolable silence. For a few seconds, there was only the incredible hush in the house that attends when something momentous has occurred. All musicians yearn for this moment: the sacred, quiescent instant when each person in the audience reconciles the experience in his soul. It's what we live for.

I smiled at the maestro, feeling profound joy and overwhelming relief. We'd done it!

He smiled back and slowly nodded.

With that, pandemonium erupted. The entire audience stood as one, shouting, clapping, pounding the floor with their feet. Offstage, Luciana held her hands high, applauded wildly, then blew me a kiss. The engineers in the radio booth brandished their fists in the air. The members of the orchestra smiled broadly and stamped their feet in approval. You could feel their ovation resonating through the stage floor. The vibration grew and grew until it seemed as though Carnegie Hall itself might come crashing down.

The maestro placed his baton on the stand and stepped nimbly down from the podium. He gestured for the orchestra to rise with a triumphant sweep of his right arm. In a return of his earlier compliment, we declined to a man.

The audience's bravos grew louder, their fervent applause now fully focused upon him. He turned, bowed to us in acknowledgment, then, slowly and humbly, bowed once more to the hall.

After a moment, he shook my hand as he had so many times before. This time, he clasped it with both of his and held it for a bit longer than usual, as if to savor our final triumph.

I looked into his eyes and saw the veil slowly return.

The audience continued to clamor, "Bravo Maestro! Encore! Bravissimo!"

The emotions in the hall were unlike anything I'd ever experienced. Love, relief, sadness, disbelief, frenzy—all found voice in the vast, surging river of applause. I felt part of something larger than myself—some cosmic validation of all we had accomplished—and at last, I fully understood.

As if recognizing my thoughts, the maestro squeezed my hand, released it, turned, bowed one last time, then shuffled offstage past his adoring musicians. It seemed, from where I sat, he just made it to Luciana's outstretched arms.

We in the orchestra looked at each other in astonishment. I could hardly believe—nor did I think they could possibly comprehend—what had just happened. The maestro had been right: from our supreme moment of fear had come the most profound musical experience of our lives. What's more, the muse had blessed everyone in the hall with her healing presence.

There would be no encore. Despite the extended ovation, the maestro did not return for another bow. Eventually, Snell signaled that I should have the musicians leave the stage. Even after the last man had gone, the bravos and calls for the maestro continued.

Backstage, by contrast, was eerily silent. The musicians huddled in small clusters outside the green room, not daring to speak. I stayed with them, attempting with little success to assuage their anxiety.

After twenty minutes the maestro emerged, supported by Luciana. It was agony to watch his feeble steps. Many of us wept openly.

"Maestro . . . ," I began.

Luciana shook her head, and I stopped. After fourteen years of marriage, I knew far better than to argue. My wife and the stricken old man I hardly recognized passed through a cordon of somber musicians toward the waiting limousine.

It took some time for Luciana to get him seated. At last he raised his hand in farewell, and the long black car slipped silently into the night.

I returned to the stage. It was deathly still, with only the conductor's spot illuminating the podium in a small pale nimbus of light. The maestro's baton still lay on top of the unopened score. I picked it up and broke it in two.

The Age of the Gods had ended.

CONVERGENCE

(A Social Farce in One Senseless Act)

"'Essentials should always be kept close at hand . . .'"

hy do people do things like this? Clarisse Renfrew thought while adding another cup of sauerkraut to her marinade.

A former beauty, only recently showing her eighty-plus years, Clarisse loathed domesticity. Life in New York and Paris had cultivated her flair for the outrageous while fueling an ever-increasing need for adulation. Indentured servitude in her brother's filthy kitchen was certainly not *her* idea of a life. She'd never felt so dreary and unappreciated.

This was the first Palm Beach season her social standing had faltered. She'd once been sought after, but this winter there were noticeably fewer invitations. Though devastated by this unexpected turn of events, Clarisse had not yet fully grasped the reason: these days, her stories were repeated far too frequently to sustain their charm.

She thought fleetingly of the two men coming to see her this evening. It had seemed a ray of sunshine when Grant and Charles had first said they'd drive up to Palm Beach. Last year, and again this season, they'd made time for her during a South Beach vacation. A couple for some sixteen years, they were new friends from Cape Cod who genuinely seemed to appreciate her. She enjoyed them, and they offered a drastic change to her tiresome routine. They took her out and indulged her, allowing her to relive her glory days back in New York, if only for a few precious hours.

As she stared out the window, Clarisse wondered why such an incongruous friendship had become so important. There was a time, not that long ago, it seemed, she wouldn't have bothered. Yet this last lonely year, whenever Clarisse telephoned or wrote, it was to Grant and Charles. She adored recounting past social and artistic triumphs that still made her feel so very much alive. These two men were gracious enough to allow her the latitude for copious reminiscences, and gentlemen enough to appear interested no matter their duration.

From the moment they'd met, Grant had seemed to understand. When she heard him play the piano and realized his talent, she made an extra effort to cultivate him. The effort had paid off. From that night on, it was as if they shared a common vision. Grant and Clarisse might have trained in different art forms, but they recognized the commonalities: the time and effort, the compulsive need to create or perform, and the elusive rewards. They discussed dark moments and joyous ones—or, better said, Clarisse did. Grant seemed content to soak up every word.

Charles sometimes looked bored or petulant, but he was merely part of the package and of little consequence in the grand scheme of things. Her kinship with Grant was what mattered. It resonated in a comfortable place inside—a place much more appealing than the "real" world she struggled to face every morning. Her thoughts often returned to their talks, replaying the discussions, refining points she'd already made, and storing anecdotes for next time.

Out in the backyard, Clarisse's younger brother, Ross, tottered into view. He'd been more off kilter than usual this week, which did not bode well for this evening. And he'd invited yet another strange woman to dine. Not for the first time this day, anger swelled in Clarisse's bosom. Ross was rude, boorish—almost childish, but he had inherited all the property and money from their parents, who had considered her irresponsible. Despite an allowance and a free place to live, Clarisse felt no gratitude toward her brother. He treated her like a servant, always disrupting her work and ruining her friendships. The more her poverty bound her to him, the more she loathed him.

Clarisse was convinced her social cache had plummeted because Ross, who insisted on going everywhere with her these days, had grown so rude and unpredictable that even family members excluded him from invitations. Citing principle, Clarisse would refuse to attend alone. Though time away from Ross would have been a blessing, she dared not offend him. The choice was, simply put, a tradeoff between living in Palm Beach with a boor and living in a room up north during the long cold winter. Clarisse was not about to live in a room, so she tread lightly around her brother and cultivated those who tolerated him. Every Palm Beach friend capable of doing so had been invited to dine this evening. Even so, Clarisse was frightfully nervous.

She'd hoped for a repeat of last year's itinerary: dinner in an elegant restaurant capped by a whirlwind tour of several hotel bars. That night had been magical. She'd been free of her brother, at liberty to order whatever she chose—and, most importantly, seen all around town with two handsome men who doted on her every word. Unfortunately, Grant had written he couldn't spring for dinner this trip. Something about their buying a loft while not having sold their condo. As if four hundred dollars for dinner would have made any difference in the long run.

It wasn't that long ago, or so it seemed, that she'd been escorted, entertained, and accommodated in her every whim. Her beauty, wit, and talent had men competing for her company. Several of them had proposed, but she'd gently turned them down, unwilling to forgo her independence.

She'd always been quite adroit at getting what she wanted. Certain she still had the knack, Clarisse had countered Grant's ultimatum with less expensive daytime activities designed to keep her in the public eye and Ross from underfoot. But Grant had remained uncharacteristically adamant. They would come in the evening, since beach time was important to Charles. Clarisse never learned that, without this concession, they would not have come at all. Reluctantly, she had offered dinner at the house. What else could she do?

Ross insisted she prepare his meal every night. Most nights, he found fault with her cooking, then badgered her into telling him everything that had happened to her that day. Once in possession of the facts, he mocked and criticized until he drank himself into a stupor. Introducing two gay men into that field of battle would be disastrous. Ross would be certain to taunt and belittle them. Concerned with appearances, Clarisse hadn't mustered the courage to explain this to her friends. She'd simply invited the others in hopes they'd distract her brother and dilute his sarcasm. A risky strategy, as Clarisse knew all too well, with only a marginal chance of success.

What other choice do I have? Perhaps Ross will be on his best behavior with this new woman, whoever she is. One can only hope. I've done all I can. It's not my fault we're dining in. That was Grant and Charles' decision. They've made their bed and will have to lie in it.

Clarisse sighed aloud, imagining her friends wending their way toward heaven knew what fate.

Janine Janowicz strode briskly down Worth Avenue, then turned left toward the beach. Everything Janine did was brisk. An aerobics instructor from Wildwood, New Jersey, she was wintering in Palm Beach, ostensibly working on a book—in actuality, hunting for a wealthy husband.

Janine had caught her first break, or so she thought, when she'd met Ross the week before at a bizarre party in an empty mansion. When he told her where he lived, she recognized the upscale neighborhood and accepted his dinner invitation with alacrity. Apparently, his family had built one of the earliest houses on the island.

"Shit!" she muttered, reaching number thirteen. "He didn't say they hadn't done anything to it since. The land must be worth two million, but the house looks like something out of *The Addams Family*! What's that over there on the terrace? A bathtub? Yup, a claw-foot bathtub. And what's that chained to the palm tree? Right by the fountain and those bizarre sculptures! It can't be . . ."

An array of rotted wooden birds in various states of collapse disrupted the otherwise understated streetscape. Transfixed by their decrepitude, Janine assessed her alternatives: a cautious advance or a hasty retreat before being noticed by Ross, who was bent over a recalcitrant weed. At the party, something about him had frightened her, and the unsettled feeling had lingered for days. She'd almost turned back twice this evening, but tried one last time to convince herself he was merely eccentric.

He might provide access to wealthy friends. It seems he's been here forever and knows everyone. I might never get another chance like this.

Even so, Janine stood transfixed just beyond the ramshackle gate.

Beresford Ashton Ryce the Third, or Bart, as he democratically styled himself, had had the good sense to be born into a prominent Brahmin family, attend the "right" schools, and cultivate a genial demeanor that deflected any possible criticism of his privileged existence. By always saying and doing the right thing in a way that never offended and was seldom even noticed, he'd fashioned a comfortable life for himself for much of his forty years.

That was his problem. He did everything so well and was so consistently nondescript that people his age often saw nothing in him at all; though Grande Dames prized him for his unflappable appropriateness—he never upstaged a soul. Recently engaged to be married and thus beyond suspicion of homosexuality, he had a distinct advantage over most other "walkers." Without Bart's realizing it, his gentlemanly attentions sustained the illusion of his companions' desirability, which further upped his social currency in a narrow but socially dominant strata. In short, Bart was something of an item in Palm Beach this season— for women over seventy, that is.

It was widely known around town that he was sleeping on the floor of his grandmother's house until it could be sold, but that was considered a charming eccentricity. There were many jokes about him "roughing it," and numerous invitations to dinner á *deux* designed to "lessen his burden."

His top-shelf existence had just taken an inconceivable turn. His fiancé, Angelica, had broken off their engagement. The actual loss of his bride-to-be was of secondary concern to the perceptions her change of heart would foster. A retreat from the ostentatious display of loving commitment at last summer's high-profile engagement party would certainly cause tongues to wag. Not the best thing to happen at the height of the Palm Beach season when the cream of Society had gathered for winter's festivities.

Angelica had been remarkably indifferent in bed, claiming all sorts of "women's troubles" that seemed, in Bart's opinion, to add up to aversion. He was too well brought up to press the issue but suspected all along he'd been quite a disappointment in that department. She'd decamped to Savannah six weeks ago, supposedly to aid in the search for her mother's dogs. All seven Pekinese were allegedly lost somewhere on the grounds of MossBank, her stepfather's fully restored, fifteen-hundred-acre plantation. Their fate still remained a mystery, at least to Bart. He'd not heard a word from her until her letter arrived this afternoon. It had been simple and to the point. There'd be no wedding. The dogs' fate was not mentioned.

Bart was so deep in thought, he failed to notice Janine standing by the gate until he nearly walked into her. He was not, under the best of circumstances, susceptible to the charms of a well-toned behind—of either persuasion. As a result, Janine's best feature worked none of its usual, if somewhat dwindling, magic. Bart remained consumed by his run of unaccustomed bad luck.

So where does all this put me? In limbo, that's where. Roped into another season of carting geriatric cases about, to say nothing of bizarre evenings with Clarisse and her whacked-out brother. I can't believe those two fags are coming for dinner instead of taking her out. Do they have any idea what they're getting themselves into? Clarisse seems besotted with one of them, but what I don't understand is their interest in her . . . but then, I'm coming to worship at the same altar. God knows why any of us do these things . . .

Odilé Clarke-Schmidt pinned a second rhinestone flamingo to her shawl, then surveyed the sparkling ocean outside her bedroom window. A gilt rococo mirror reflected her albino skin, blonde-white hair, and the rolling contours of her ample hips and bosom. Odilé had developed a unique mode of dress over the years that would have been considered ludicrous if adopted by anyone with less money— "unique" being the most charitable description of a costume that varied in hue, but never in style or composition. Silk, rayon, and velveteen layered over one another in a cascade of texture, much like a sofa draped with several throws. The effect was one of softness bordering on vulnerability, which on a smaller person might have suggested timidity. On Odilé's capacious frame, it suggested a pile of discount prayer rugs. Her pale makeup often received the same reaction as the first glimpse of a poorly embalmed body. As disconcerting as it might be, Odilé's mask was intentional, consistent, and inviolate. From behind it, she projected the bored indifference of the ultra-rich, creating an additional layer of aloofness. Her carefully constructed vulnerability was simply a conceit. She was used to getting her way and would tolerate nothing less.

Odilé scowled at the wedding picture on the Louis Quinze bureau. Her husband Wolfram, resplendent, if slightly dazed, in a white, *Saturday Night Fever* ensemble. She never had understood why he wouldn't wear a tux to the wedding. The thought still plagued her after more than thirty-five years of marriage. She'd had many more worries since then, but always tallied her husband's failures sequentially from the very first infraction, like a rosary. That inappropriate wardrobe was the first bead of many.

From the wedding night on, Wolfie's indiscretions had been forcefully dealt with. These days, he always wore tuxedos—if not tails—to dress events.

Odilé feared he'd embarrass her tonight in front of "those two nice boys." Wolfie was awfully tough on Clarisse, but for some strange reason, she still wanted him to meet them. Odilé thought that rather odd. Usually, Clarisse tried to keep Wolfie as far away from her conquests as she could. Perhaps inviting him tonight was simply a matter of having enough bodies to neutralize Ross's nonsense. But then, Clarisse had also cajoled Odilé into buying the food, so perhaps she felt an obligation to invite Wolfie as well. Odilé didn't waste much time analyzing the situation. Her thoughts quickly turned to the luscious piece of salmon she'd bought at TooJay's.

Imagine being invited to dinner at someone's house and having to buy the food, to say nothing of the wine! Still, it's a night out, and Clarisse is supportive of the benefit, which is coming up fast. If Ross still refuses to wear the gorilla suit, it'll be a big problem. People expect it after all these years. Some even expect his ratty old cat to be perched on his shoulder. A cat on a leash . . . at a charity gala of mine!

Odilé dabbed just a touch more powder on the tip of her nose.

Well, I'll take him on any terms if he'll just wear the goddamn suit. It wasn't my fault it was eighty-five degrees last year and he got dehydrated. Clarisse needs to bring him around. Maybe the salmon will tip the scales. Salmon—scales—ha!

Downstairs in the butler's pantry, Wolfie, the perennial source of Odilé's vexation, grabbed a pack of ginger beer from the fridge. Then he poured a large tumbler of scotch and downed it in a single gulp. His impeccable white linen shirt covered a trim but sagging chest, complementing his pure white mustache and mane of snow-white hair. Anyone else his age would have looked washed out, but his tan was perfection, and he knew it. Self-study occupied most of his free time, except when Odilé's plans intruded, as they had tonight.

Dinner with Clarisse . . . mein Gott! That old cow hasn't said anything new in the last twenty years.

He had to go. He couldn't snub Clarisse; she'd known him in New York. Even after all these years, he couldn't afford to alienate any of his wife's crowd. They might rat him out, and Odilé would not take kindly to tales of his life back then. It had been bad enough trying to shut up Clive Barrows at the Sailfish Club last night. The old soak had one too many and came damn close to including Wolfie in his tales of orgies at the Y. You'd think he'd have forgotten them after forty years. They were good, but not that good.

Wolfie had never been forgiven for sneaking away while Clive and two other friends were hauled downtown in disgrace. Nor had Wolfie's subsequent marriage to Odilé set well in that quarter. Clive had actually called him a hypocrite to his face, and all his gay friends had boycotted the wedding. Aware of what even a single rumor might cost him, Wolfie tread lightly around anyone with a New York connection.

His thoughts derailed by his wife's shrill insistence, Wolfie replied in rapid fire to the three most recent of her all-too-frequent directives.

"Yes, dear, I'll get ze car. Yes, dear, I'm only bringing ginger beer. Yes, dear, zaht's all I'll drink."

Why do I do these things? Wolfie thought, not for the first time, as he hurriedly downed another Scotch.

Back on Flagler Avenue, Janine and Bart met at Clarisse's gate. She'd been adjusting her outfit in the side mirror of a parked Rolls Royce, choosing the driver's side in hope passers-by might think it was hers. The mirror reflected an athletic, wiry torso with perky breasts and a face that mirrored her physique—taut to the point of hardness. The initial onslaught of wrinkles at her throat hinted of her real age, though her body kept the secret in a constricted fashion that betrayed an intense, even slavish dedication to halting the ravages of time. There was no real beauty here, more adroit fabrication and sheer force of will. To a close observer, the steely glint in Janine's eyes revealed she'd stop at nothing to achieve her goals.

It had just dawned on her that no one who could afford a Rolls would ever think of primping in front of it when Bart said hello in a soft, unassuming voice. Caught off guard, Janine replaced her sunglasses, turned, and took inventory. Her smile was only slightly forced, bright enough to mask the calculating effect the mirror had captured, yet still tight enough to fend off an unwanted advance. Bart maintained his state of detached politeness, unaware and unaffected. Belatedly, Janine recognized him from the strange party in an empty mansion they'd both attended the week before. She was still unaware he'd been the host.

"Oh, are you coming to dinner, too?"

"Why, yes," Bart replied, pleased at least one other straight person under seventy would be attending.

He paused, seemingly in search of something else to say as Janine quickly thought, *White shirt? Necktie? He's either old money or a CPA. Worth finding out which, just in case . . . I guess I'll go in.*

Clarisse rose from the porch swing where she'd been awaiting her guests. She'd not associated the primping woman at the end of the walk with the evening's festivities. Bart was a different story. He was a devoted acolyte whose attentions she jealously guarded.

"Welcome! You're the first to arrive!" Clarisse shouted in an overly enthusiastic voice. "Grant and Charles are due any minute. We'll hold the hors d'oeuvre until they get here, but there's champagne here on the porch. Do come up and help yourself."

Well here we go, thought Janine, already resenting the old woman who'd ruined her chance to chat up the nice man in the white shirt.

Eighty-five-year-old Ross was still pulling weeds. At the sound of Clarisse's voice, he stood slowly, then saw Janine.

It's that piece from the other night. What's her name? Jocelyn? Janice? Janine? That's it. Janine! I'll be damned . . . She actually showed.

Ross's invitations were seldom accepted, especially by young women, who seemed to sense his intentions at forty paces. For this, like all other setbacks in a life fraught with rejection, he blamed Clarisse. She'd already meddled with his plans for Janine by insisting he take her to a concert after dinner.

No doubt it's so Clarisse can be alone with those two fags she harps on all the time. The concert would have been alright, except she's arranged for that eunuch, Bart, to tag along. It won't be easy to ditch him. At least the gal's here, which is something. Better look my best. Who knows, I may get lucky.

Ross lurched to the back door. Had he given it more thought he might have realized a shower, shave, and change of clothes could not overcome his death's head appearance nor stabilize his drunken gait. One could count on Ross to never consider such things. He was Don Juan incarnate, if only in his own mind.

The traffic on I-95 was dreadful, turning Grant's mood from expectant to grim.

"What the fuck is wrong with this state? They were working on this same stretch of road last year. Not a goddamn thing has changed!"

Grant had just called Clarisse to say they'd be late and had been dismayed to learn she'd invited Odilé and Wolfie. The visit he'd anticipated for so long was becoming a carnival event.

Grant had met Odilé on his first trip to Palm Beach. Having prattled on about gorillas for most of the evening, she'd not impressed him as a scintillating conversationalist. Grant supported conservation, but not to the same extent as Odilé. Building a three-hundred-acre enclosure in Guatemala for one gorilla was not at the top of his list as long as there were whales to be saved. As for Wolfie, Clarrise had told Grant more than he ever needed to know about his predatory ways.

The night was shaping up to be a colossal bore; not that Grant took a superior view of social obligations. He preferred his "quality time" with Clarisse. It was always best when they talked only to each other. And about the only time in his life he felt truly understood.

He was quite certain it was the same for Clarisse. Even so, she remained a paradox. She would often make discerning artistic judgments, but then display a shallow side that undermined their impact. Palm Beach "Society" dominated most of her correspondence during the winter months. She never painted while in Florida. Only on the Cape. She was talented, supposedly well known, and had lived—to hear her tell it—a rich creative life. Why would she have thrown it all away to winter with a bunch of brain-dead snobs? It just didn't make sense.

Meanwhile, Charles drove stoically onward, silently rehashing last year's visit. It had been quite the night: first the stares at Taboo when he and Grant entered on the arms of the outrageously dressed Odilé and Clarisse. (Weeks later, Charles had been tickled to learn from a TV show that the restaurant was a prime watering hole for gigolos and their wealthy clients.) Then there was the after-dinner tour when Odilé drunkenly parked her brand-new Lincoln on the sidewalk in front one of the finest hotels in town. Later, at the Breakers, Clarisse insisted on showing Grant the circular dining room where she'd celebrated Thanksgiving as a child. Her updo tenuously secured by glittering strands of silver tinsel, she tugged him across the stage in front of a vocalist, backup band, and audience. Finally acknowledging the crowd, she proceeded to dance the shimmy before dragging him into the dining room. Charles relished the crowd's unbridled astonishment almost as much as Grant's discomfort, until, capping off the evening in grand style, Odilé—all three hundred pounds of her—passed out on a banquette in the middle of the ornate lobby. Charles watched helplessly as she slid slowly to the floor. It took three bell-boys to help him get her to her feet.

Given that bizarre expedition, he was gravely concerned about tonight's dinner. He knew how important Clarisse was to Grant. Even so, Charles had insisted on scaling back the time they'd spend for reasons beyond his love of the beach and the constraints of two mortgages. He feared Grant was besotted with an illusion and would inevitably become disenchanted. Ever since that bizarre night at Taboo, Charles had recognized Clarisse's self-deception and anticipated disaster. Grant's disappointments always ran deep. If his artistic bubble burst, he'd have a hard time getting past it. Far better if he came to this realization gradually—and on his own terms.

Mutual friends had informed Charles that Clarisse cooked only one meal. He suspected this worked as a powerful incentive for guests to take her out to eat. Nevertheless, money was tight this trip, and courage was called for. It was a shame. A good dinner would have made a hell of a lot of difference and perhaps softened the blow, which he was fairly certain would come tonight.

No doubt she'll have the same ghastly pork dish she serves in Hyannis Port. Oh well, noblesse oblige . . . I guess.

The two men crossed the causeway, then drove down a palm-flanked boulevard and turned right on Flagler Avenue. They parked in front of an old-style bungalow that must have been captivating when it had an unobstructed view of the ocean. It had been well-sited astride an ample tract of land that allowed it to take advantage of cooling breezes from three points of the compass. The rambling porch still had its original windows with their thin metal cranks and tattered bamboo shades. A small table and chairs in an open area beside the porch overlooked a garish modern mansion that had appropriated every ocean vista. The bungalow's second floor must have once featured spacious water-view bedrooms, but gaudy, clashing curtains in every window betrayed its dissection into tiny rooms.

The appearance of Clarisse's family home was one of an off-the-wall stage set. The same friends who had revealed Clarisse's meager culinary skills had also speculated that Ross ran an illegal rooming house. A torrent of salsa music from a car on the lawn confirmed as much. Three men sat inside, passing a joint. On a coquina-stone terrace, an enormous Easter-Island-like statue competed for space with rusted chaises, overgrown tropical plants, and decayed wood carvings. Water spurted at an alarming rate from a large carved pineapple atop a massive fountain. A feral cat sat astride the pineapple, drinking in greedy gulps. A refrigerator was padlocked to one of several unkempt palm trees. The bathtub that had so flummoxed Janine was topped by a sheet of plywood. Pressed into service as an outdoor bar and littered with a slapdash array of near-empty bottles, it presided over the courtyard, both incongruous and strangely apt.

Grant jumped from the car and gave a wave he immediately considered effeminate and overdone.

"Hi, Clarisse! The traffic was dreadful! Sorry we're late."

His overblown enthusiasm was short lived.

Shit. There's that fellow. What's his name, Bart? That's it. What's he doing here? I thought it was just Odilé and her husband. Bart's sitting exactly where he was when we arrived last year, as if Clarisse just threw a dust sheet over him for the summer. How weird is that?

Grant tried to recall something—anything—about him. Hadn't Ross and Clarisse acquired him on some barrier island in the Carolinas? The woman next to him couldn't possibly be the fiancé they'd met last year. Even if the braces had come off and she'd gone blonde, she couldn't have lost that much weight. Had Bart actually bailed after the lovefest in the Hamptons Clarisse had described in such painstaking detail?

So Odilé, her husband, and now these two . . . There was no point in having driven all the way up here for this circus.

When Grant reached the porch, Clarisse stood, embraced him warmly, and kissed him on the lips. Touched by guilt, he struggled to restore his enthusiasm.

Well, we didn't do the reception at the Breakers with John Silber. And we didn't play croquet at Mar-a-Lago. So whatever this evening is going to be, it's got to be better than the alternatives—please God.

"How nice to meet you, Janine," Grant said when Clarisse made introductions. "You're writing a book? How fascinating . . . Oh, on exercise . . . Isn't that interesting?"

He spoke quickly, trying frantically to shore up his mood, which was deflating rapidly.

What do you call a gay man who cultivates older women, he thought, *a "hag fag?"*

"Bart, nice to see you again. What a coincidence we're all here a year later at precisely the same time . . . Your fiancé is helping her mother find her dogs? How long have they been missing? Six weeks? My, that is determination!"

Didn't Israel wage war for only six days? Charles thought, growing more concerned that Grant was rapidly losing his capacity for small talk. Not a good sign so early in the evening.

"We'll wait for Odilé and Wolfie before we have hors d'ouevre," Clarisse said in a regal tone. "I saw her earlier today, and she told me she'd be a bit late. I'd have expected her by now, though."

Is there any food at all? And, if so, why do we have to wait for other people before we get it? Janine thought.

Just then Ross, dressed from head to toe in dingy white, tumbled through the screen door. He careened into the table, knocking it over and demolishing Janine and Bart's champagne flutes. The guests stared in horror as the wine fizzed out of its bottle and trickled between the slats of the porch floor.

He looks like a character from The Jackie Gleason Show, Grant thought. *If the camera zooms in from the ceiling and everyone starts making patterns on the floor, I'll know this is a dream.*

"Ross, mop up that mess, fix the table, then get more chairs. And get something from your stash to replace what you ruined," Clarisse ordered. "No, not those chairs, the other ones." She turned to her guests. "Shall we sit on the terrace instead?"

Oh great, next to the bathtub and refrigerator, Janine thought. *Watch the owner of the Rolls come out and spot me sitting there with these wackos.*

"No, let's stay here," Grant said, fearful of whatever dark mysteries the terrace might contain. "We can all fit."

Bless you, thought Janine as Ross stumbled across the terrace and unlocked the refrigerator. Grant was stunned to see it was completely filled with unopened bottles of champagne.

"Essentials should always be kept close at hand," Celeste said, as if launching a lecture on household management.

Then she started the social ball rolling, ignoring the gathering crowd of boarders who stared wide-eyed at her guests.

"Janine is writing a book on exercise."

"How interesting," said Bart. "Are you a proponent of juicing?"

Grant squirmed in his astoundingly uncomfortable chair.

What the hell is juicing? It sounds like something prohibited by the NFL.

Janine assumed the role of author much too prematurely for the actual effort expended on her book.

"Oh yes. It's an important part of my regimen."

"Juicing helped Angelica tremendously, didn't it, Bart?" Clarisse said, nailing the topic solidly to the wall before turning to Janine. "Bart helped his fiancé, Angelica, get well through juicing. She was very ill and it solved all sorts of problems for her."

Not all of them, thought Bart, recalling their grim sex life.

Even Clarisse knows what this juicing thing is, thought Grant, not realizing the conversation was repeated every time Bart and Clarisse got together.

"Yes, it was a great help."

Bart's tone was obviously distracted. Even so, Janine feigned interest.

"Do you juice, too, Bart?"

"Not as regularly as I should," he said with a sigh.

"I simply don't have the space to grow the wheat germ," Clarisse said, sounding bereft.

Heaven forbid. You'd have to get rid of the bathtub, thought Janine.

A shrill scrape of rubber against curbstone overpowered the salsa music as a long, shiny Lincoln lurched to a halt.

"Oh here's Odilé and Wolfie, at last!" Clarisse said, shading her eyes with her blue-veined hand. "I wonder what took them so long."

As her guests watched expectantly from the porch, the crowd on the lawn did an about face. Seeming jealous of Odilé's grand entrance, Clarisse hurried inside.

Maybe she's gone to get food and we can finally eat, thought Janine.

It spoke volumes when her aggressive matrimonial agenda was supplanted by such mundane considerations.

The crowd on the lawn gesticulated wildly as Odilé approached the porch. Her slow, rolling gait lent a certain majesty that transcended her garish ensemble as well as the observers' raucous commentary. Odilé seemed indifferent to the uproar. A signature plastic camellia tilted above her left ear, she looked like an elderly Mae West in the wardrobe of an equally ancient Dorothy Lamour.

Mae had a better rinse, Grant thought. *Odilé seems happy to see us. It must indeed be boring in this town. And here is the much-rumored husband . . .*

"Mmm . . . vhat have ve here? Delighted to meet you, deeelighted," murmured Wolfie as he held out his hand and stared seductively into Grant's eyes.

Charles and Grant shared a startled glance.

Reluctantly, Grant shook Wolfie's hand. He'd thought Clarisse's tales of predatory manners had been exaggerated, but the man in front of him was a bizarre meld of the features of Ricardo Montalbán with the voice of Leon Askin. What's more, with his suggestive gaze and arch smile, Wolfie seemed more than ready to head for the bushes.

Charles struggled to suppress a grin.

This is going to be one hell of a night, he thought.

Clarisse returned from the kitchen with a large platter.

"Look at the lovely salmon Odilé contributed!"

There is a God, thought Janine.

Once introductions were complete, talk turned at lightning speed to the black community and reparations for slavery. Wolfie and Ross, appropriately seated to everyone's right, front-loaded the topic for an eternity and then grilled Charles, a historian and liberal Democrat, on his views.

Charles tried to make the case that one of the many significant differences between sweatshops and slavery was that people were less likely to be hunted down and killed for leaving a sweatshop. His argument went nowhere. It merely provoked inaner statements of ever more questionable taste. Mortified, Grant sought refuge in the dingy kitchen, knowing there'd be hell to pay on the ride home.

"Tell everyone to come to the table, and to bring their glasses," Clarisse yelled just as he walked through the door.

"Can I help with anything?"

"Yes. You can bring these in."

Clarisse handed him two plates piled high with a gray, rubbery substance.

Oh great, sauerkraut. As if the old kraut on the porch isn't enough.

"Come to dinner, folks. And bring your drinks," Grant yelled.

You'll need them.

He speculated that, save Janine, Charles, and himself, the social parody playing out on the porch occurred with astounding frequency during the so-called season.

What brought them together? Loneliness? Boredom? Clarisse's strength of will?

"Let me help, too," said Janine, who had suddenly appeared, looking flushed.

Grant guessed correctly that the conversation had deteriorated even further since he'd retreated from the porch. What was old ground for Wolfie, Ross, and the passive Bart had proved too crass—even for Janine's aggressive matrimonial agenda. This said a lot. She had four weeks of expenses left before her "sabbatical" would be over. There'd be no funds left to support another bout of fortune hunting. The book would remain unwritten, and her forty-fifth birthday would be all too close at hand.

"I've never been in here . . . iz a wonder zis place iz still standing," said Wolfie as he finally sashayed into the dining room where the rest of the party stood waiting in awkward silence. The carved cherubs atop the wicker dining chairs were disfigured by oily blackness, with missing limbs and tortured gouges in their pudgy torsos. One particularly malevolent one-eyed cherub seemed to leer at Grant.

"Now that everyone's here, are we going to say grace?" demanded Ross.

"Just a minute. Let everyone sit down first," said Clarisse, her voice heavy with loathing.

Everyone scuttled to his or her seat.

"Dear Lord, we thank you for this food and company here tonight, and we sincerely hope no one at the table has herpes."

"Ross!" shrieked Clarisse, "I'll have none of this at my table—you are at dinner, for Christ's sake!"

Wolfie, who had begun to eat during the prayer, spoke with a mouthful of food. "She's dried out ze pork. I knew she'd fugidup."

My God, he sounds just like Arnold Schwarzenegger, thought Grant.

Janine pondered the guests around the table, her face pink with mortification.

This is Palm Beach Society? There are better manners in Asbury Park.

"There's plenty," announced Clarisse, with feigned enthusiasm. "Eat up!"

Janine surveyed Clarisse's empty plate, then said, "You don't seem to be eating at all."

"It's because she dried out ze pork too much," mumbled Wolfie.

"I can't eat after all this," replied Clarisse. "I'm just going to drink this lovely wine that Odilé brought. It's simply scrumptious, and I get so tired of champagne."

That's a bit much even for you Clarisse, isn't it? thought Grant as he surveyed several of Clarisse's masterful paintings hanging in the room. Almost against his will, his gaze left them and returned to Odilé's unnerving gorilla "portrait," which his hostess had brought to his attention on their way out of the kitchen.

This dubious work had been strategically placed on a jog in the dining room wall that blocked it from the view of most seats, save Grant's. Clarisse had apparently found it politic to display the painting, despite its shallow, almost childlike rendering. The gorilla towered over its jungle surroundings much like King Kong, its paws raised as if it were playing volleyball. Perspective was clearly not Odilé's strong suit.

Clarisse announced a new topic with a flourish and a soupçon of insistence that attention be paid.

"Bart had the loveliest party at his grandmother's house. It costs sixteen thousand a month in maintenance and sits there empty, so he had the *marvelou*s idea of throwing a party to get some use out of it."

"Well, she *is* dead, after all. There's no pressing need for furniture."

Per usual, the petulance in Bart's voice went unnoticed by his fellow guests.

"I must say, Bart, the caretakers don't do much for the money," said Clarisse, leaning coquettishly toward him. "I leave messages for you, and they just hand them to you whenever they feel like it. But the party was lovely."

Now comfortably ensconced as the lady of the manor, she turned her focus to Grant.

"Bart called me for lamps and things, but I wasn't available to provide them, I was getting ready and didn't hear the phone. But you had more than sixty people, didn't you, Bart?"

Bart rubbed his forehead as if a migraine were in the offing. "Yes, and the Swedish princesses. It was quite the crowd."

I guess he's not a CPA, thought Janine, smiling graciously across the table at the red-faced Bart. He's a little nerdy, but sixteen thousand a month—that's a lot of wheat germ.

"Bart and I have been playing croquet at Mar-a-Lago. It's very amusing. Trump owns the place, you know," said Clarisse. "Croquet is a socially acceptable way to vent your frustrations and be evil."

God, Bart really is as boring as he looks, thought Grant.

"Is zere more bread?" interrupted Wolfie. "I have to eat zomzing."

The conversation was strained, privileged, and so stilted one would have thought they were seated at Mar-a-Largo instead of in a dilapidated boarding house surrounded by old cars, moldering statues, and discarded bathroom fixtures. Parties and fundraisers were discussed. The merits of the neighboring communities were debated and found wanting. Finally, it was time for Bart, Janine, and Ross to leave for the concert.

Their impending departure offered Grant one last ray of hope. On other occasions, in the sated afterglow of a good meal, Clarisse had warmed to a discussion of creativity and the rigor of perfecting one's craft. She'd readily described stellar moments in '50s-and-'60s New York, spinning an enticing tale of creativity and artistry. Grant had enjoyed hearing stories of alleged friends who were now icons: Dylan Thomas, Dizzy Gillespie, Leonard Bernstein, Andy Warhol, Miles Davis, and Norman Mailer were all described with wit, warmth, and the ease of timeworn repetition.

Clarisse claimed to have been with Norman in Provincetown when, in a drunken stupor, he'd mistaken a police car for a cab, clambered into the back seat, and instructed the officer to drive him home. She'd also supposedly introduced Dizzy to the glories of the Metropolitan Museum on a languid Sunday afternoon, and declined an offer by Andy to paint her portrait.

Beyond her stories, Grant saw in Clarisse's work the expression of an observant creative spirit. Her painting of a seagull hung over the fireplace in the living room. Vivid against a pale blue background, the gull seemed to soar on an updraft, sunlight illuminating its white feathers, its dark eyes vibrant with intent. The bird's taut energy and focused gaze commanded the room, adding panache to otherwise shabby surroundings.

The combination of talent, experience, and humor Clarisse often displayed had given Grant a lot to think about. He'd considered her a role model until this evening had revealed how dependent and constrained her once-glamorous life had become. He pondered the impact on her talent and spirit.

What would the future hold for her? Did she even have a future?

Grant flinched when a shriek from Clarisse interrupted his thoughts.

"Ross, don't you have a cravat or something?"

"Just a minute, I'll get one," Ross replied, seeming satisfied at having achieved the group's attention.

All stood waiting by their chairs as he lumbered from the room. There was something genuinely unlikable about the man. His childishness, combined with his prejudices and overbearing personality, cast a tangible pall. Time had stood still in anticipation of his departure; now the delay caused by this new development was nearly intolerable.

At long last, Ross completed a complex operation on a grimy piece of fabric.

"OK, I have a cravat. You finally satisfied, Clarisse? If so, it's hi-ho, off we go."

Ross shrugged Bart aside in order to claim Janine's arm. Bart fell complacently behind the couple while she stood as though facing the guillotine; her steely confidence replaced by grim resignation. When Charles shot her a sad smile, Janine shrugged helplessly.

"Let's go on the porch where it's cool, now they've gone," said Clarisse with a feeble attempt at enthusiasm.

Her words fell flat. Ross's pall had not yet vacated the house. The group slowly found their way to the cluttered porch in grim silence.

"Odilé, why not sit over there," Clarisse instructed. "Will that chair be comfortable enough for you, my dear?"

"Yes, it's fine," said Odilé, as she slid cautiously into an amazingly low sling-back chair, not sounding a bit as though she meant it.

She looks like a beached whale, stretched out on her back like that, Grant thought

The remaining guests took their seats. Odilé remained sprawled at some distance while Grant and Clarisse sat at right angles to each other. Charles sat beside Grant. Wolfie had chosen to sit legs apart on a rattan sofa strategically across from him. The location had the added strategic benefit of being out of Odilé's field of vision.

Grant turned to ask Clarisse a question, but was interrupted by Wolfie's demand for an after-dinner drink.

"I'm sorry, I have nothing to offer you of that nature," said Clarisse, with a touch of chagrin. "I'd be delighted to offer it had I anything in the house."

"Forget it," Wolfie said, smirking, then winking at Grant as if they were comrades in deprivation.

Clarisse launched into a meandering anecdote about Clive Barrows, whose "walker" had left him high and dry.

He'd spent the last fifteen winters in a guest cottage on the woman's estate, renting his house from November to May to supplement his meagre retirement income. Now, much to Clarisse's amusement, he was homeless. Speculation about the woman's health, mental state, and heirs followed in rapid order. Several candidates for Clive's services were proposed, ranked, and dismissed in a tortured solo performance. The topic, while going nowhere, seemed inexhaustible. No one else said a word for several minutes until Wolfie, scowling, finally interrupted.

"So vhere are you guyz staying tonight?"

"We're heading back to South Beach," replied Grant.

"Oh, no! Zhat iz too much!" said Wolfie, showing the most animation of the evening. "You must stay viz us. Is too much to travel so far so late at night. I have some very old brandy and some movies I *know* you vould like."

As Wolfie leered at the stricken Grant, Charles clenched his fists and spoke through gritted teeth. "Thank you so much. It is so kind of you. But we do have to get back. It really isn't so bad a drive. We're used to driving back and forth from Boston to the Cape."

"I've got a couple of friends I can invite over to join us. You'd really *enjoy* zem."

"Thank you. No."

When Grant did not even trouble to disguise his loathing, Clarisse bristled.

How dare Wolfie hit on my friends, in my home, and in front of his wife! He's the absolute limit.

It was a decided breach of manners to proposition Grant in front of his partner, never mind in her own home. Something must be done. What would the "boys" (ages forty-eight and fifty-three, respectively) think of her if she let Wolfie's rudeness stand unchallenged?

Clarisse recalled all of Wolfie's snide comments over the decades. She'd stored them away like tinder, never having dared to jeopardize her friendship with Odilé by confronting him. With this appalling affront to her hospitality and the copious amount of alcohol she'd consumed during dinner, the tinder caught flame. She stared pointedly at Grant, then at Charles, before turning her attention to the unsuspecting Wolfie.

"I don't know if I've ever mentioned this . . . I knew of you in New York, Wolfie. Before we met here. I worked for Amalgos at his gallery, and Clive was his partner back then, as you well know. They both knew you. Quite well, it appears."

"Oh, don't talk about zose days, no one vants to hear such ancient history," Wolfie replied, his body tensing. "By ze vay, I've been meaning to say how vonderful the dinner turned out."

Wolfie was stymied by this sudden turn. If the rules had somehow changed, he must make amends, and fast. What had brought this on?

"I was talking with Clive just the other day," said Clarisse.

"Oh, you never can trust vhat he says," interrupted Wolfie. "He and his fancy curtains and Limoges . . . You know all zose boys around him? Zey steal from him left and right."

Clarisse glanced around the room for a moment, then seemed to come to some sort of decision.

"Yes, I am fully aware of that. It's old news. Even in New York, those sorts of things happened. I met him in Europe and then his other two friends back in the city; all independent of each other, but there was one thing they all had in common . . . you." She paused dramatically, seeming to gauge the impact of her words. "It appears you all had a narrow escape in New York, Wolfie. I was fascinated when Clive told me all about it. Honestly . . . in public like that? You could have gone to jail if you'd been caught. I'd love to know Odilé's opinion of that little episode . . ."

Clarisse stared at Odilé, waiting for her response. There was none, save fitful snoring. Charles studied her reclining figure. He wasn't entirely convinced anyone could fall asleep in such an uncomfortable position. Her flabby hips poured over both sides of the chair, her knees splayed in a way that could not possibly be comfortable and was nearly indecent.

She looks like a tanker run aground. How is it she hasn't fallen out of that chair? Why are there leather chairs on a porch anyways? They're all cracked and rotted from the sun. Is this a Southern thing?

Clarisse sat coiled on the edge of her seat like a cobra ready to strike—her eyes two fiery specks. Salmon or no salmon, she'd had enough.

Wolfie's tan features paled as he wondered what had set Clarisse off. Surely not some dried-out pork?

Clarisse took a deep breath and slowly stood to rouse Odilé. The porch was eerily silent. Even the salsa music had finally stopped.

"Is she asleep?" hissed Wolfie, unable to see where Odilé lay stretched out like a mountain range.

Charles nodded slowly. Wolfie stood up abruptly and cut in front of Clarisse, nearly knocking her over.

"Odilé, dahling, vake up, you must be tired, my dear. You fell azleep."

"Oh, it's just the wine," Odilé said in a leaden voice.

"Ve should be going, my sveet. It's late.

"Thank you again, my dear Clarisse, for ze lovely evening and ze fabulous dinner. Nice to meet you guys. Perhaps ve will visit you on the Cape this summer."

Great, thought Grant, *that would impact tourism for years. Run while you can, Wolfie . . . Clarisse is winding up for another pitch.*

As the Lincoln sped off into the night, Clarisse turned to her two remaining guests.

"Well, now it's just the three of us . . . Alone at last."

She felt a sudden letdown. The situation was distressing, yet she couldn't muster the strength to repair it. She was too tired to sustain her anger. Instead, she began to prattle.

"Wolfie gets nervous around me because I know all he got up to in New York. He met Odilé through her mother, who was a renowned beauty. Odilé is fragile. Despite all her money, she needs someone to protect her from the world, but she could have done better than that fraud. In any case, I thought it would be amusing for you to meet him."

Amusing as dental surgery without anesthetic, thought Grant.

"It's a shame you didn't hear Silber speak this afternoon," said Clarisse, her voice flat and distant.

Why did we need to? We had Herr Goebbels spouting propaganda at the table all evening, thought Charles.

"Which makes me think of this book I read about the Cultural Revolution in China and how it impacted education for a generation."

God no, not the education speech again, thought Charles and Grant as one.

"The point is," said Clarisse.

There hasn't been a point to the entire evening, dear, but why not give it one last try before we abandon this looney bin, thought Charles, while continuing to smile at his beleaguered hostess.

His hopes for the evening in ashes, Grant stared down at the floor, then slowly raised his right hand to his forehead. A maudlin, wine-abetted recognition emerged as he saw the real Clarisse for the very first time. He felt the aching loneliness that haunted her days and sensed the toll taken by Ross's constant sarcasm. Grant understood everything save the devastating impact of the decision not to take her out to dinner. Lowering his hand, he mustered a smile, turned to her, and found his mind a total blank.

For her part, Clarisse had been so long without genuine affection she could no longer conceive of friendship without exploitation or social advantage. It never occurred to her to share her circumstances. She merely soldiered on as best she could.

As she brought forth one well-worn phrase after another, Clarisse thought back to other nights rife with witty conversation that had effortlessly sustained itself until dawn. The gifted artists and musicians; the legions of talented men who adored her and catered to her every wish; where were they now? All dead and gone. And was she any better off? She might have lived longer, but was this living? Squawking like a parrot in some forced monolog no one wanted to hear? How had things ever come to this?

This evening, the person she'd tried so hard to be— the one Grant so greatly admired—had proved to be little more than a moth-eaten costume, unsustainable and forever relegated to memory by harsh, unyielding reality. There was no other life than the horrible one she now inhabited. Why bother to pretend there was?

She pondered her narrow escape.

Thank God Odilé was asleep. Wolfie won't dare say a word, so everything will be alright. I'll call her tomorrow and promise to make Ross do the benefit with the cat and the gorilla suit. At least he wasn't here for this fiasco. I won't have to relive that altercation with Wolfie over and over again the way I would have had Ross been here to witness it.

Clarisse studied Grant with sadness. His disappointment was evident in his pursed lips and lifeless eyes. He was disillusioned with her and—much, much worse—bored. A bitter ache took root as Clarisse confronted the inevitable and lost the thread of her story.

"Much as it grieves me, I know you must get back," she said, bringing her jumbled soliloquy to a close.

She rubbed her face with her hands, then passed her fingers through her hair.

"Yes, I'm afraid so," said Grant with barely disguised relief. "Thank you for a lovely evening . . ."

Charles approached Clarisse tentatively, as if expecting her to have more to say. She tilted her head to one side in anticipation of his kiss. Grant followed suit, and she responded in the same mechanical fashion. Then she forced her mouth into a thin smile as the men stood waiting expectantly. When she made no effort to rise, they showed themselves out.

And so, independently, yet concurrently, an impasse was reached. Grant and Clarisse's friendship would never be the same. Both parties realized it and neither made the slightest effort to salvage what they had once so deeply cherished.

Within minutes, the rental car was off the island.

"Why do people do things like this?" asked Grant.

Charles kept his own counsel and drove on through the night. He found little satisfaction in having predicted this debacle. Friendships built on false expectations were inevitably doomed. How could one this incongruous have possibly turned out any other way?

Back at the house, Clarisse sat on the darkened porch savoring the cool ocean breeze. The full moon illuminated a wizened old man in white staggering up the front walk. Ross was returning home alone. The concert could barely have reached intermission. Apparently, his date had gone awry.

No surprise there, she thought.

As her brother struck out blindly at a low-hanging branch, Clarisse stepped quickly into the shadows. She dared not risk his wrath by showing herself. She couldn't bear it after all that had just happened. Fortunately, she need only wait on the darkened porch for an hour or so. Ross would soon drink himself into a stupor, providing a short respite before morning, when the interrogation would begin. Every detail of the evening would be analyzed, critiqued, and derided for days to come.

How would she handle the altercation with Wolfie? Best to say nothing and remain as vague as possible. She depended on Odilé far too much to tell Ross a single word. He'd certainly file it away and make use of it at the first embarrassing opportunity. Besides, Clarisse could no longer recall exactly what it was that Wolfie had done to provoke her.

She shuddered at the thought of tomorrow's inquisition. How long could her life go on like this? At eighty-seven and in robust health, she could reasonably expect to live another ten years. Could she continue to bear life under these conditions? Did she have any choice? Ross was younger, in excellent shape, and apt to live at least as long as she did. He wouldn't leave her a cent. That die had already been cast. And, if his recent behavior were any indication, he would become more difficult and even less likely to see reason as the months and years wore on.

Whatever should I do?

She couldn't bear to think.

Clarisse stared longingly at the full moon. Once, she'd have raced for her palette to capture its burnished-gold perfection. As a single tear trickled slowly down her face, she lay down on the leather chair and pulled a dew-laden blanket to her breast.

THE
HONOREE

"Good old Mayor Moron. How many times have I sat on this very stage and listened as he spouted the same silly platitudes."

The day has finally come, thought Wanda Atkinson, dean of the prestigious Briarwood School, *after all these years . . . Let the play begin. Act one, scene one. Curtain up.*

As was often the case, a small group of young boys lay in wait outside her private suite. Stepping into the gilded hallway, she engaged them with a bright smile.

"Jimmy, Louis, *and* Bobby. Aren't you supposed to be at my farewell assembly? It's about to start."

"Well, Dean Wanda," young Louis began, "we sorta dep . . . dep . . ."

"Deputized," coaxed Bobby.

"Yeah, we deputized us."

"Ourselves," the dean corrected. "You deputized yourselves to do what?"

"To ask you to stay," replied Jimmy. "Briarwood won't be the same without you."

"How sweet," Dean Wanda said, making sure they held the rail as they walked down the imposing marble staircase. "But I've given this a lot of thought. Old folks should step aside, so younger folks have a chance to move up in the world. What do you think things would be like for you if they didn't? Don't forget, your teachers will still be here, and Dr. Pickens is staying on, too."

"He's no fun. He's boring," the group sang out as one.

"Now, now," the dean said, silently agreeing with them. "You really shouldn't speak that way about Dr. Pickens."

She was touched by the boys' concern.

I guess, despite it all, I've accomplished something in the past twenty years. It's not been easy. Sort of like navigating a ship through uncharted waters, always watching for the next sign of danger, hoping there's enough time to chart a safer course. Life certainly is strange. I never expected to be running a school, and if someone said I'd have mixed emotions when the time came to leave, I'd have laughed them out of the room. That said, I've gotten more joy out of working with these young boys than I ever anticipated. If only they didn't grow up to be teenagers.

"Well, it's true," Louis said, seeming reluctant to relinquish the topic. "You get it. He doesn't. He's an old stuff shirt."

"Stuffed, not stuff," Dean Wanda said, having come to the same conclusion herself on numerous occasions. "Boys, I *have* considered it, and I'm certain to miss you three most of all, but my mind is made up. I can't keep everyone waiting. Let's go to the assembly. You can be my official escorts."

Once seated on stage, the dean studied the crowd with smug satisfaction. There were only a couple of empty chairs. Given recent developments, she'd been a trifle concerned.

Mayor Laurence Moran, emcee for the festivities, strode to the podium. The sight of his outlandish mustache and portly form produced the kind of rustling from the audience that anticipates a lengthy monolog. From her place of honor, the dean empathized. Smiling graciously at the crowd, she recalled her pet name for him.

Good old Mayor Moron. How many times have I sat on this very stage and listened as he spouted the same silly platitudes. Speaking of a "stuff shirt," that man could bore the birds from the trees. If I didn't need him where he is, I'd run for his office just to put an end to his pontificating.

She did need him. Yesterday's board meeting had made that all too clear. Only his political machinations had prevented the demise of her refinancing plan. Mortgaging the school and grounds to raise much-needed capital was to be her swan song. Despite her compelling case for the state-of-the-art sports center and library, a new board member's aversion to risk had threatened to undermine all she'd worked so hard to accomplish.

Of course there's risk. Life is full of risk. My original board knew that all too well. For decades, they've left things alone—as well they should—and never once been disappointed. That foolish court order and all the hype surrounding it must have something do with this new fellow's reluctance. I'll bet he's been following the story for months—like everyone else in town, whether they'll admit it or not.

Death had recently claimed a board member and the newly installed replacement had introduced a tiresome level of additional scrutiny at just the wrong time. The dean had gotten nowhere with him during the meeting. What's more, some of the other board members had suddenly developed cold feet. Things were at an impasse until the mayor called a special session for Thursday to revisit the proposal after further study. Yes, the old windbag had bought her the time she needed to twist a few arms and get things back on track. The dean would be sure to look enchanted with every inanity Mayor Moron uttered today.

She surveyed the crowd a second time, then returned her gaze to those on the platform. The board member in question, Dr. William Langley, sat placidly at the far end of the row. He was a recent transplant from New York City, one of an influx of retirees making Crossroads their home as baby boomers reached their "golden years." Dean Wanda felt, yet again, a twinge of frustration with this demographic shift. Until quite recently, Crossroads had been a static Maine community: a few summer residents in the big houses on the coast, a cluster of homes in the village center, many used only on weekends, and good, solid farming folk on the outskirts who left well enough alone. When she'd founded the school, the dean had culled anyone lacking a year-round commitment from her inaugural board. This mandate had held sway for two decades.

It was the right thing to do then, and it still is. What's the point of having a board that's only around in the summer when school's not in session?

The auditorium door opened to admit two late-comers. The first to enter, Marguerite Maidstone, stared at Dean Wanda with obvious loathing and received an equally dark look in return. The audience reacted to the exchange with muted whispers and expressions of surprise.

The dean struggled to maintain her composure. Last she had known, Marguerite was vacationing at her villa in Greece. It was inconceivable she'd come all this way without some new trick up her sleeve.

And who is that young man in black that came in with her? He looks familiar, but I can't place him. No doubt they're in cahoots.

As her nemesis leaned against the wall and smiled her odd, tight smile, the dean's thoughts wandered back to their first confrontation, at the reading of old Luthera Maidstone's will. Even though Marguerite had inherited the bulk of her grandmother's estate, she was furious when Briarwood, an elaborate gilded-age demesne, was left to Nurse Wanda, as the dean was known back then.

"You took advantage of my grandmother. There had to be something wrong with her. She would never have signed this in her right mind," Marguerite had screamed when the bequest was read.

Even when Garrison Walker, the family attorney, stated under oath he was satisfied with Luthera's mental state, Marguerite would not back down. She'd refused to vacate what was now Dean Wanda's house until Garrison convinced her to consider the adverse publicity if she were forcibly removed. The dean recalled the ugly scene as if it had happened yesterday.

It all started then—all these years of persecution and discord. I've tried everything to appease Marguerite, even offering to sell her Briarwood before I founded the school. The amount she offered was an insult to my intelligence. She was a young woman then, in Birkenstocks and peasant skirts. Now she's a middle-aged matron, tufted and meticulously made up and, if possible, even more obnoxious. Far be it from me to show prejudice, but since she's taken up with that women's studies professor from Smith, Marguerite has gotten much worse. She'll never give up until she's driven me out of the place. That's all everyone's been thinking about from the moment she walked in.

When Luthera Maidstone, doyenne of the fabulously wealthy Maidstone family, had died from a fall, rumors had overrun the town: Nurse Wanda had pushed the old woman down the stairs; Nurse Wanda was having an affair with Garrison Walker; the Maidstone estate was sitting on oil deposits, and Nurse Wanda was the daughter of the engineer who had discovered them . . . Such speculation would have been laughable, if it hadn't created such awkwardness at the very time Wanda was yearning for friends by her side. She'd waited things out, though, and stayed on, doing good deeds, bringing people around one by one. In short, she'd held her own.

The next clash occurred when Marguerite, claiming her grandmother's will had been forged, sued to block the sale of the estate. In response, Dean Wanda announced plans to convert the property to a nonprofit corporation. With Briarwood under the aegis of a hastily assembled board of directors, Marguerite's lawyers lost momentum, and a significant amount of moral ground, just as the case went to trial. After weeks of testimony by scores of handwriting experts, the suit was dismissed. When it became known that Dean Wanda would get nothing but a modest salary out of her inheritance, talk died down. It always did in time, as if the good people of Crossroads, lacking a collective attention span, were all too willing to move on to the next scandal.

Undeterred, Marguerite threw even more money at her lawyers, who huddled and strategized like an invading army, laying siege and accruing thousands of billable hours as the dean went about the day-to-day routines of the fledgling school. Every few months saw another appeal in what eventually became the longest-running, costliest litigation in the history of Hancock County.

The attacks escalated in venom over the years. Marguerite's most egregious sally had been the exhumation order filed less than a year ago. Despite Garrison's testimony about Nurse Wanda's great affection for Luthera, and months of legal wrangling, the Supreme Judicial Court had finally sanctioned a disinterment. Marguerite and her lawyers were thought to have orchestrated this costly exercise solely for the humiliation it would bring. The family mausoleum was on the grounds of the estate, so every student at the school—and their parents—soon knew why the police had cordoned off the opulent gardens just when the roses were at their peak.

As she sat attentively listening to the mayor's speech, the dean still struggled to mask her annoyance.

Such a selfish child, despite her hundreds of inherited millions. I worked so hard to provide proper care for Luthera. You'd think Marguerite wouldn't begrudge me some sort of reward, given she was nowhere to be found when she was needed most. Imagine having your grandmother dug up and cut into bits just to get your own way. It's a disgrace to the memory of a fine lady. I still can't get over it.

Jason Pomeroy strode to the podium. As he stumbled through the usual platitudes, his brow damp, his nasal, down-east accent ensuring the letter *r* never crossed state lines, the dean smiled with genuine regard.

Getting Larry Moran to push through a zoning variance, and selling Jason that marshy acreage by the ocean, had been a masterstroke, sealing her credibility with the locals and generating enough cash to build the dormitories out past the gatehouse. When word got out about these luxury accommodations, students had come rolling in. For the last fifteen years, wealthy New Yorkers had sent their sons to Briarwood knowing they'd get what they needed to graduate in an atmosphere of sympathetic encouragement. Not for the first time, the dean congratulated herself on choosing Jason to build the dorms. It had further bound him—and the town—to her cause.

That's the best way to get things done. Find a couple of hungry mutts and toss them a bone. They'll hang around waiting for another scrap and protect the house for free.

As Jason left the stage, she blew him a kiss. Much to the audience's amusement, Rob Johansen feigned jealousy as he made his way to the microphone. Rob's revenue projections were the cornerstone of the refinancing proposal. His wizardry had impressed finance committee and auditors alike. Dean Wanda had discovered him years ago, and he'd been worth every penny. An audit had not been a concern for years. Rob's speech was witty, short, and charming. He knew how to finesse every situation. The dean blew him a kiss as well, to chuckles and a smattering of applause.

All too soon, Mayor Moron returned to the microphone.

"A paragon of inspiration," he bellowed, now well warmed to his task, if not half baked, "Dean Atkinson is beloved by this community. It's no understatement to say she has joined the pantheon of local saints."

An acerbic laugh sounded from the rear of the hall. The dean, expert in the rascality of unruly boys, sought its source until Steve Cafferty's eyes met hers with a defiant glare. His behavior was appalling, but she might well have expected it. Despite her promises to settle his account as soon as the refinancing was in place, Cafferty, an electrician, had continued to threaten a lien for nonpayment. The dean had withheld payments several times before but had always caught up in the end. This time, he'd sought out fellow contractors for a class action lawsuit.

It's a proven business practice to delay disbursements when a nonprofit faces a financial challenge. What other options are there? Close things down and toss out the students and faculty? As a businessman, he of all people should understand my situation. Marguerite must have gotten to him. Fortunately, Garrison says we've got enough on Cafferty's youngest son to make the case dry up like rain in a desert.

It had been a smart move to keep Garrison on retainer all these years. His fees were high, but not unreasonable, given all he had done to support Dean Wanda's efforts. He was a trusted ally, so in tune with her she seldom had to spell out her intent before he knew just what action to take. In this case, he already had everything he needed to show Cafferty the error of his ways.

I'm so glad I hushed things up when the boy left the scene of that hit-and-run. At the time, I saw no need to tarnish the reputation of a local student who'd gotten in with the wrong crowd. Besides, keeping a little something in reserve is often useful—as this case proves yet again. Garrison understands that, all too well. Cafferty's campaign will fizzle when he learns certain school records might just find their way to the press.

At the thought of the press, the dean stifled a laugh. She'd first known Theresa Longacre when she was just plain Theresa Harrington, housekeeper of the Longacre estate out on Four Mile Point. Helping her discreetly when she got in the family way had certainly been a smart move. It had saved Theresa's engagement to old man Longacre— paralyzed from the waist down by a stroke—and insured Dean Wanda excellent coverage once Theresa inherited his newspaper. Not one negative word about Briarwood had appeared in the paper since the old man's mysterious death. One look confirmed Theresa's undying gratitude; she beamed at the dean from her seat with the board.

Folks in town openly joked that Dean Wanda got more press in the *Crossroads Observer* than the president. She certainly could get her story out whenever she wanted. The same could not be said of the *County Link,* a web-based news service recently launched in Hancock County. Steve Cafferty had used the website to round up other unpaid vendors, but that was the least of it. A series of articles and interviews about Marguerite's most recent shenanigan—a court-ordered DNA sample—had been a much greater concern. That story had not died down like the others, and rumor had it Marguerite was funding its longevity. She seemed to take sadistic pleasure in using her money to hunt down Dean Wanda as hounds might chase a fox.

The dean studied Dr. Langley again, certain that with a few words in private, she could get him to discount the rantings of some Internet-based rumor mill. Until the most recent story in *The Link*, she'd remained stoically silent on the subject of Luthera's death, demonstrating character as well as respect for the deceased. Agreeing to an interview with those muckrakers two months ago had been her only public response to any of Marguerite's accusations. Dean Wanda realized she either had to share her side of things or be prepared to put up with an endless stream of negative commentary. In the interview, she'd explained that she and Garrison had contested the order solely to draw the court's attention to decades of harassment. All she asked was to be left alone to complete her life's work.

Most of the community, with the apparent exception of Dr. Langley, had received the dean's comments favorably. Even so, the dean had lost her case on appeal, though two of the judges spoke sharply about a visible pattern of harassment and strongly advised Marguerite to desist. Convinced the order was another calculated annoyance, the dean had grudgingly submitted the sample. Once again, nothing had come of it.

Dr. Pickens, chair of the faculty senate, rose to speak.

"Happy teachers make for happy students," he said, opening his tribute with the dean's best-known quote.

This brought back memories of the school's first year, when the dean had taught that inaugural class all by herself. Now there were thirty teachers, the newest having come on board six years ago. She'd always done everything in her power to recruit the right faculty. More importantly, when they came, she made sure they stayed. "Happy teachers don't move their retirement funds," was a far more accurate sentiment.

"Dean Wanda's integrity, passion for education, and unwavering commitment to this community are known to one and all," Dr. Pickens intoned, "but on this auspicious occasion, I feel compelled to elucidate a few of her many accomplishments since founding the Briarwood School more than twenty years ago . . ."

As her colleague droned on, the dean recalled walking the footpath to the Briarwood mansion for the very first time. It all came back to her: the imposing size of the house, Mrs. Maidstone's eccentricities, and the way they had bonded like mother and daughter within a few weeks. Luthera was full of humorous reminiscences and so profoundly disappointed in Marguerite, who'd recently vanished from sight. Nurse Wanda was embraced as family almost from the start.

Dr. Pickens rambled his way to his last page of notes, smiled a thin-lipped smile at the dean, and, at long last, vacated the podium. Much to the dean's chagrin, Mayor Moron took his place.

Surely it must be time by now for the presentation. Dr. Pickens' historical harangue, on top of Mayor Moron's loquacious rambling, has turned this simple affair into an endurance contest. Politicians and academics are so alike: talk, talk, talk, and nothing to say. No, I forgot Garrison Walker; there's his speech remaining. It should be a beaut.

Pondering the odd ways of academics, Dean Wanda recalled the school's tenuous beginning. For the first few years, she'd worried about a misstep. In the end, she got by on old-fashioned common sense. All her teachers came to her for help at one time or another—even Dr. Pickens. And she was always able to handle the students.

Yes, I overstated my credentials a bit. There wasn't time or money to start the school and get yet another degree, but I did well by my students and faculty nonetheless. That's it in a nutshell. I've always been able to hold my own by paying attention to the little things. The people of Crossroads want to think well of everyone. They believe in my noble cause and don't care to know the details. To endure in this town, all one has to do is be consistent and anticipate your adversary's next move.

The strategy had paid off. Even Marguerite's monstrous accusations were finally overshadowed by Dean Wanda's accomplishments.

Garrison's oration reached its thundering peak without Dean Wanda's attention. She'd spotted Louisa Crossley, her faithful assistant, desperately attempting to catch her eye. When the dean nodded discreetly, Louisa held up a sheet of paper whose scribbled message proved unreadable from such a distance. Annoyed in the extreme, the dean waited for Garrison to finish, then stepped brusquely down from the stage and marched into the great hall just as Mayor Moran returned to the podium.

Louisa tottered toward her. "Oh Wanda," she whispered morosely, "I don't know *what* to do."

"What is it?" The dean asked, as she wondered if poor old Louisa was off her medication yet again.

"There's a man in the office with a search warrant. He wants to see the books as well as deeds and mortgages for the school."

"Tell him to wait. I'll be there as soon as the ceremony ends."

"That's just it, Wanda. I told him you were busy, but he says I'm to comply immediately, or he'll arrest me for obstruction of justice. He gave me five minutes to get your permission. What's going on?"

Though the dean still couldn't place the young man in black she'd seen earlier with Marguerite, she now suspected he was behind this surprise attack.

"Take me to him. Quickly," she whispered, trying to calm Louisa's breathless frenzy by example.

At that very moment, Mayor Moran concluded his verbal marathon, or "mayorathon," as folks often described his prolonged orations.

"And now, ladies and gentlemen," he bellowed, "a few words from our honoree . . ."

The audience erupted in raucous laughter. The old windbag had droned on for five minutes without realizing the guest of honor had left the stage. Mortified, the dean considered her options: saying yes to the auditor and going on with the show, or racing to the office to confront him, which would spread speculation through the crowd like a prairie fire. The mayor made the decision for her, seeking her out and escorting her back onstage.

Once at the podium, her speech was characteristically modest. She briefly thanked people for coming, declared the testimonials gross exaggerations, then directed one and all to the great hall for punch and cookies.

During the reception, as well-wishers crowded round, the dean continued to worry; not about what the auditor might find, but rather his reasons for looking.

How tiresome that this day, of all days, I should be distracted by yet another of these petty annoyances, to say nothing of this mysterious guest. To paraphrase Lady Bracknell: "To intrude during an assembly is disrespectful; to do so when I'm the honoree, unforgivable."

Marguerite stood by the fireplace speaking to Cafferty. Her porcine face was surprisingly relaxed, and the two seemed on extremely friendly terms. Cafferty caught the dean's probing eye with an arrogant but amused glance. Turning away, she made a mental note to ask Garrison if he'd heard what scheme those two were hatching next.

Cafferty escorted Marguerite to the punch bowl, then left the room. Dean Wanda recalled the last time she'd seen the two of them together. Four months earlier, she'd encountered them in the parking lot of the Crossroads Inn. While unlocking her car, she smelled a waft of expensive perfume. Even before she turned around, she knew it was Marguerite, her voice slurred and brimming with suppressed anger. Cafferty was lurking behind her.

"I believe congratulations are in order, Nurse Wanda. I hear you're stepping down."

The dean did not even bother to be civil.

"I resent your stalking me like this, Marguerite. You must know by now I have nothing to say to you."

Marguerite dismissed Cafferty like an errant dog, smiled her tight smile, and moved closer; the scent of gin overwhelming the lush fragrance of her perfume.

"Let's skip the usual catfight and get right down to business. You've had your fun. Sell Briarwood back to me."

"If you recall, I made you that offer more than twenty years ago. You're a little late to the table, Marguerite. A great deal has happened since then."

"Look, Wanda, I may have been foolish enough to deny my heritage during my youth, but I don't want my daughters cut off from theirs because of it. Surely we can come to some sort of compromise. I do realize you've put your whole life into the school. If you can't bear to sell me the big house, sell me the land around the mausoleum. My grandmother wanted to be buried with all our relatives, including those to come. I can't believe she ever thought things would turn out like this."

Dean Wanda, realizing Cafferty might still be within earshot, lowered her voice and struggled to remain calm.

"Marguerite, we've been over this a hundred times. Despite what you may think, I loved your grandmother.

Her instructions were clear. She was to be buried in the mausoleum at Briarwood. The house and grounds were to be kept intact and put to good use.

"Now you say you care about your heritage. What utter nonsense. You turned your back on your only relative. Your grandmother was your heritage, not some pile of bricks and mortar. You abandoned her, which devastated her. She left the place to me because she trusted me to preserve it. I promised I'd honor her wishes as long as I lived, which is why Briarwood remains under my protection—as will her resting place. Much as you may think to the contrary, your gripe has never been with me, Marguerite. You've persecuted me for half your life as if I'm to blame for your lack of a moral compass. If you'd just shown the slightest consideration for your only living relative, you'd have had Briarwood years ago and been free to do whatever you wanted with that godforsaken mausoleum.

"Face facts for once in your life. Briarwood is no longer your family home, it's an institution. As such, it's bigger than any one of us: there are students, faculty, and staff— even groundskeepers—who depend on it for their education or livelihood. You can't buy the place back unless the board votes to shut the school down.

"No disrespect to your grandmother, but I happen to care more about the living than the dead. That said, how can you possibly excuse what you've done to her remains, having her carved up like that to sustain your vendetta against me? You're a spoiled, vindictive child who should realize by now you can't buy everything you want in this life. As long as I'm dean, the Briarwood School will continue to fulfill its mission. The board won't be selling to you or anyone else—at least not on my watch. And that's my final word on the subject."

As Marguerite stomped away, Cafferty sidled closer.

"Take the deal, Wanda. You can pay your bills, with something left over to retire on. Everyone wins. All those employees you're so worried about and all the folks you owe so much money to. I don't want to put you through another court battle. You must be getting tired of them after all these years."

Dean Wanda had never felt so angry.

"Tired of them! Of course I'm tired. Slander and misrepresentation; constant assaults on my good name; distractions everywhere I turn. Who wouldn't be? Even so, if you think for one instant I'm going to give in, particularly after the indignities that overly entitled emotional cripple has foisted on me for the last twenty years, you don't know me at all!

"Steve, I strongly advise you to stay away from Marguerite. She has a history of instability. You don't have to side with her. You'll get your money as soon as we refinance. There's nothing personal about all this. It's a cash flow issue, and I don't like it any more than you do. Trust me, she's become unbalanced by the consequences of her own behavior. It will only be a matter of time before she turns on you."

A court order requiring the dean to submit a tissue sample had arrived within the week. Marguerite was still in the game, and Cafferty was still on her side.

Returning to the present, Dean Wanda studied the man in black as he huddled with Marguerite. Catching the dean's puzzled stare, he nodded and smiled cordially. Embarrassed, she turned back to her well-wishers and abandoned any further attempt to identify him. He wasn't worth the effort. She could tell that much by the company he kept.

Her guests were in high spirits. It was a glorious day, and most had nowhere else to go. As the reception dragged on, she made progress with Dr. Langley, who expressed willingness to discuss his concerns privately. While he was unable to come for dinner the next evening, he promised to check his schedule for the following day and get back to her immediately.

Flush with satisfaction, the dean watched him walk away. Nothing worked better than a little arm-twisting after an excellent meal in Briarwood's luxurious dining room. It was essential that board members see things from her point of view, and she was now certain she'd have him back in line before the meeting on Thursday. With that, her legacy would be secure.

Cafferty returned to Marguerite and the mysterious man in black. There was a whispered conversation, then Marguerite looked over at the dean, laughed, and left the hall.

Dean Wanda, unnerved, took a moment to compose herself, then sought out Garrison. At her request, he cornered Cafferty, giving her a discreet thumbs-up when her warning had been delivered. She felt relieved and slightly dizzy.

This is the limit, bringing such venom to Briarwood on a day of celebration. Much as I regret having to act in kind—today of all days—once again, they've forced my hand. I didn't want to do it; he brought it on himself by siding with her.

Louisa returned to say that the auditor had proved gracious once given access. He'd studied the books briefly, then left without a word. The dean shook her head.

Another tempest in a teapot! Just like that court order a few months ago. No doubt Cafferty's accusations are behind this little incursion. He's taken a page from Marguerite's book. That man in black must be one of the auditors. He certainly is tight with those two. Well, they won't find anything untoward in those accounts, whatever they may be looking for. Rob is the best money can buy.

The dean scanned the room and found Rob huddled with Milton Hager, the bank president. When that conversation ended, Rob sought her out to whisper that approval should be forthcoming within a week, if Thursday's meeting went well. It was time to set her plan in motion.

I'm stepping down at just the right time. Things are bound to change as more professionals retire to Crossroads. Langley was just the opening salvo in the fusillade that is bound to follow. Nothing can prevent it. Much as I've come to love the school, it would be increasingly difficult to continue as before. Better to be done with it and get out while the getting's good.

With Rob's departure, no one remained in the great hall but Cafferty and the man in black. The dean was not about to wait *them* out.

As she climbed the stairs toward her quarters, the man overtook her. When he turned to face her from the step past her own, his massive frame towered above her. Filled with apprehension, she clasped the railing to steady herself. His swarthy complexion and close-cropped facial hair added to his sinister appearance, but his tone was kind—almost apologetic.

"Congratulations, Dean Atkinson," he murmured, staring at his feet. "I hope you enjoyed your send-off. That certainly was quite the crowd."

"Why thank you, young man. How kind of you. I must say, you seem familiar, but I'm afraid I can't recall your name." She felt curiously touched and much less anxious. "Are you a former student?"

"Yes, ma'am. I was in your first graduating class. Wally Harrington is the name. I wanted to be sure to thank you for the education you gave me. It made me who I am today."

"Ah, yes, Wally. Now I remember you. A fine scholar and an excellent athlete. How sweet of you to come to see the old dray horse put out to pasture. Where have you been living? What are you doing for employment these days?"

"I was in the service, but I've been in Portland for the last fifteen years or so . . ."

The dean barely heard him over the cacophony in her head.

Such a tiresome day. Oh well, soon this masquerade will be over for good. Thank God for Garrison. He hates Marguerite as much as I do, if not more. It must have been infuriating to be about to marry into all that money and then have her run off to a lesbian commune. I suppose I should be grateful she did. His desire for revenge has made so much possible. From the moment I told him Luthera had early Alzheimer's, he's been invaluable.

The dean stared blankly at her former student. His mouth was moving, but she couldn't follow his words.

With the house in Andorra ready, my time has come at last. Langley will buy in. I can taste it. I just have to hold on a few more days until the loan comes through. Then a simple wire transfer, and I'll be on my way. And no extradition treaty with the States . . . It certainly pays to research things thoroughly.

All's well that ends well. Marguerite will finally get her precious family seat back—for five times what it's worth. Contrary to what Rob's books show, there's nowhere near the revenue to meet payments on such a large loan. The bank will have to foreclose, pay off all the creditors, and sell the place to Marguerite to recoup their losses. Everyone will get what's due them, especially me, but at her expense. It's a roundabout way to get what should have been mine from the get-go, but it'll work.

After that conversation a few months ago, I'm positive she'll spend twenty million more than the place is worth just to get her own way. Briarwood has become an obsession for her. What's really rich is that once she has it back, she won't be able to enjoy it because the only thing she'll be able to think of is how I put one over on her. That will drive her stark, raving mad. Serves her right. She should have bought me out ages ago when I gave her the chance, the stupid cow.

The dean's attention finally returned to her former student, who was still standing above her on the stairs. He seemed to be repeating himself, as if she'd not answered a question.

"As I said, ma'am, I work for the Portland police these days—in homicide. I want to be sure you understand. The samples taken from under Mrs. Maidstone's fingernails at the time of her exhumation were analyzed again, this time using new state-of-the-art techniques from the FBI. The traces of DNA, blood, and tissue found are an exact match when compared to the samples you provided the court. I'm afraid you'll have to come with me."

Dean Wanda stared into his dark, troubled eyes. Her knees quaked. She gripped the banister with both hands to stop from falling. As if watching a movie from a great distance, she suddenly saw her younger self and Mrs. Maidstone on the second-floor landing—just as they'd been on that fateful day. The old woman had lost her balance and instinctively clutched her nurse's arm to prevent a fall. Expecting rescue as so many, many times before, Luthera had clung frantically to her beloved caregiver, who stood rigid and impassive, a distant glint in her eyes.

At first, everything seemed to happen in slow motion. The old woman's gnarled hand slowly traversed the length of her nurse's arm; past the elbow, then the wrist, and finally the limp, unaccommodating fingers. Luthera's eyes widened in surprise that gradually turned to anguish. There was a moment of comprehension that seemed a lifetime, then Luthera Delano Maidstone, chatelaine of Briarwood for more than sixty years, hurtled down the curved marble staircase to her death.

Shifting her gaze from the landing to the steps in front of her, Dean Wanda struggled to comprehend all she'd just heard, but her mind refused to cooperate.

It was a spur-of-the-moment decision. Once Luthera signed that will, I never intended to do anything but wait her out. When she began to fall, it seemed a mercy somehow to just let her go. How strange a single untoward impulse could change everything for years to come. Strange, too, how a single moment can retain such clarity despite being suppressed for so long. I'd never have let her fall had I realized she might be in any way aware of her surroundings. I'll never forget the look of betrayal in her eyes. With that, there could be no half measures.

Luthera's grasp had been so feeble, the mark she left behind so innocuous—a slight red line on the skin, a scratch on the wrist, easily masked with makeup and a long-sleeved blouse—there'd never been a moment's cause for concern. In fact, all traces had completely disappeared in a few days.

I never gave that scratch a thought from that day on. Now all of a sudden, this. If I'm convicted, the will becomes invalid, and Marguerite will get everything as next of kin, despite how hard it's been, how carefully I've planned, and all the good I've done . . .

With great deference, Detective Harrington escorted Dean Wanda down the stairs to an unmarked police car, where Marguerite stood holding its open door, smiling her odd, tight smile.

LAST
CHANCE

"*I'm not the greatest authority on feminine wiles, but even I can tell she's quite the package. No doubt, she'd make some guy truly happy—until she killed him, that is.*"

"**D**etective Lieutenant Beston, you simply **must** understand,** it was never about the money," she says, her husky voice resonant with enough sincerity to assail, but not assuage, my suspicion. "I agreed to sail away with Vaughn because I love him, and trust *he* loves *me.*"

There's a slight chance she's telling the truth, though my bet is she'll never set sail again—or see a cent of his money. The evidence is piling up.

Amanda Mulher is one complex lady. Somewhere between thirty-five and forty, she poses a slew of contradictions for a guy like me. Her understated, classic wardrobe broadcasts good taste, yet a smoldering sensuality just below the surface suggests so much more. If you take a good look, those expensively tailored suits are hiding something. And that's what I'm paid to do, take a good look at every last detail. I'm damn good at it, too—and I'm not talking fashion.

She's not a high-priced call girl—old news given the hordes of working "ladies" here in Grand Bahama. She's not one of their "altar" egos, either. By that, I mean the hordes of trophy wives holed up in gated communities along the shore. No, Ms. Mulher's in a class by herself. Like no one I've ever met. Because of that, I can't scuttle a hunch she's not who she says she is. Maybe I'm out of my league, but my instincts tell me there's more to her than I've gotten out of her. Yet.

I've seldom seen a woman so comfortable in her own skin. Even after hours of questioning, every glance, every gesture, is captivating. Not studied or provocative, just charming and incredibly self-possessed. She's more than at ease; she's savoring every moment life has to offer—even while being grilled for hours in this dump.

There's fun to be had with Amanda Mulher. That's for sure. She's got a terrific wit, she's smart, and she treats me as if I'm the only man in the world. I'm not the greatest authority on feminine wiles, but even I can tell she's quite the package. No doubt, she'd make some guy truly happy—until she killed him, that is.

What I'm trying to say is I'm pretty damn sure she murdered Vaughn Kreisler. He's been missing for nearly two weeks and things don't look so good for him making a comeback. According to the Boston FBI, he left one hell of a life behind, a multimillion-dollar company he started from scratch, a society wife with an impeccable pedigree, a waterfront house in Marblehead, Mass., a townhouse in Boston, and a winter getaway in Kauai. The way I see things, it would take one hell of a woman to get him to slip his mooring line. I think I know who, and, the more time I spend in Ms. Mulher's company, why.

Kreisler's disappearance is a sensation back in the States. The tabloids run something on the case almost every day. It all began when his wife found a note at the summer place that said, "Forgive me." That was it. They'd recently separated, but even before that she'd paid little attention to his frequent absences, so she just figured he'd had an attack of remorse.

Three more days passed before she stumbled onto the fact that he'd vanished without a trace—at least that's what she told the Feds. She found a hell of a lot when she finally put two and two together. He'd closed his bank accounts and sold his shares of the company, as well as several investment properties. What's more, all proceeds had been wired offshore.

There was some consolation in the midst of all this: a brokerage account in her name with a recent deposit of fifty mil. A pleasant surprise for most folks; but it appears the little woman isn't satisfied. When you think about it, why wouldn't she try for more? If he's proved dead, she gets it all. If they divorce, she could get as much as half. Seems worth the extra effort to me.

With all the cars accounted for, no trace with private jet services or public airlines, and his fifty-footer still moored off the Corinthian Yacht Club, the wife was at a loss. Then a yacht broker called to ask how they liked their brand-new eight-eight-footer, the *Last Chance*.

Dawn over Marblehead, as the saying goes. Lois Kreisler called the police. The locals got lucky right from the start. They learned *Last Chance* was delivered at night—fully provisioned down to the last detail—and departed at dawn the very next morning for points unknown.

Apparently, an old duffer overnighting at the next mooring got up early to hang it over the side. Midstream, he was taken aback to see a tall, beautiful, buxom woman board *Last Chance*. As he finished up and settled in to watch, the goddess raised her sails, dropped the mooring pennant—tossed it from the bow like a bridal bouquet is the way he told it—then, with no help, tacked through a harbor crowded with high-end yachts. All this without auxiliary power, against the tide in a light breeze, just as the sun rose, as if she had something—or someone—to hide.

The theory is Kreisler was below decks. The question is why wasn't he at the helm of his brand-new yacht? Lots of millionaires get kidnapped for ransom, and some don't live to tell the tale. As a result, the Feds consider him a missing person—until he turns up somewhere dead or alive, that is. This makes the woman sailor a person of interest to the FBI and, subsequently, yours truly. How much do you want to bet the babe at the helm was our Ms. Mulher?

According to the Feds, Lois is furious about the other woman and insists Kreisler's still alive, or—if you read between the lines—will be until she kills him herself. I don't mean to sound so negative; it's just I've learned to expect the worst. An occupational hazard, I guess. As some smart-ass once said, "An optimist is frequently disappointed, a pessimist sometimes pleasantly surprised." I'll take pessimism every time—you've got no place to go but up.

In any case, Lois claims her husband moved his funds offshore and fled the country to avoid a divorce settlement. She's already initiated proceedings for her share of the seven hundred million she says he's worth. So Kreisler's in the soup with the FBI *and* a pissed-off wife. Maybe he should have given more thought to his choice of crew—or should I say first mate?

When *Last Chance* hailed the marina at Old Bahama Bay, I raced from Freeport to West End to take Kreisler into custody. The FBI wanted him on ice until they decided whether charges were warranted. In a rare example of inter-agency cooperation, Customs held the yacht in quarantine until I got there.

Ms. Mulher, the only person on board, greeted us on deck like the Queen, offering the grand tour as if she did it every day. We searched the whole boat, even the crew quarters in the bow, but no Kreisler—just some monogrammed men's clothing and a shaving kit. Quite the yacht, by the way: electric winches, power thrusters. Despite the size, a seasoned sailor could single-hand her. In fact, my late sainted grandmother could have managed it from her rocking chair.

Desertion, divorce, adultery, they're not my bailiwick, but a missing person case often ends up as a murder investigation—my specialty, as it so happens. The facts in this case shout foul play: there are minute traces of blood on the lazarette and the sheath of a long antifouling knife. The knife is missing, and there's no tender in the davits.

No one sails any great distance without a tender, so where is it? I've got a hunch. If the murder took place in an inflatable Zodiac, a few slashes and the body, the knife, and all blood traces—save the two I found—would be safely at the bottom of the ocean.

I ask again about the missing items.

"As I told you yesterday, *and* the day before, *and* the day we met," Ms. Mulher says, with a touch of weariness that borders on the theatrical, "it was dead calm before dawn. I was awake, but still in my cabin. We must have caught a net or line on the rudder because I heard Vaughn lower the Zodiac. He *had* to have taken the knife with him. It was in the lazarette the day before—I saw it there.

"As you already know, a rain squall overtook us. As I *also* told you, the autopilot was on, the sails were up, and *Last Chance* took off like a shot. I felt her heel, then came up on deck. The Zodiac was gone, and Vaughn was nowhere to be found. I reefed the sails and hove to, but by then visibility had deteriorated. It stayed that way for several hours. I searched and searched but found nothing. Finally, I made for Old Bahama Bay."

"And you didn't radio his disappearance because?"

"Vaughn wanted to start a new life. He made me promise there'd be no publicity, no matter what. Besides, I just know he's alive. He's an excellent seaman. He's done several Atlantic crossings by himself. What's more, the Zodiac was extremely seaworthy. He must have made for shore. We were only a few miles off West End, after all. Those waters aren't exactly isolated."

And yet he didn't radio to tell you he was safe, and he wasn't waiting for you when you came ashore, I say to myself, seeing a hole in her tale big enough to steer the *Queen Mary* through. This lady hasn't deviated from her story one iota. It has the same flaws every time.

"You're quite the sailor yourself, Ms. Mulher," I say instead.

Again, I ask myself, why didn't she call for help?

She tosses her blonde locks, then runs her fingers through them.

"Why thank you. How kind of you to notice. I've sailed for years. That's how Vaughn and I met."

"Say more about that."

Amanda Mulher's background check has come up blank in the States—no record, no identity. Nada. Except here in the Caribbean, where she has several Customs entries and hotel stays on various islands.

"Nothing much to say. I've been a sailor most of my life: transatlantic crossings, the Mediterranean and Pacific, and, most recently, the Caribbean. I met Vaughn when my boat was moored next to his at the Corinthian in Marblehead. He was kind enough to help me replace my solenoid."

I'm not going to ask what that did for her, in case it's some mainland euphemism I haven't heard of yet.

"Your personal information seems a bit sparse," I say instead, hoping my research will shake something loose. "The folks at the Excelsior said you had only a passport when you checked in—no other photo ID."

"Oh, that! My purse was stolen the first night you let me go ashore. Fortunately, my birth certificate and passport were still on board."

She looks me right in the eye as she says this. No doubt about it, she's one cool customer. Her casual, confident tone gets my guard up. We're not chatting at the country club; we're talking about a missing person, possibly a murder. She should be nervous, and she isn't. There's something off about that. I can't put my finger exactly on what. Yet.

Perhaps she figures she's gotten away with it and just needs to let the clock run out. It's worth a try. I can't keep her indefinitely without evidence. I don't have a body, just the FBI dossier. There's no official suspicion of foul play, only my instincts, which are decidedly unofficial. She could pass the hours playing dodge 'em with me and get off scot-free if I don't catch a break soon. I wouldn't put it past her to think that way. Given our proximity to the Gulf Stream, there's little chance Kreisler's body will wash ashore. Even so, it's a high-stakes gamble on her part, but then, as I've said, she's not your typical suspect.

"OK, that's it for today," I say, more intrigued than ever, but not wanting to overplay my hand. "Check in with me tomorrow, in case there are any developments. In the meantime, stay on the island and make sure I can reach you."

I find it useful to string suspects along with multiple interrogations over extended periods. Even if they don't show it at first, the pressure to keep their story straight day after day wears them down. Sooner or later, they slip up or crack. Works every time.

Ms. Mulher pouts a bit as if it's a minor inconvenience: like breaking a nail or finding a run in her pantyhose.

"Oh sure . . . No problem. Where can I go? You've impounded the boat at the marina and my passport at the hotel. You have someone tailing me night and day. It hardly seems the time for a trip to Paris."

Ha. I'll have to swap out Fawkes for someone else. She's pretty slick, this Ms. Mulher, or whoever the hell she is. Fawkes is a real pro, and no one has ever made him before.

Standing to leave, Ms. Mulher extends her hand palm down as if expecting me to kiss it.

"A pleasure as always, Lieutenant. I've come to enjoy our little chats. Same time tomorrow?"

I shake her hand instead—with a strong grip. She doesn't even wince.

"Sure, why not," I say. "I've got all the time in the world."

"Aren't you fortunate," she says with a mischievous glint in her eye.

I smile in spite of myself.

With that parting shot, she turns and sashays out of the room as if she's walking the red carpet. Every head in the squad room turns to watch. Three cops collide in a rush to open the door for her.

Though I don't particularly care for women in the sack, it's beginning to make sense why Kreisler tossed everything over for this one. You have to admire her guts, and if she's half as good in bed as her sexy vibes suggest, she'd be well worth weighing anchor. Even I can see that. That said, I can't get past this hunch she's one of those "black widow" types. You know the MO: seduce the man, get in the will, do the poor bastard in, and move on to the next one. It would explain why I couldn't trace her in the States. Those gals go through so many married names and false identities it'd be easier to find Jimmy Hoffa than track one of them down.

Along those lines, I wonder if Kreisler had any idea what he was getting into. I could make a joke about him going overboard for a pretty face, but given the circumstances, it seems in poor taste.

Next day—two thirty on the dot—Ms. Mulher's seated in the waiting area. It's time for another round, except she's learning more about me than I am about her.

After weeks of sniveling phone calls, Javier, my all-too-embarrassing ex, has brought his world-class brand of psychodrama to my office. Appeals for another chance echo around the squad room as I try to act as though it's just another interrogation. My ploy is failing miserably. His flame is so bright you can see it from Uranus. What's more, he's outing me in front of the change of shift, and no matter what I say, he refuses to tone it down. Not a good thing.

Finally he storms out, leaving a sibilant trail of Spanish in his wake that makes Carmen Miranda sound like John Wayne.

Ms. Mulher waits a moment, then knocks.

"Handsome fellow," she says as I escort her in.

Surprisingly, her tone is devoid of sarcasm. She seems inclined to spare me further embarrassment.

"Handsome isn't everything," I reply with a taut smile.

Until moments ago, I was on the DL. Now Javier's floorshow has blown the door off my closet, which will mean problems—lots of them. Ms. Mulher is likely to be more sympathetic than most of the assholes on this godforsaken island, so why not be civil? After all, she didn't murder anyone I know.

Wait. Now there's a thought . . . I wonder if she'd take on a client.

"Neither is money," says she, interrupting my mafia moment. "Shall we take up where we left off yesterday? If I recall, you were accusing me of doing away with Vaughn for his, were you not?"

As I offer Ms. Mulher a seat, Chaela, my unofficially adopted niece, sticks her head through the open door. She's off to the College of the Bahamas in Nassau and is all smiles and excitement. The sight of her makes me go warm all over.

"Hey, Unca!"

"One moment . . . Do you mind?" I ask Ms. Mulher as Chaela holds me tight—somehow a mature young woman and a little girl all at once.

"Not at all. I'm delighted to see you aren't always the cold, calculating ace detective."

Chaela's brown eyes dance.

"Cold and calculating, lady? You must not know him very well. This guy's an absolute pussycat. A prince. As good as they come."

Ms. Mulher beams as if she's found me out. It's supposed to be the other way round.

Chaela shines her light back on me.

"So, Unca. I got the check and just had to say thanks. As if you haven't done enough for me already . . ."

"It's nothing. Don't sweat it."

It's lovely to see Chaela, but this scene doesn't exactly give me the upper hand with my interrogation. Still, she's all I've got in the world. If she needs time to say good-bye, Ms. Mulher can just cool her Pradas.

Strangely enough, that's not what's happening; the diva looks fascinated, blatantly studying us as if researching an article for *Family Life*.

Chaela rattles on about college. She wants to major in marine biology. Ms. Mulher asks a number of questions and sits patiently through the answers as if she came specifically to hear them.

It breaks my heart Chaela isn't going to UCLA or Rutgers. She was accepted to both, but I can't hack the expense—even with the scholarships they offered. I know I've let her down, but she's never once complained. As Chaela talks with Ms. Mulher—Amanda—I learn things I never knew about either of them. I decide to take a backseat and let them chat until it's time for Chaela's ferry.

Once she's gone, I take a moment to pull myself together, then study Amanda through misty eyes. She has the strangest look. It's radiant and energized, as if she knows exactly what Chaela means to me. I try mightily to regroup, but Amanda beats me to the punch.

"Before we begin today's inquisition, do you mind if I ask a few questions about that lovely young woman? She doesn't appear to be a family member, yet the love between you is palpable."

Amanda sounds genuinely interested. I fight the urge to tell her what it means to me that Chaela's setting out on her own. It's hardly an appropriate topic for a murder investigation. Still, there's more than one way to get at the truth. I decide to play the soft touch and see where it takes me.

"It's a long story," I say, knowing already I'm going to tell it.

"It's not as if I've a lot of places to go," Amanda says with a half-smile.

I'd better start talking—and fast. It's part of the job to be immune to charm, and I'm not doing so well at the moment. I tell Amanda of my first case as a detective. Adrian Moon, Chaela's father, was an informant of mine. He and his wife were killed in a home invasion after someone on the force—we've never discovered who—tipped off the drug runner I was investigating.

"Thank God, Chaela was at boarding school when it happened," I say, failing to completely mask the catch in my throat.

"How horrible. The poor child."

One look and I know Amanda means it. She doesn't need to tell me; I've lived with the price Chaela's parents paid every day since.

"She moved in with her aunt after that, but I've sort of looked out for her."

"Ah, I see. I can tell she thinks the world of you—and you of her. I find that touching. She could easily have blamed you for her parents' death."

I nod, knowing all too well.

"And the drug runner?"

"We got him."

The truth is he was tried, convicted, and executed the very next day. I like the personal touch. I'm sure as hell not getting into *that* story.

"May I remind you you're here today to answer questions, not ask them," I say, trying gently to regain the upper hand.

Amanda laughs.

"That's right. Please *do* forgive me. How *could* I have forgotten?

"You've already had enough drama for one day. I promise to behave during today's interrogation. If you *must* ask the same questions all over again, we might as well get on with it. I know them by heart. Shall I just recite my answers to save you time?"

I know she's busting me, but the way she does it makes me smile. One cool lady; that's all I can say. Suddenly, I feel defensive about doing my job.

"Look. I'm sorry, Amanda, but I've got to ask you this stuff. There are things about your story that don't add up."

"Such as?" she asks, her arched brow revealing more humor than inquisitiveness.

Her eyes are dark green and sparkle like emeralds. I see the laughter in them, but her glance isn't mocking; it radiates carefree enjoyment. I just don't get it.

I've been saving this tidbit, but this is as good a time as any. Besides, putting the screws to her will take my mind off my career, which is self-destructing as I speak.

"I've had word from the FirstCaribbean International Bank of Barbados . . ."

For the first time, Amanda seems taken by surprise. It's not much, just a slight catch of breath, but it's progress.

"There are regulations forbidding disclosure of financial dealings outside proper channels . . ."

"There certainly are," I say, chuffed at how quickly I've turned the tables on her and wanting her to know I'm enjoying myself, too. "Fortunately, I was able to call in a favor from a friend."

"Ah, I get it," she says, placing her thumb under her chin and leaning forward. "The gay boys' network! How could I have forgotten sex in the islands? Nobody does it in their own backyard. Where'd you two meet? Rumrunners?"

"You certainly *have* been around."

I'm struggling to play it cool. Not one woman in ten thousand would know the gay club in Bridgetown. And as a matter of actual fact, she's right. My "friend" is a sometime playmate who works at FirstCarribean's data center. It can take weeks to gather this kind of information if you can get it at all, so I'm determined to use it while it's hot. Besides, no matter how smart she is, I'm the man in charge, so I get to say when playtime's over.

"Just between us, would you care to explain why you are a joint account-holder with Vaughn Kreisler of assets amounting to nearly eight hundred million dollars?"

Her body language doesn't change. Not one bit. I've already accused her of murder, for God's sake, and now I've dished up an impressive motive. How can she just sit there as if we're having tea at the Ritz?

Amanda pauses, leans back, crosses her legs, then stares me down.

"Vaughn insisted. He said we were soul mates—two sides of the same coin—and that we should share all we have."

"But sharing wasn't enough for you, was it?"

I admire her poise. Her situation is getting worse by the moment, yet she's calm and confident—almost indifferent. I've never seen anything like it. She should be cracking like an egg by now.

"It's more than enough. It's everything," she says, her jaw tightening a bit.

Another small triumph, but I'll take what I can get.

It's short lived.

"Perhaps if you'd truly connected with someone just once instead of bed- and island- hopping every free moment, you might have the slightest clue as to what I mean.

"I've had enough for now, Lieutenant. You've had a tough day, and after your illegal invasion of my privacy, so have I. If you want to arrest me, do so. Otherwise, you know where to find me."

With that, she gets up, grabs her purse, and strides to the door.

"Take care, lady. OK? Stay put. Don't do anything rash," I say, feeling like we've had our first spat.

For my trouble, I get a pert wave over her left shoulder.

The rest of the day is a nightmare. At first, it's just teasing—a couple of guys swishing around the office with limp wrists and swaying hips. Then I catch Scavela egging the others on. He and I have never gotten along, particularly since my promotion. I'll have to watch my step, but not only with him. Word spreads fast and homophobia runs deep in the islands. Gays get killed for walking down the wrong street at the wrong time. I know; I've seen the bodies.

Thanks, Javier, you neurotic son of a bitch, I say to myself, watching huddled cops laugh as Scavela puckers his lips and points my way. These goons are working themselves into a frenzy. And that's not good. I know what they're capable of. I've heard their macho shit a thousand times.

I've fucked up my life and the case with it. Thank God Chaela's not around to witness it.

Next day, I'm so distracted I can't accomplish a damn thing. Two thirty comes and goes with no sign of Amanda. I didn't actually expect her, but to my surprise, I'm disappointed she didn't come of her own accord. Not that I have a thing for her per se, but right now, her wit and sophistication are the sole bright spot in my otherwise pathetic life. Sitting alone in my office, I feel as though I've lost my only connection to the outside world—and maybe even a friend.

Three days pass without word. Each morning, I wonder whether I should call her in. With no progress on the Kreisler case, there's little point. I tell myself to let her wonder what's going on. It may make her more pliable in the long run.

Then the strangest thought comes to me: is this a strategy for an investigation or a romance?

The morning of the fourth day, Charlie, the new guy tailing Amanda in Freeport, still has nothing. Her routine never varies: breakfast in the Excelsior dining room; reading by the hotel pool all day; a single vodka and tonic on the terrace overlooking the bay; then dinner at Kelso's Bistro in the hotel. The same waiter tends her every night. He's the only person she speaks to all day.

I've known Charlie since I moved to West End. We used to hoist a few brews and compare notes. Now it's all business. He won't look at me when he reports in and doesn't seem to be making his usual effort with detail. For all I know, he's waltzing me.

It may be my distraction, my loss of respect from my peers, or a genuine lack of evidence, but this case is as dead as disco. I can't detain Amanda much longer without just cause. What's worse, the more I think about it, the less confident I am she killed Kreisler. As things stand, I can't decide whether she's blowing smoke up my butt or telling the truth. I'm not used to being in a quandary like this. My instincts are usually impeccable.

On the fifth day, I'm listening to tapes of Amanda's interviews—looking for something I might have missed—when Charlie calls to say he's lost her. He waited in the lobby for her routine to start, but she never showed, so after a couple of hours he checked out her room. It was empty, though her clothes were still in the closet. He's spent four hours watching the elevators, but she hasn't returned.

It almost doesn't matter. I still don't have enough evidence to make an arrest. Besides, I'm a short-timer with problems much closer to home. Even so, Amanda weighs on my mind.

Charlie is no sooner off the phone than it rings again. It's Chaela, calling from Nassau.

"What's wrong, honey," I ask, my heart in my mouth.

"I'm not sure anything is, Uncle Paul," she says, as I catch my breath. "That beautiful lady who was in your office the other day? The one who asked me all the questions about college? I just got back from lunch with her."

"What?"

"She had me summoned to the dean's office, then took me to the nicest restaurant I've ever been to in my life. I had the best time. She's great."

"What did she want?"

"That's the strange part. I can't tell if she wanted anything at all. We talked about lots of different things. Mostly she listened. The time passed so quickly; I couldn't believe we talked for four whole hours."

"Now, Chaela, listen to me. This is extremely important. What did she ask about me?"

"That's the thing, Unca. Nothing much. She already knew what happened to Mom and Dad. We talked some about that. I told her how you've always been there when I needed someone. She did ask about Javier, though."

"What did you tell her?"

"I told her the truth: you're an amazing, loving person who's never been able to find a man worthy of you."

Christ. I was positive Chaela thought Javier was just a roommate. Who's the detective around here, anyways? I must be losing my touch.

"Did she say anything else?"

"Yeah. And that's why I'm calling. She asked me to tell you to trust your gut and meet her at Kelso's at eight tonight."

That night, I drive to Freeport, dismiss Charlie, wait outside the terrace bar, and, when Amanda arrives, rise to meet her as if we're on a date.

"Why Lieutenant," she says, a sexy lilt to her voice, "I see you got my message. I'm delighted. I've missed our little chats. And how thoughtful of you to dismiss the new man who's been following me; it must have been *such* a long day for him with nothing to do but lie in wait in the lobby and pretend to read the newspaper. Shall we go in?"

She's calm as ever. As if certain I'd be there. It takes an effort to act like the cop I'm supposed to be.

"What the hell do you think you were doing? You weren't supposed to leave the island, never mind pry into my personal life."

To tell the truth, I'm impressed by her guts, but I can't let her defy my orders without putting up a bit of a fuss.

"I know you'll find this hard to believe, Detective Beston, but I wasn't prying. When I met her in your office, I found Chaela to be a fascinating, bright young woman. When you told me what happened to her parents, I wanted to learn more about her."

"Why?"

"I thought I might be able to help her."

"What?"

"She was accepted into some pretty prestigious schools, but couldn't afford to attend them."

"That's a bribe."

"Oh, for goodness' sake! Of course it isn't. Stop being such a stick-in-the-mud. She's no relative of yours."

"That's putting a fine point on things."

"Now, look here. How I want to spend *my* money is *my* business. I won't have you making inferences when there are none to be made. And, since you're so suspicious, don't worry; my charitable foundation is an independent corporation. Should you get me convicted of murdering Vaughn, she'll still get the money."

Amanda's grin is a silent challenge. Do I push back and cost Chaela a world-class education or roll over and become indebted to a suspect? I have no proof there even is a charitable foundation, though I should be able to find that out quickly enough. I decide not to decide, but to bring some pressure to bear and see what else I can learn.

"You left the island in violation of my instructions."

"And I'm back."

"I should arrest you right now for unlawful flight."

"There's one flaw in your logic, Detective. I'm standing right in front of you."

"And bribery."

"Have I offered you any money?"

"No, but you did to my niece . . ."

"She's not your niece. Besides, she doesn't know a thing."

"But she's someone I care about."

"Really?"

Amanda taps an expensively lacquered fingernail against my chest.

"Yet you have a problem if an independent charitable foundation awards a full scholarship to a bright young student whose parents were brutally murdered? That doesn't seem like caring to me. It seems like putting your ego ahead of the needs of a deserving young woman. Please explain how helping someone in her situation is a bribe? I'm dying to hear."

I know I should say something, but I'm at a total loss. I sense Amanda won't tolerate silence for long, so I brace myself for another salvo.

"If you're so sure you've got me pegged," she says, her eyes full of mirth, "you can damn well arrest me whenever you want. If that's what you're planning, though, let's have a drink first?"

She's just loving this sparring match and, funny thing, so am I—even as I raise the white flag.

"Chaela gave me your message, and here I am. It's a lovely evening, you look gorgeous, and I haven't had a night out in months. I guess we might as well go in.

"By the way, I haven't asked why you invited me. What is it you wanted to tell me, Amanda? That you killed Kreisler or that you missed me? I've been on tenterhooks since I got your message."

For once, my smile isn't just part of the game. It's like I'm teasing an old friend. I struggle to understand why I'm enjoying myself so much. Then, given the fact I'm probably off the force within a week, I wonder whether I even need to know.

"That's it, exactly," she says, her green eyes dancing. "I've been dying to tell you just how much I've missed your warm personality and delightful repartee. As for the other business; you have my story, and I'm sticking to it.

"Just a moment," she says, turning to the waiter who's leading us to the best table on the balcony. "How are things, William? Did you find that lotion?"

The waiter's smile is radiant.

"Yes, Miss Amanda, and it worked! Made all the difference! Everything is wonderful. Like heaven. Many, many thanks to you!"

"A pleasure. I'm delighted to hear the good news. The usual for me, please, William? And you, Lieutenant? Off duty or on?"

After today's events, I need a drink. I stare down at the table like a shy kid on a first date.

"Hendrick's and tonic. Double, with cucumber."

"Why Lieutenant, that's quite the opening gambit, even for someone who hasn't had a night out in months. Is something troubling you besides my little expedition today? Might it be your dismal social life?"

"Nothing so simple."

Amanda leans toward me.

"It's that drama queen I saw in your office, isn't it? I totally agree with Chaela. You could do *much, much* better.

As we discussed just the other day, neither looks nor money is everything. Seriously, given his theatrics, it must be hell in the squad room."

"Forgive me, but that's none of your business."

There's an odd catch in my throat. I'm sort of wishing it were. Chaela's gone, my colleagues have turned against me, and isolation is staring me in the face. I don't do lonely well.

"Now, now, Lieutenant, I simply won't tolerate taciturn behavior this evening. As you said, it's a lovely night. Besides, with your drink order, you've declared yourself off duty. C'mon now. Tell me what's going on. I'm a damned good listener."

Just then, William returns with our drinks. It's record time for the Excelsior. Even at the high-end places, drinks usually arrive on island time, if at all, for cops like me. Most waiters think we'll scare off the drug runners who leave much better tips. I often get such subtle reminders I'm not wanted. Like everything else on this goddamn island, I'm used to it.

"Here's to better days with better lovers," Amanda says, tapping my glass and looking me dead in the eye. "Don't get discouraged, Detective. *Most* men are dogs," she says with a wan smile. "Women know that intuitively, which is why *some* of us have to be bitches now and then."

The first Hendrick's is followed by a second—just a single—then a third. Amanda meets me measure for measure. When she orders yet another round, I'm so relaxed it barely registers. Some interrogation. Some detective. I'm enjoying the view and wishing for a better life, when I should be ripping her alibi to shreds.

Amanda talks fondly of the islands: her favorite harbor, the best beaches, and the most spectacular views. Inconsequential stuff like that. I can tell it's a glossy cover designed to put me at ease, and it works. Her web of intimacy draws me in; her warmth envelops me like a cocoon. I listen and respond when appropriate, but mostly wallow in the sultry cadence of her voice. I can't help but think if this were Paris back in the day, she'd have made one hell of a courtesan. The whole scene makes me yearn for someone of my very own who would treat me this way.

Suddenly, as if reading my mind, she pulls me up short.

"Let me tell you something, Detective Beston. Listen closely: never settle in life. Not ever. Cultivate your own company, become your own best friend, love yourself with all your warts and blemishes, and *only then* put what you can out into the world. Once you've done that much, all you have to do is wait. Once you find a way to love yourself, the world will love you back."

"What are you trying to tell me, Amanda?"

"You're a handsome, intelligent, earnest man—generous, caring, and fundamentally decent, despite the untold horrors you encounter every day. You've helped a young girl survive a tragedy that might well have destroyed her, earning her admiration and love when she could just as easily have blamed you for her parents' death. Some folks let an entire lifetime pass without having that kind of impact on another person. Can't you see that?

"Why do you stay on this soulless piece of coral where you are loathed for who you really are? Don't tell me you're hanging around for that two-bit Charo who outed you in front of your fellow officers?"

"You know, for a classy lady, you sure know your gay lingo. Where'd you pick it up? You don't seem like any fag hag I've ever met."

Amanda responds with a peal of laughter.

"Who says I'm not? But don't deflect! What is it that keeps you here so far beneath your potential? There's a whole world out there for you to conquer."

"It's a long story."

"A perfect topic for a dinner conversation. I know just the place . . ."

She summons the waiter and whispers in his ear. He's still beaming when he sees us to the rear entrance, and it's not because of the generous tip. He clearly worships her.

She must have solved one hell of a problem for him, I think, wondering what it was and why she bothered.

Once a detective, always a detective. I open a new line of questioning in the cab.

"So what was William's problem? An allergy?" I ask, thinking the topic innocuous enough for the ride.

"A rather personal one. In fact, a challenge of significant proportion."

"You make it sound so mysterious. I thought it was a case of dry skin."

"In one way you're right, but in another, you're way off the mark. That surprises me, you being a detective and all. Let's just say he was having difficulty expressing the full depth and breadth of his passion to Victor, his new boyfriend. William is madly in love with the fellow, who, at the first sight of his artillery, sealed his borders tighter than China before Nixon."

"You've got to be kidding! A waiter told you that! Not that *I'd* consider it a problem."

I glance at the rearview mirror. Two brown eyes stare back. As I return their probing gaze, the driver flashes a knowing grin, then licks his lips. It figures—just when I'm about to be ridden out of town on a rail . . .

The cab pulls up in front of Vittorina's, a little hideaway with the best food in West End.

"How the hell do you know about this place?" I ask, relinquishing the luscious driver's attentions with regret.

"Friends. As I told you before, I've spent a lot of time in the islands," Amanda says, handing the cabbie a fifty and some free advice. "Jean-Paul is a good man, Louis. Remember all you've built together over the years. It's well worth honoring at all times. Keep the change and pick us up in three hours."

Brown-Eyes looks like Momma caught him with his hand in the cookie jar.

So much for my chances later on. Thanks a bunch, Saint Amanda.

At Vittorina's, good food and a laid-back atmosphere go hand-in-hand with ample cover. Guys on the DL skirt island prejudices and socialize without fear. Straight couples in the first blush of an affair dance cheek to cheek. It's one of those joints no one ever admits going to. Sort of the Rick's Café of Grand Bahama, though without a Bogey or Bergman, unless it's me and the femme fatale on my arm. There's a laugh. "Here's looking at you, kid."

It says a hell of a lot about Amanda that she brought me here—about the only place on the island where I can safely let my hair down. The staff obviously know her. We're seated at the best table again. Once the wine is poured, I continue my line of questioning. Half in the bag, I can't resist.

"I've got to admit I'm dumbfounded a waiter would tell a classy lady like you about a problem like that."

Amanda shrugs.

"They love each other. Of course they'd want to consummate their relationship. William was understandably distraught, and I don't blame him for seeking advice."

This is said in such a matter-of-fact way I'm impressed. I should be so nonjudgmental. But then if I were, I'd be fired.

"Even so, why did a waiter tell *you* about something so intimate? And why would you care?"

"Why wouldn't I care? Don't write William off because of his accent. He's a good man, well educated, and the best student of human nature I've ever met. I so enjoyed talking with him the first time he waited on me, I requested him as my regular waiter. One particularly slow night, he seemed distracted. When I asked what was wrong, he poured his heart out. I'm the kind of person people talk to. You should try me."

She stares deep into my eyes and says, "OK, copper. Out with it."

So I try her and it's as if I fall under some sort of spell. She focuses those emerald eyes on me, leans forward in encouragement, and my words just pour out.

"I hate what this island is doing to me. You haul someone in for dealing, and somebody else takes over the next night. Last week I broke down a door to find a woman had been battered unconscious. She's still in a coma. Why? Because she wouldn't give her husband money for drugs. She wanted to feed her six kids instead. I can't begin to tell you how many gay people I've seen beaten within an inch of their lives, and how many times I thought it could have been me. The cycle just keeps repeating and repeating. It all seems so hopeless, I can hardly see the point of caring anymore.

"Perhaps I'd feel different if there weren't so much corruption. You can't get a goddamned thing done without greasing palms. Most folks are scrambling to get a crumb while a handful of rich bastards gorge themselves. It makes me sick.

"I see things other people don't. And way too much at that. I can't seem to make a difference, and now after Javier's theatrics, my business is in the street. It's only a matter of time before someone comes after me."

"Tell me something," Amanda says, her voice empathetic, but surprisingly forceful. "Why would you even *consider* staying here now Chaela's gone?"

"I guess I'm afraid I'll have the same experience wherever I go. That I'll only see the underside and nothing else. People are the same all over the world—one guy's foot on the other guy's neck."

"What about your family? Are you close to them?"

"I ran away from home at an early age and never looked back. My parents' hatred for each other left no room for me. When Chaela needed me, I found I needed her just as much, if not more. She's been my family for the last few years."

"Your language, Detective . . . Your language . . . Since we sat down, you don't sound as much like a dumb flatfoot as an earnest, decent man with a brain in his head. You've changed. What's that all about? Something tells me there's more to it than just the booze."

It's strange. I don't feel criticized, and I'm not testy about Amanda's advice, which is rare for me. Instead, I feel safe— even loved. I must be drunk.

"Is it that obvious?" I ask with some hesitation as I collect my thoughts. "I've felt most of my life as though I'm fronting for someone else, but I didn't realize it was so transparent. I learned early on to act like all the other guys to avoid being singled out. I guess I've been doing it most of my life. Acting tough and not too smart is certainly the easiest way to get by on the force. It's sort of like a locker room thing. If you're the gay guy on the DL, you become very aware of what you need to do to fit in. It must rub off in good company."

Amanda nods. She gets it.

"Well, don't hold back on my account. If I'm going to be arrested for murder, I'd rather it be by an intelligent man than a Troglodyte. But getting back to you; don't you think the best course is to just be who you really are? How else will you meet someone you can be satisfied with?"

"When I first began to realize I was gay, I knew my father would kill me if he found out. I used to fantasize about a sort of Prince Charming, who'd carry me off to a better place. One day we'd meet, and the next he'd take me away to his castle in a distant land where we'd love each other and live happily ever after. I can hardly even remember the naïve little twink who thought that could ever happen."

"C'mon now, don't go maudlin on me," Amanda says. "Here's a newsflash: you're not the only handsome, idealistic, caring gay man on the planet. There have to be a few more around somewhere. And I just know there are better places to find them than West End."

"If you say so, lady."

"I'm not saying anything earth shattering. It's just a matter of giving life a try on your own terms. Why are you making that so difficult? Have you always lived under a rock like this?"

"Now that you mention it, I suppose I have. I've always preferred to watch from the sidelines and figure things out from a distance. That's why I liked working security on a cruise ship; it was great people watching with no commitment. The passengers always got off the boat. If there was a hassle with a crew member, you put in for a transfer, and that was that. All nice and tidy.

"Seven years ago, when I took the West End job, I thought I'd find the life I'd always wanted and someone to share it with. Instead, I've had a string of washashores, all running from something only to find their baggage waiting when they arrive. I've never found anyone I could be close to. Ever."

"Especially Javier, by the looks of it," Amanda says with a sly grin. "He's about as far from Prince Charming as you can get. Even on this pathetic pile of coral. That voice! What *could* you have been thinking?"

I laugh with her. She's not making fun. It's a statement of fact and strangely encouraging. She understands me so well it's scary. If only I understood myself half as much.

"I should never have taken up with Javier. My gut told me not to, but he wanted a relationship so badly I finally gave in. Perhaps in my own way, I was desperate, too. I didn't want all that much, except someone to be there when I came home. And look what happened: my shit's all over the island. I can't believe I ever thought I'd find more than a parking place with that asshole."

I lose track of time as I ramble on. Amanda comments every now and then in a silken, empathetic voice that sustains her spell. I know, without her saying a word, she's lived a similar life, and somehow that makes it OK for me to tell her the whole pathetic tale. A couple of times I question her motives, but it feels so damn good to get things off my chest, I don't dwell on them.

"You have it all," she says, when I finally stop, emotionally drained. "You just don't trust it. You stay put because it seems impossible to start over. You're afraid of failing. And afraid of what it might mean to truly love someone. Trust me, I've been there, too."

"I can tell."

I can—and it's not the booze talking.

"You'd think, looking at you, that everything was handed to you, Amanda. Somehow, I don't think that's the case. You've fought like hell to become the woman you are."

She looks away, but not before I see a wistful glint in her eyes.

"You're right. I started with nothing and built up . . . a bit of confidence . . . and, ah, set out to . . . to tackle the world on my own terms."

There's too much uncertainty in her voice. For the first time since we arrived at Vittorina's, my cop's instincts kick in, and in a flash, I'm back in interrogation mode. I feel that predatory edge—a sort of zeroing in for the kill—that always kicks in when I sense a lie. Then it hits me: I've poured my heart out to a murderer; I've crossed the line. I have to get back in the driver's seat.

Amanda looks at me questioningly, but only for an instant before her gaze drops to the table. Without a word, she signals for the check.

Nearly three hours have passed. Our cab is waiting. A surly queen demands a ride as Louis sits patiently ignoring an avalanche of sibilance. For an instant, I feel loathing for those simpering faggots who make stereotypes of the rest of us. One look at me, the queen gives up and minces away. That's right, Mary, you never stood a chance.

"Where can we drop you?" Amanda asks, looking worn, as if the evening's sudden turn has sapped all her energy.

Or did she notice my reaction to the queen? I suspect she'd have a problem with that. See what I mean? Reading someone else's thoughts is tough. Your mind never stops trying to figure out if you've got things right.

"That's OK, I'll walk. My place isn't far."

"As you wish," she says in a monotone, without even a wave this time.

I wobble down the street a bit, then look back. The cab hasn't moved.

The fifteen-minute walk to my house is surreal. Given the significant amounts of liquor I've consumed, I'm not all that steady on my feet. Besides, my thoughts are a train wreck.

Even if I were straight, what would a classy dame like her want with the likes of me? This whole empathy thing is just a ruse to get me to back off on my investigation. So is Chaela's scholarship. This is hard to take. Without Amanda, I have no one in my corner. But I just know I'm right. Another triumph for the great detective.

When I reach my street, it's lit up like daylight. My house has been on fire for some time, but the fire department is nowhere to be found. A small crowd of neighbors has gathered, laughing and joking, in the front yard. Whoever has done this has gone to considerable lengths: a clothesline stretches between two palm trees; all of my briefs and jocks hang from it like carnival flags, looking oddly effeminate. Then there's the piece de resistance, a giant banner that spells out "FAGGOT" in gold letters that glisten in the firelight.

The roof collapses, provoking a short gasp, then a smattering of applause. After that, there's a hush—almost a religious silence—broken only by crackling flames. As I scan the crowd to see who's responsible, a neighbor spots me and word fans out.

A shadow moves in my direction. It's Scavela. No surprise there. His face is furrowed with hatred, his eyes black slits, brimming with rage. I tense, ready for a fight—welcoming it, in fact. What the hell do I have to lose? I step into the street. He's halfway across when a car races between us, horn blaring. Its headlights blind me, so it's only when the rear door opens that I realize Louis and Amanda have followed me home.

"Get in. Now! No macho bullshit!"

Amanda's tone brooks no refusal. I doubt I could even land a punch in my drunken state, but I sure as hell want to try. I hesitate, determined to have it out with him at last. Amanda grabs me and pulls hard. I topple onto the back seat. Scavela pulls open the other door.

Amanda yells, "Louis, get us out of here. Now!"

There's a squeal of rubber as the cab picks up speed. As I watch in what seems slow motion, the door knocks Scavela to the pavement, then slams shut. Amanda's arms encircle me. I feel relief, then rage, then nausea. Her lips graze my forehead; then everything goes black.

I wake around eleven in a huge, comfortable bed. The ocean sprawls below like a string of sapphires. I'm in Freeport—the penthouse suite of the Excelsior, no less. As I stare out over the ocean, it strikes me, not for the first time, it's a crime such a beautiful island is so full of bullshit. This is a typically lousy thought to start a brand-new day. And with a first-class hangover, to boot.

Towels, a razor, and shaving cream have been set out in the bathroom. I shower and shave. Only then do I see the note on the washstand, held in place by a bottle of expensive cologne.

Dear Detective Beston,

Good morning (I hope). It seemed a good idea to let you sleep. Forgive my absence. I have several obligations that make for a busy day.

Please accept my hospitality as you plan your future. The place is yours for a month. On me. I insist. Charge all food, beverages, clothing, and necessities to your room. Refurbish your wardrobe downstairs with Pierre at Van Wyck's. I took the liberty of picking out a tuxedo he will alter immediately after your fitting. Would you be so good as to wear it for dinner on the terrace at eight this evening? Until then, might I offer a word of advice? Especially at a time like this, don't give in to suspicion and negativity. Instead, seize the day.

By the way, call Chaela. She's got news.

Fondly,

Amanda

PS: Under the circumstances, I'd suggest you stay within the hotel grounds and maintain a low profile, but I'm sure I don't have to tell you that.

I'm stunned. At this point, I don't care if she orchestrated the Saint Valentine's Day Massacre; this strange, sexy woman is the only friend I've got.

I call Chaela, and she's ecstatic. She's heading to Rutgers tonight—first-class, all expenses paid. I'm not the only one who's got a friend in Amanda. I spend the rest of the day buying clothes and luggage, working out, and getting a massage. I guess I'm a kept man, but with no alternatives, I just suck it up and deal.

Promptly at eight, I saunter into the terrace bar with my hands in my pockets. In my new tux, I feel a bit like Cary Grant and more than slightly cocky.

My entrance is wasted. Amanda's not there. William escorts me to the same table as last night, though it feels a million years have passed. He brings a Hendrick's and tonic without my asking. Recalling Amanda's praise for his gentle ways, I'm oddly touched.

"How are things going, William?" I ask, realizing a moment too late there's more than one answer to *that* question.

"Fantastic! That Miss Amanda, she a miracle worker. I thank her in my prayers each night, and so do Victor!"

I'll bet he does, I tell myself, savoring humor for the first time in what seems an age.

At twenty past, Amanda's still missing in action. William brings another Hendrick's. I scan the terrace, filled with couples engaged in amorous conversation, and worry what might be keeping her. For all I know, Scavela may have sent some goon after her for knocking him down like that.

William takes a call at the bar, hangs up, then returns to my table. He seems slightly troubled.

"Miss Amanda say she be very sorry, but she be detained and won't make it for dinner."

I search his dark brown eyes. There's no trace of deception in them, but I'd swear in court he's anxious about something. I down my drink and signal for another.

William is back in a flash. He serves my Hendrick's, then hovers nearby, watching me closely, until, feeling like a charity case, I wave him away.

At eight thirty, as I'm wondering if I'm no longer Amanda's flavor of the month, a handsome man in a tux strolls to where I'm staring out at the bay.

"Detective Lieutenant Beston?" he asks in a deep voice that immediately catches my attention.

"Yes?"

"I believe Ms. Mulher has already sent her regrets. She's desolate she can't make it this evening and was kind enough to suggest I take her place. Might I sit down."

He doesn't ask as much as tell. I study him as he pulls out a chair: a man near forty, with piercing hazel eyes and the slightest hint of gray around the temples. His body is in fantastic shape. He looks oddly familiar.

"Sure, why not," I say, still trying to recall where I've seen him before.

"I'm a paltry substitute for Amanda, I know. She's well, but caught up in urgent business. If you'd be good enough to settle for me, it would satisfy her wishes. Always the wisest course of action, I've learned." He sticks out his hand. "I'm Vaughn Kreisler, by the way. Amanda has told me a lot about you."

It takes a couple of seconds for me to digest what he's said. At first, I think he's messing with me, but when I recall the photographs from his FBI file, I realize he may well be the genuine article. If so, I've spent days trying to indict an innocent woman. If Amanda decides to sue, I'm fucked.

"You're Kreisler?" I ask, my voice just a trace too high. "Where the hell have you been?"

"All will be revealed. First, might I order a drink?"

Head still reeling, I summon William and introduce them. Kreisler orders a vodka and tonic. I signal for a much-needed refill. By now I've lost count.

"OK," I say. "What happened on that boat?"

"Before getting into that," he says, with a captivating grin that telegraphs, 'I appreciate your frustration, but you can't pull rank on *me*,' "I'd like to make sure you're satisfied there's been no foul play. Amanda did everything she could to find me. What happened was simply a fluke. And entirely my fault . . ."

"OK, I'll grant that for now. But I still need you to corroborate her story."

I feel stupid for having assumed the worst. The evidence seemed to add up, but now I've got to figure out how far off the mark I was.

"Well, to put it bluntly, I was incredibly stupid. We were sailing on autopilot in light wind. Overnight, we snagged a long net. I broke every rule in the book when I went out at dawn to cut it loose."

He tells me how he rowed so as not to wake Amanda. His story matches her description: the squall, her trying to turn *Last Chance* around—it all ties out perfectly.

Apparently the engine wouldn't start, and he rode the Gulf Stream until a fishing boat picked him up the next day. If he's to be believed, the crew was making a connection off Jamaica and refused to take him ashore until the deal was done. After several days, they dropped him off on Little Inagua on their way back to God-knows-where. Evidently, he was smart enough not to ask.

"Where've you been since then?" I ask, partially convinced, but needing more proof.

"I gave the fishermen the Zodiac by way of thanks, so it took quite a while to get to civilization. When I reached a phone two days ago, I tracked down Amanda and learned *Last Chance* had been impounded. She sent money, and I island-hopped my way up to Nassau. Yesterday, I caught a ferry to Freeport, and here I am."

"You mean she knew you were OK and went along with my interrogation without saying a word?"

It sounds a bit farfetched to me.

"I've learned the hard way never to try to explain Amanda's actions," Kreisler says with a sheepish grin.

"Do you have any ID? I have to file a report with the Feds."

"What would you like? Driver's license, birth certificate, or passport? I snuck on board and retrieved them from the secret compartment early this morning. Or perhaps you want to bag my glass for fingerprints? If so, just let me finish my drink."

"I'm not likely to be a cop for much longer, so I'll take your word. For my own peace of mind, just let me see your license."

With that, he opens his wallet and tosses me a Massachusetts license. I study it carefully. Everything seems in order. The photo is his, the eye color matches, height seems right. No, it's Kreisler, alright.

"One more question . . .," I say, not so much to learn more, but to keep him talking for reasons that suddenly don't feel all that professional.

I'm stunned my whole theory has collapsed. It's never happened like this before, but I'm getting the oddest hunch I should be glad it has.

"There was blood on the inside of the lazarette," I say, trying to remain objective while surveying Kreisler's lithe body and handsome features.

He grins as though applauding my observational expertise. His glance is coy, which makes me wonder if he's caught me checking him out.

"I scratched my shoulder on the latch when I reached down for the antifouling knife. It was a minor scrape, and it's nearly healed by now. I'd be happy to show you if you need more proof."

"No, I guess I'm satisfied," I say, trying to maintain a shred of professionalism. "But I'm still curious about a few things back in the States."

"Sure. Shoot."

"Your wife's issued a divorce summons for desertion and adultery. Amanda was spotted sailing the boat out of Marblehead Harbor, so Lois may have a damn good case for at least half of all you've got. From what I've heard, she's thoroughly pissed."

I expect him to tense or get angry, but he just laughs.

"Other than the fact that Amanda was seen, I'm not surprised in the least. I expected Lois would try to break the prenup despite the fifty million I left her."

"What do you mean?"

"There's an ironclad prenuptial agreement. When we met, I had all the money. Her family had the pedigree, but would have had to retrench in a major way if she didn't marry well. They were in no position to bargain back then, and I've come to suspect over the years the only reason she married me was to shore up their cash flow.

"I doubt if Lois even remembers what's in the agreement. I left her five times the agreed-upon amount, which is enough to keep the whole lot of them in the style to which they're accustomed. She's done better than she had any right to expect—not that she could prove adultery with Amanda in the first place."

This strikes me as odd. What's he saying? You don't sail off to the Caribbean with a sexpot like Amanda and not give at least the appearance of adultery. But then, maybe he's right. How could it be proved? They were the only two on the boat.

He changes the subject.

"I understand Amanda was of some help last night."

"Some help? She saved my ass and has been generous beyond belief with *your* money."

"It's not my money; it's hers, too. She's a soul mate—the other side of the coin—and anything I have is hers."

Just what Amanda said less than a week ago. Obviously, this guy has feelings for her.

I feel a bitter, empty spot inside, which makes no sense—no sense at all. Why would I be jealous? And if I were, of which one?

I slip into interrogation mode to ground myself. It's second nature: detached, analytical, and externally focused. The safest space I know. Incursions into emotion are always dangerous for me. As I learned from the murder of Adrian Moon and his wife, when I lose my objectivity, bad things happen.

"So where's Amanda?"

Kreisler seems nonchalant when he replies, "As I said, she's tending to something rather important."

I sense a little hesitation, though. Amanda must have mentioned my suspicions. I decide to tackle the issue head on.

"I suppose she told you I accused her of murdering you."

"Oh yes; she *certainly did*."

He smiles. I find myself captivated by his eyes. They're a rich hazel color. I've never seen eyes like them.

"There *is* a certain logic to your theory, but if you knew Amanda as I do, you'd know for sure it was off the mark."

"You probably won't believe this," I say in spite of myself, "I was coming to that conclusion. Something about her intrigues me. I confess I used the investigation to get to know her better."

Vaughn looks surprised.

"So you find her attractive?"

"She must have told you about me. I'm not into women."

"I thought we had something in common besides Amanda."

Vaughn looks right at me as he says this. It takes a second for me to get the picture—the guy who ran off with the "other woman" isn't into women. Either.

"You mean you're . . ."

"As a goose. Which reminds me . . . William! Another Grey Goose and tonic?"

Kreisler holds up his glass, grinning from ear to ear.

"Wow, I finally said it!"

"'Another Grey Goose'?"

Kreisler laughs. His voice is very, very sexy.

"No. That I'm gay."

"Well, technically, you didn't."

I'm pretty sure it's him, not the booze, that suddenly has me at attention. There's laughter in his eyes, as if he knows, too.

"I'm not going to quibble. It's been a long haul getting this far, and if you won't let me celebrate, then you're not half the catch Amanda says you are."

With that, he colors a bit. It's charming—almost innocent.

"She said I was a catch?"

This is beneath me, though given what's been happening lately, I'm not too proud to fish for a compliment.

"Not in so many words. She said you were a good man suffering untold indignities."

"I appreciate that. Coming from her . . ."

I stop, not wanting to sound infatuated or needy, which I realize to my embarrassment has already happened.

"Let's give Amanda a rest, OK?" Vaughn says with a satisfied smile. "I'm certain my filling in at the last minute is more than happenstance. I want to say right now that I truly regret wasting your time. How can I make it up to you?"

I look over at Kreisler. He's thinking the same thing. I just know it.

"The kind of apology I'm looking for is best made in private, my friend," I say, holding out my hand. "Before things go any further, Vaughn, the name is Paul.

"William, check, please?"

Vaughn finishes his drink. I toss mine down, stand up, and head toward the elevator.

Amanda would love the way I'm taking charge of my life.

The morning after is a revelation. For once, the night wasn't just sex. It was the whole package—conversation, affection, exploration, laughter—everything I've always wanted and never found until now. To be honest, it was even more than that. We couldn't get enough, finally falling asleep in each other's arms at five in the morning. Or should I say Vaughn did. I just lay there, watching him sleep, trying to convince myself it wasn't all a dream.

Now, in the light of day, there are choices to be made: thank you and out the door; a little dance about another date; or another round to keep reality at bay for a few more hours. Then, of course, there's the most unlikely option of all . . .

I feel Vaughn's eyes on me as I walk back from the can. I stop, give him a good look, and wait to see which route we're taking.

"Paul, you know, I never realized . . ."

He pats the pillow beside him. I hop into bed and pull him close.

"Realized what?"

"That men could connect like this."

"From a plumbing standpoint?"

It's obvious I'm dodging the issue, but Vaughn chooses to ignore my feeble attempt at humor.

"As men. With no shame or regret."

"Isn't that why you ditched your former life? To come out as a proud gay man?" I ask, wondering why love didn't claim Vaughn Kreisler ages ago.

Then I think about his relationship with Amanda. If there isn't sex between them, what's their bond? From the way they speak of each other, they clearly love each other very much.

"That's part of it," he says. "There's no question I should have accepted myself, with all my warts and blemishes—say nothing of my complexities—years ago."

"I covered every inch of you at least three times last night and, except for that scrape you told me about, there were no warts or blemishes. Far from it. As for complexity, only time will tell."

He flashes a lusty grin. There's a thank you in it.

"You wait, Detective. You just wait. I'm your toughest case yet."

"OK, Vaughn. I think we're in total agreement, but first there's work to be done. We don't have a moment to lose. Go get changed. Where we're going, you can't be seen in a tux."

He looks crestfallen, as if he's being tossed out on his ass, though nothing could be further from the truth. I reach under the covers, squeeze just the right spot, then chuckle when his eyes roll to the back of his head.

"It's good, Vaughn, damn good," I whisper. "Worth fighting for, which is just what we're going to do."

He jumps out of bed and stretches, looking heroic. While feasting my eyes on the magnificence of this man, I find myself thinking of Amanda.

Should I feel guilty for coming between them?

Island bureaucracy being what it is, there's no doubt I'm still an officer of the law. Even so, I'd be lying if I say I'm relaxed when Vaughn and I stride into the squad room. Conversation stops. All eyes turn toward us. It's gratifying to see Scavela's face swathed in bandages. The dark bruise on his forehead gives me that warm, fuzzy feeling that always comes with justice served piping hot. He starts to rise from his chair, but before he can get to his feet, I've got my hands around his throat and have pushed him back down.

"You motherfucker. Someone could have been killed in that fire you set."

I relax my grip just enough to let him speak. The rest of the squad jumps to their feet. They're tense and uncharacteristically quiet.

"You can't prove nuthin'," Scavela says, his swagger falling flat.

"Maybe he can't," says Vaughn, moving to my side, "but I can. I've got seven witnesses who either saw you douse the house in gasoline, light the fire, hang the banner, or heard you brag about it to the crowd."

"Who the fuck is he, Beston? You his batty boy?"

I tighten my grip. Scavela slumps, gasping for breath.

"This is Vaughn Kreisler, recently discovered *very much* alive and well. Mr. Kreisler, this is former officer Scavela, who was playing with matches last night."

"Ah yes. Mr. Scavela," Vaughn says, "your reputation precedes you. I'd be more careful about those you consider friends. They gave you up for an average of fifty dollars apiece on the fire, and three hundred apiece on that business with Adrian Moon and his wife."

Adrian Moon?

Scavela's eyes shed all trace of bravado. Now there's fear in them. Somehow, Vaughn's gotten the goods to put him away for a long time.

"Charlie," I say, tightening my grip on Scavela while wondering why I don't just get it over with and break his neck, "get the chief. Now!"

Vaughn catches my eye. He shakes his head as if he's read my thoughts. The movement is nearly imperceptible, but it's enough to get through, and I stand down. Charlie, once my best friend on the force, hesitates, looks around the room, and then, thank God, does as I ask.

When the chief arrives, he surveys the scene with a puzzled gaze. This is my biggest gamble so far. He's island born and bred; a decent, devoted family man. Until recently, I've had his respect. He must know by now I've been outed. That, I know, will change everything.

"Chief Rolle, may I introduce Vaughn Kreisler? Vaughn Kreisler, Chief Rolle."

The chief shoots me a quick questioning glance, but steps up readily enough.

"Mr. Kreisler, I'm delighted no harm has come to you. Would you be kind enough to tell me what happened to you?"

"With pleasure, Chief. But first, if you don't mind, I'd like to swear out a statement against Officer Scavela. He's guilty of arson, intimidation, reckless endangerment, and attempted homicide. He's also an accessory to the murder of Mr. and Mrs. Adrian Moon."

Chief Rolle takes a step back.

"How do you know all this?"

"A private investigator has been working the Moon case for a week now with enough money to pry the story loose. This piece of slime plotted to discredit Lieutenant Beston when he was first promoted to detective. When sabotaging the drug investigation didn't accomplish his goal, Mr. Scavela bided his time. Recent developments rekindled his hatred and offered an opportunity. He burned down Lieutenant Beston's house two nights ago and tried to assault him in the street."

"You have proof of these accusations?"

"Undeniable proof on all charges from sworn witnesses. You'll find their depositions with Gowrie, Smythe, and Co., the solicitors in Freeport. George Gowrie is waiting for your call."

The chief seems stunned, but I know he'll do the right thing. He's worked with Gowrie for years and knows he's on the level.

"Thank you," I whisper to Vaughn as we wait for the chief to reply.

"Not me. Amanda," Vaughn whispers back. "That's what she was up to last night. She's rather tapped into this island, you know."

No kidding.

"Charlie," I say, "lock up Scavela, then get Gowrie down here."

Charlie looks to Chief Rolle, who slowly nods his head.

Scavela struggles to break free. I tighten my grip, but he escapes and lunges toward Vaughn, who doesn't seem concerned in the least. Just before his hands reach Vaughn's neck, I knock Scavela over, then sit on him, grab his arms, and pull them behind his back. The entire squad looks on without anyone making a move. This sucks. I can't keep this up forever, and it's clear none of these bastards will help me.

"Enough," says the chief at last. "Remove the prisoner to the cellblock."

With that, Charlie and three others finally step forward. In less than a minute, Scavela is cuffed and on his way.

"Faggot whore," he growls as he's dragged past Vaughn.

"Perhaps," Vaughn replies with a wide grin, showing no signs of anxiety after his near escape, "The big difference is, I get to choose. At Fox Hill Prison, you won't get to pick *your* dance partners. Drop me a note in a year, batty boy, and we'll see then who's the bigger whore—if you can bear to sit down long enough to write it."

Scavela exits the room to mocking laughter. The squad may not like me, but realizing he's the traitor in their midst, they like him even less. Small satisfaction, but I'll take it.

"Chief, there's one more thing . . ."

I grasp his elbow as he starts to leave. He glares, frozen at my touch. I remove my hand as naturally as I can. This is all I need to know my days on the force are at an end.

"As you know," I say, acting as if nothing happened, "I impounded Mr. Kreisler's yacht during the investigation. Obviously, there's no need for that now he's returned."

The chief's response is rigidly formal. He tells Vaughn he's free to go, but must leave the island at once—under police escort.

This news hits me hard. I'd expected we'd have time to find out if last night was the real thing. In contrast, Vaughn's face is a mask. If the order came as a surprise, he's not giving anything away. Perhaps I was wrong. For all he said to the contrary, maybe last night meant more to me than to him. With his new life and his glamorous fag hag to keep him company, he can go anywhere in the world, first class. If he's changed his mind about the two of us, I'm going to be lucky to get off this island alive. Scavela may be out of commission, but no doubt he has friends who'd enjoy making my life a living hell—until they ended it.

Vaughn is fingerprinted. The prints match. Then he makes a couple of quick calls. While we wait for the Feds to sign off, I wind up some paperwork, pack up my personal effects, then call the Excelsior and release Amanda's passport as my last official act. No doubt, she'll leave on *Last Chance* with Vaughn.

At last, we're free to go. I'm not surprised to see a cab waiting. I *am* surprised to see Louis behind the wheel. Charlie's cruiser pulls up to escort us, and we're on our way. Our first stop is the Excelsior. Vaughn tells Louis to wait, then turns to me.

"There's no need for you to go in; I won't be a moment."

His eyes seem to avoid mine. I shrug my shoulders in reply, trying hard to appear indifferent, then stare blindly as he jogs up the stairs to the lobby. For a while, I battle the sense of inevitability that's slowly overtaking me. If Vaughn had wanted me to go with him to Barbados, this would have been the perfect time to retrieve my luggage. Then I give up and face facts. The final act will be nothing but a big kiss-off.

At Old Bahama Bay, there's a flurry of activity around *Last Chance.* Customs takes time, but eventually the paperwork is completed and the impound removed. Now there's nothing left to keep Vaughn on the island. I sense his agitation and prepare myself for the big brush-off.

"Take a walk?"

"Sure."

We head toward the dock where *Last Chance* is berthed, majestic and eager.

I tell myself he'll start with, "It's been great."

"Paul, it's been great . . ."

Can I call it or what, I think as we stroll past the quaint buildings, so idealized and sterile. Welcome to paradise, sucker.

"Meeting you is the best thing that's ever happened to me. After last night, I'm finally comfortable being myself."

"Yeah, talk about a transformation. One night with me, and you come out to a room full of cops. Quite the debut!"

I feel like an ass before the words are completely out of my mouth.

"You could say that, I suppose . . ."

He's ignoring my sarcasm. We could have worked. I need someone to let me be the idiot I often am. He continues, seeming in dead earnest.

"But I see it a bit differently. There were signs throughout my life I wasn't being honest with myself, but I suppressed them. Everything came together for me last night, and I'd be a fool not to realize that."

One look, and I can tell.

He stops walking and turns to face me.

"I don't have any right to ask."

"Ask away . . ."

"You mean you'll consider it?"

"Considered and decided—just waiting for the invite. I was brought up that a gentleman needs a proper invitation."

"Really?"

"Not really, but it sounds good, don't you think?"

Vaughn pulls out his cell phone.

"William, Jean-Paul's waiting behind the clubhouse with Mr. Beston's bags. Bring them on board and unpack them in the second port stateroom. And William, cancel Mr. Beston's reservation at the Excelsior as well, please?"

My curiosity gets the better of me.

"Not the same William who waited on us?"

"Uh-huh."

"He's everywhere."

"Uh-huh."

"You knew him already?"

"Amanda did. Don't you remember? You introduced him to me last night."

"Is he crew, or onboard entertainment?"

I sound like a bitch, but Vaughn overlooks it again. We're going to be a fabulous couple.

"Amanda tells me he's quite the sailor. His family ran charters to the Exumas for years. In addition to captaining the boat, he'll be our valet and assistant.

"We'll also have a crew. It was too long a wait for visas to the States, so I figured we'd sail to Grand Turk and pick them up there. Once she heard from me, Amanda had them fly here instead."

"So William wasn't part of the original crew?"

Once a detective, always a detective. Once a jealous queen, always a jealous queen.

"William is a new addition, and so is Victor, his partner. They're our valet and cook, respectively. A live-in *couple*."

Vaughn shakes his head. I just know he's getting a kick out of my possessiveness. OK, that's it. I'm hooked. Just reel me in, please?

"Amanda told me they dreamed of living together openly, so I thought, why not?" Vaughn says to me with a coy smile. "There's plenty of room on the boat. On Barbados, there's a private cottage on the grounds that will suit them well."

"You amaze me. *Last Chance* is a Noah's Ark for gay men."

Vaughn chuckles. "You ain't seen nuthin' yet. Wait till we get home and you meet the rest of the staff. Everyone is gay save Bruno, the chief of security. She's a lesbian. I feel extremely safe around her. You will, too, once you get used to how macho she is. She makes Rocky Balboa look like Quentin Crisp."

As Vaughn gives the tour, I can hardly believe what's happening. *Last Chance* is even more spectacular than I remember: three staterooms, a gourmet galley, a book-lined salon, separate crew's quarters, and, most rare, an elegant dining room behind sliding doors. Everything is teak and polished brass. A framed photograph of Amanda at the helm rests on a shelf in the salon.

I reach for the door of the last stateroom and find it locked. I'm surprised, given the rest of the yacht is wide open, and ask why.

"That's Amanda's berth. She always locks it when she's away."

"She's not sailing with us?"

"No, she's going on ahead to make sure the workers have cleared out of the new house."

Nice of her to give us some time alone, I tell myself, appreciating the fact there's been no fuss about the two of us. Yet.

"A new house?"

"That was the point of sending everything to Barbados. I wanted a comfortable, isolated setting to use as home base for a whole new life. I hope you'll like it."

"If it's big enough for two and the neighbors aren't pyromaniacs, I'm sure it will be fine."

"I think you'll find it suitable," he says with a smile.

Cute.

The crew from Grand Turk is pleasant and, even better, another gay couple. They cast off, back expertly out of the slip, and motor through the narrow channel as if they've manned the yacht for years. Once we're under sail, Vaughn leaves to consult Victor about dinner. I watch Grand Bahama recede into the distance, until at last, Vaughn returns.

"Dinner's at eight. Black tie. William and Victor are making quite the fuss, so we should do our part, don't you think?"

"Fine with me."

Vaughn studies me closely.

"Penny for your thoughts?"

His arms slide around my waist. It feels as if he's held me that way for years.

"To hell and good riddance, to be perfectly honest."

"No regrets?"

"Only that I didn't pound the shit out of Scavela and give him something to remember me by."

"He'll remember you well enough every time he's forced to bend over in the shower. Don't give that bastard a second thought."

Victor is everywhere at once in the galley as William puts the finishing touches on the table settings. The two men greet me as if hosting a party in their own home. Silver candlesticks, fine china, and a spectacular crystal wine decanter on silver gimbals grace the table. William, resplendent in black tie, pulls out my chair.

A formal dinner for two at sea. I could get used to this.

As a Chelsea ship's clock strikes eight, I hear a stateroom door. Amanda is a vision in a low-cut purple gown—simple, but elegant. An enormous diamond nestles between her breasts like a captured ray of sunlight. Then there are the matching bracelets and earrings.

I stand.

William pulls back her chair.

She sits.

I sit.

Silence.

"Vaughn said you weren't aboard."

My voice sounds accusatory, but I'm too rattled to tone it down.

"I wasn't."

"Come again?"

"I wasn't aboard until two hours ago, give or take a few minutes."

"What do you mean? Where's Vaughn?"

"He's not here right now."

"What?"

"William, please give us a moment? I'll ring."

Amanda smiles as if to telegraph all will be well. William excuses himself. As he draws the doors closed, his brow creases with concern, and my gut starts to churn.

I was right. She *is* a black widow. She's thrown Vaughn overboard, and I'm her next victim. She won't get away with this.

"Paul . . ." Amanda says, with a slight note of censure, then pauses as though waiting for something to sink in.

"How do you know my first name? I never told you . . ."

"Oh yes, you did."

I study her face.

"Amanda . . . your eyes."

"Yes?"

"They're hazel."

"You're very observant."

"You're not Amanda."

"Oh yes, I am."

"No, you're not. You're Vaughn!"

"Imagine that."

Shit! I get it, but then again . . .

OK, so I overreacted. I've still got more than enough to worry about. Sorting through all our discussions and interrogations, I search for something—anything—that might have clued me in. I can't find a damn thing. Even so, I doubt I'll ever get over being played for such a chump.

"You mean I accused you of murdering . . . of murdering yourself?"

Amanda, or should I say Vaughn, places her (or is it his?) hand on mine.

"You could put it that way, but I'd rather say that given the facts you had, you were seeking justice."

"Why the hell did you lie to me?"

I usually interrogate with more finesse, but I need answers, and fast.

"At first, because I feared repercussions."

This is said as if to chasten me.

"You were in touch with the States, and could have caused a great deal of embarrassment for me. Enduring your daily interrogations seemed easier than risking exposure. I could always appear as Vaughn and shut things down if absolutely necessary, but something unforeseen happened. I—Amanda—began to fall in love with you."

I watch the decanter level as the boat heels ever so slightly. After a minute or so, when Amanda (or is it Vaughn?) speaks again, it seems as much for himself (herself?) as for me. I decide to listen politely. Confrontation in the early rounds never gets you anywhere.

"I stayed away to gauge my feelings. Once certain they were genuine, I sought out Chaela to find out more about you. I didn't have to ask much; she was so full of love and gratitude, the answers came spilling out on their own. I could tell instantly you'd worked wonders with her. She spoke eloquently of your compassion, courage, and integrity."

Bad move to bring Chaela into all of this.

"Before you call me on it, Paul, I had good reason to contact her. The attraction you and I felt for each other needed to be dealt with. You knew that, too. You didn't come to the Excelsior just to ask questions. There was more to it than that."

"Well . . . yes . . . that's true, there was. Although I didn't think of it in quite those terms."

"But this morning, with Vaughn, you certainly did. You said we were worth fighting for. Though now you know the nature of the battle, you'll probably reconsider such a brash statement."

"Now, wait. Don't go expecting the worst. Maybe I just need some time to adjust. Give me a minute, for Christ's sake."

This may require more than a minute. It could take strong drugs and years of therapy. I've dealt with drag queens before as part of the job, but I've never been had by one before, never mind in bed. Let's just say I'm not thrilled with the wardrobe Vaughn chose for dinner and leave it at that. I can tell he, or better said she, knows this deal is a long shot. I'm glad not to be considered a pushover, but I'd rather we just have it out like men.

"Let's take one thing at a time. I need to get my head around all this. Didn't you say something once about 'a perfect topic for dinner conversation'?"

"Ah yes, that *was* me, wasn't it? I have trouble keeping track sometimes."

Her smile is pure charm. Something inside me softens. As far as I'm concerned, she's still the same Amanda. That, at least, is progress.

She presses a buzzer on the underside of the table. William enters with her vodka and tonic and, much to my relief, a Hendrick's. He serves us silently, then departs, closing the doors without a sound.

"You certainly owe me one hell of an explanation," I say, struggling to keep my voice down.

"Absolutely." A trace of guilt clouds her features. "Let me start by apologizing for deceiving you and turning up unannounced like this. I'll be forthcoming from now on. It's only fair, given the way I've dragged you into all this—if you'll pardon the pun."

All this Glinda the Good Witch stuff is beginning to get on my nerves. Nobody can be this poised and mannered all the time. Nobody real, I mean. But then she's not, is she? I manage a half-smile. It's the best I can muster.

"Let me try to explain, Paul . . . When Vaughn realized he was in love with you, he decided to tell you about me right away; even though it might ruin everything. This morning, when Vaugh went to get dressed, he had William make a reservation at Vittorina's for just that purpose. If you need corroboration, William can attest to the fact. He was worried how you might react."

I shake my head. I believe Vaughn's intentions. It's hers that bother me. I suddenly wish I was a more gullible sort; if I were, I'd be home free about now—the way I thought I was just five minutes ago.

"Go on," I say, deciding petulance isn't going to do me any good.

Amanda stares at me intently, as if looking for something, then continues.

"Chief Rolle's ultimatum changed everything. I know my appearance just now was a shock, but we did the best we could on such short notice: Vaughn invited you on board, and I showed up for dinner. Just as I invited you to dinner last night, and he showed up instead."

"No one has the right to deceive someone just because they can."

I mean it. These machinations don't sit well with me, say nothing of the fact my plans for the evening are shot to hell. A gourmet meal followed by mind-blowing sex beats playing twenty questions with a transvestite every time.

"Suck it up, Detective," Amanda says with a smirk. "You're not here forever unless you want to be. In two days, we'll land at Grand Turk. If you wish, you can leave then."

"But I'm stuck on this boat until we get there?"

"Unless you find the situation so repellent you want me to charter a helicopter for an immediate escape. If so, I'll call for one this instant."

"I may hold you to that."

"And I wouldn't entirely blame you if you did," she says, relaxing ever so slightly into our usual give-and-take. "This has to be a huge shock. Especially after last night."

"It's one hell of a second date."

"I'll bet."

Amanda seems to be putting on a brave front for my benefit. Looking closely, I can see her jaw is tight, her body tense. Her right hand toys with a linen napkin.

"Well, what do you have to say for yourself?"

"Paul, I could recount a million stories, recite a million heartaches, but it all comes down to the fact that I'm both Amanda *and* Vaughn. God, it feels good to tell you at last."

"Is this more of that 'true to oneself' mumbo-jumbo?"

"Yes, as a matter of fact, it is, though I'd prefer you not be so crass when discussing something so intimate. It took a lot of effort for Vaughn to come to grips with his sexuality."

"It didn't seem all that difficult for him last night," I say wistfully, as arousal and revulsion course through me.

"For Vaughn, accepting his gay self was harder than accepting my femininity. Perhaps it was all the corporate constraints, but it was just too much for Vaughn to admit he was gay on top of all that. Until you came along, that is. Then everything fell into place."

"It certainly did. I'm still sore."

Not a great time for a bad joke, but I guess I'm wishing I could see even a trace of the man I thought was my own personal Prince Charming. Instead, all I see is Snow White.

Amanda's the one smiling wistfully now, and I feel some empathy for her. Even with all that money to keep the bullshit at bay, it must have been one hell of a ride. Some of her dough was well spent, though; her makeup and wardrobe are flawless. Why the hell am I thinking about makeup at a time like this? This isn't *RuPaul's Drag Race,* for Christ's sake.

Fascinated in spite of myself, I continue to search for traces of the man I was planning to seduce after dessert. I see similarities, of course, but there are significant differences once I look closely enough. Shadows and accents that play down the masculine and subtly elevate the feminine. The low-hanging necklace is a brilliant choice. It redirects attention from an unobtrusive Adam's apple—a dead giveaway—to an ample rack guaranteed to hold most men's undivided attention. Having dissected the visual, it's time to probe the psychological. Perhaps a show of empathy will help get me where I need to go.

"I can see why Vaughn would have had a tough time. Gay life is hard enough as it is without this. Why take on all of it in the first place?"

She takes a deep breath.

"I'm fully aware you may find Vaughn attractive even as Amanda may repulse you."

"Thanks for understanding that. Since we're being so honest, I will confess that Vaughn works for me. *Really* works for me, as in the man I've dreamed of all my life."

"And Amanda?"

"I do genuinely like her."

What a ringing endorsement. God, this is a weird conversation . . . all so tentative and polite. I can do better than this. I hope.

"I feel a sense of fun and comfort with her . . . Ease is the word. I enjoy matching wits, I envy her warmth and admire her compassion. Even so, I think of Vaughn and Amanda as two separate people—two different friends. I'm not sure I could ever relate to them as one person."

Amanda nods, then says, "I gave up on that one years ago."

"Say more."

"When I'm Amanda, I think of myself as Amanda. When I'm Vaughn, I think of myself as Vaughn. I see us as separate individuals, so why shouldn't you?"

She must read frustration in my features, for suddenly the old Amanda returns with an impish grin.

"One more thing, Detective—just to send you over the edge. I was never married to Lois; Vaughn was. I simply won't let you assume we had a lesbian relationship on top of whatever else you may be thinking at the moment."

Despite myself, I laugh aloud. Amanda joins in, although her features remain guarded.

"Now, if all that's perfectly clear," she says, after our mirth has faded into an awkward silence, "I'll try to explain. Only when I accepted Amanda as one part of myself, and Vaughn the other, separate part, did things come together for both of us. Does that make sense?"

"I guess so."

I'd pay good money for a scorecard of who's talking and what happened to whom, but I make the best answer I can.

"What I think you're saying is you're two in one. 'Two-Spirit' as Native Americans would describe it."

"Paul, you've no idea what it means to me . . . to us . . . to hear you say that. It's been rough, knowing the world, or should I say *worlds*—as in gay *and* straight—would always consider us freaks."

"But you've got all you need to keep those worlds at bay."

"In a way, you're right. Even so—and I want to be sure you hear what I'm saying—without someone to love, we're missing out just as much as you are."

"But it's not the same thing at all. Anyone who gets involved has to relate to both of you. I'll be damned if I can see how it could work. It's a love triangle with two people and three personalities. Any poor bastard who tried would be outnumbered two to one from the get-go."

"That's exactly what you're up against. I couldn't have said it better myself," Amanda says, without even a trace of sarcasm.

"I'm not sure it would work."

"Don't hesitate to say that, Paul. Until Vaughn met you, we didn't think it could work, either. The odds of both of us loving the same man seemed way too high. I'm walking a fine line here . . . I don't want to talk you into anything against your will, but you've got to believe me when I say we could have one hell of a life."

"Aren't you really saying it's all up to me?"

"No, not really. I'll do anything, and Vaughn has already proved his commitment in a rather convincing manner, don't you think?"

Don't let her spin a web, I tell myself. You're vulnerable.

Her eyes seldom shift their gaze from mine. She's doing the sales job of her life despite all she says to the contrary.

"Tell me something?" I ask, still determined to get inside her head.

"Anything you want."

"What do you get for all this effort?"

"My life. On my terms."

Who doesn't want that? I think of my DL years on Grand Bahama. I've got more in common with that sentiment than not. Her solutions are hard to fathom, but her desires make a certain amount of sense.

"And you've achieved that?" I'm genuinely intrigued.

"Up to a point," she replies, blushing ever so slightly. "Although the more Vaughn and Amanda evolved, the more they yearned for someone to share their lives."

No arguments there, either. There truly aren't—if you get past the obvious complications. In fact, it's what I've always dreamed of: to be sure of a man, catch my breath, lay down my burdens, and just love him. Note the last word in that sentence. Him. It sticks in my mind even as I recall Vittorina's, when Amanda and I spoke of anything and everything. I liked that. A lot. Then there's Vaughn— no slouch either. An insatiable, powerful man—an equal at last—with his tight muscles, magnificent cock, and tranquil masculine presence. No surprise I like that, too. Put them together and . . .

But I can't. I just can't envision it.

C'mon. Get past it, I tell myself. You're bigger than this. So there's a bit more to this deal than you expected. Accept it and move on. Just try to think of it as a two-for-one special. You ordered the beef, and it came with a side of fish.

This lame approach bombs in less than a minute, so I seek refuge in interrogation mode, where I can feel smug and superior even while deceiving myself.

"Why is playing dress-up so damn important?"

There's silence for a moment, broken only by sounds from the galley and the steady gurgle of water against the hull. The sun has begun to set, and the ocean is alive with color. Gold, red, and deep purple sparkle between the cresting white of the waves. It's breathtaking. A part of me wishes that Vaughn and I could have had at least one night of this. Yes, I admit it, I'm acting as if the bridal suite was double booked on my wedding night, but can you honestly blame me?

Amanda takes a deep breath as if she's going someplace she'd hoped to avoid.

"It expresses a duality Vaughn has felt his entire life. We all have facets of ourselves we bring forward, and others we suppress. Look at you with your 'tough guy' talk. That's not who you really are, but you created a persona to protect yourself. Is it really all that different?"

I take a moment to consider what is actually an excellent point. Making use of the silence, and, I suspect, wanting to check on Amanda, William enters and serves a lobster cocktail. She smiles broadly as if we're having the time of our lives. Once he departs—less convinced than she might think—her smile fades. Completing my deliberations, I decide to change the subject. My defense mechanisms are off-limits.

"How did Vaughn handle all this? He had a pretty good life as it was."

Amanda seems reluctant to change the topic. She pauses for a moment, looks at me as though she knows what I'm up to, then answers in a slightly petulant tone.

"Not as good as you might think. He faced a huge dilemma when he finally found the courage to be himself. He wanted it all. Both of us—both lives. He wouldn't hear of surgery. Even I couldn't bear the thought. He looked forward to his new identity as a gay man just as much as achieving the freedom to be me."

This is the best piece of news I've had since I sat down. I try to suppress my excitement and search her eyes for confirmation. She certainly seems sincere.

"The more time I spent as Amanda, the better I got at passing, and the clearer things became for both of us. The less time Vaughn spent with Lois, the better he felt, too."

I can relate to that. I've always pictured Lois as the woman in *American Gothic*. Funny thing. Though I've never met her and have little information other than what's in the FBI report, I'm damn sure if I woke up one day and found myself married to her, I'd flee the country, too—though probably not in a dress.

"Abandoning his old life couldn't have been easy," I say.

"It was difficult, to be sure, but so rewarding. For the first time, Vaughn began to like himself."

That must be nice. I wonder what it feels like.

With that maudlin thought, the tension in my gut becomes a stomachache. I expect those I interrogate to get worn down, not me. I've never bought anyone's story without getting all the facts first. And I'm not starting now. Especially with corroborating witnesses who just happen to share the same body. If I apply my detective's training, this nonsense about two personas is nothing more than textbook psychosis. What's more—and I hate to say this—part of me considers her a freak. What a hypocrite, but there it is. Even so, I hang in and ask if there were any surprises along the way.

Amanda seems to weigh her answer carefully.

"Yes. A few. As my persona evolved, I gradually became what Vaughn was not. Where he was driven, I took my time; where he was so focused on making money, I yearned to give it away. In time, I became his 'better angel,' doing things he had been unable or unwilling to do on his own. I don't think either of us expected that."

She hesitates again.

"Since you ask, and I've promised to be forthcoming, there *was* one totally unforeseen development. As Vaughn's life expanded beyond making money, I grew more sexual, though he continued to hesitate. We struggled with this for a long while, and, I'm dreadfully embarrassed to say, eventually rented the comfort I craved. The hustlers—and there were only three over the years—seemed to understand. They treated me like a lady and never confronted Vaughn. After a time, they shared their tricks of the trade and explained what it would be like out there for someone like me."

I have to give her credit. Most people would have skipped over such intimate details. Even so, I can't ignore the fact that she (or is it really they?) bought whatever was needed. Then I wonder if this conversation isn't cut from the same cloth, which gets me thinking—big-time.

"Why didn't you just hire a hustler instead of coming on to me? With your money, you could easily find somebody full-time. Maybe not Prince Charming, but someone well equipped to scratch your itch, and even Vaughn's, for that matter."

As far as I'm concerned, it's a valid question. As I see it, there are two possible scenarios. The first is I've found what I've been looking for—albeit with a few unexpected extras. And as for the second option? Well, let's just say it'll involve an exchange of certain core services for cold hard cash.

Amanda clasps my hand, making me strengthen my defenses.

"Paul, think about it for a moment. Knowing this character was only in it for the money, how could we ever trust him? Without trust, there could never be love. We fell in love with you in part because we trusted you. It's just that simple."

I wish it were. Funny thing, trust. As far as she's concerned, it seems to be a one-way street. I'm fascinated she should place such a high priority on trust when all she's done is lie to me since the day we met.

Amanda interrupts this thought, which is probably a good thing. I don't like where it's coming from. She leans close, her hazel eyes shining.

"Can't you see how important you've become to us? Last night, we got a glimpse of how life could be—not two to one, but two *plus* one. Though now you know the truth, I'm scared to death you'll . . ."

"You're jumping to conclusions. Don't tell me what I might do. Just answer my questions. Why leave the States, when you'd be safer there than anywhere else? Why take on the risk of fake passports and everything else? If you were so lonely, why not just stay put and send out for a piece of ass whenever you felt like mussing the sheets?"

This is a cheap shot, but her passion for whatever the hell "two plus one" might be is really getting to me. I can't cope with such powerful expectations. I'm just not that kind of guy. One look, and I can tell she's finally gotten that much. Then I start to worry I've disappointed her. Weird, huh?

When Amanda finally answers, there's an edge to her voice I've never heard before.

"That remark is beneath you, Paul. The answer is simple. Vaughn was a corporate celebrity of sorts. I'd have been found out in no time if we'd stayed in the States. We wanted to start over again on an equal playing field with a new home, new friends, and new identities. Vaughn had a passport forged in my name, which I used to establish a paper trail in the Caribbean and pave the way for our new life."

"Which is why I could find traces of you in the islands but nowhere else," I say, feeling a kick in the nuts as I'm struck by the enormity of her deceptions: a spouse, business partners, investors, the police, the FBI, several governments, and untold acquaintances. Quite the rap sheet.

"Exactly," Amanda says, her eyes reflective, her voice softening. "I established my identity in those places to which I'd want to return. In some ways, it was the most glorious time of my life: the sea, quiet islands, beautiful sunsets, and the freedom of wind in my sails. I nearly convinced myself friendship and a fair breeze were all I needed from life; that I could go it alone, charting my course, navigating wind and tide, leaving all else behind. The elements don't care what you wear. They challenge all you've got no matter what."

I can see what she means. The sun has set. The candles' light aligns with a shimmering trail of moonlight glistening across the rolling waves. It's like a magic portal to some better place. I struggle to capture the image in my mind, realizing I'll probably never see something so beautiful again.

"And that was all so compelling you thought you'd just leave everything else behind?" I ask.

"We could hardly wait to do just that. Finally, the day arrived. It was essential I be an equal partner, so that spectacular dawn I hoisted the sails, took the helm, and *Last Chance* slipped out of Marblehead Harbor unnoticed, or so I thought. It was just a coincidence that man saw me, Lois got jealous, you got brought in, and Vaughn had to reappear to prove he was still alive."

"An unfortunate development," I say. "At least, you always knew right where to find him if you needed him."

"Yes, it seemed unfortunate at the time," Amanda says, with a trace of a smile. "Though I bless it now. If I hadn't been seen, Lois might have taken things better. From what I understand, she's mostly upset about Vaughn leaving her for me, the poor dear."

I catch myself returning a conspiratorial grin. I certainly do admire this feisty broad who has the right answer for every occasion.

"If Lois hadn't been so jealous, I suspect there might have been no summons, and I might never have met you. I'll treasure the time we've shared, Paul, no matter whether you decide to go or stay."

"Can we just chill with the 'big decision' bit," I say, extricating my hand and jiggling my glass for another drink. "I'm still here, and I'm still listening. Can't you give me some credit for that?"

"I'll do more than that. I'll give you equity."

Amanda pushes the button for William, then reaches into her purse and hands me an envelope. Inside is a statement with a two-million-dollar deposit to my FirstCarribean account. I'm not as surprised as you might think. It's the cornerstone of option two, after all, though the amount is a stunner, I'll grant you that.

Option two it is. The most likely outcome of all this thrashing about in angst and embarrassment. Nothing says commitment like cash on the barrel. Perhaps I haven't lost my touch after all. Maybe I'm just a little slow out of the starting gate.

Amanda watches me intently. The tension in the room grows oppressive, like a game of high-stakes poker. I feel cynicism, born of a lifetime of suspicions proved true, rise up inside. Emotionally drained, I clench my fists and let loose.

"What the hell is this?"

"Now, listen to me," Amanda says, locking her eyes with mine. "Don't get your back up. I've got plenty of money and don't need for a thing."

Except a man on a string, I think.

"If we're ever to be together," she says, her voice taking on a tensile edge, "as unlikely as it may seem to you at the moment, I'd be worried money would be an issue. This is a gift from your friends Amanda and Vaughn, whether you go or stay. It's meant to ensure your independence and give you a shot at the life you deserve—with or without us. Don't go all hidebound and moralistic on me now. There are damn good reasons to want equality in a relationship."

"Yeah, right. That sounds so noble, but your offer still reeks of manipulation."

When she slams her fist on the table and glares at me, I sense I'm finally getting someplace.

"Paul, get a grip, for God's sake. I'm not trying to be noble *or* purchase your affection. I could have manipulated the shorts off you, and you'd never have been the wiser. I've been dealing in good faith since I came to the goddamn table—even before that. I transferred the funds so you could leave the island because it was the right thing to do, and that was *before* I thought we might ever be together."

Glinda seems to be giving up on the charm offensive. That's another good sign. I decide to up the ante and see what more I can shake loose.

"That's all well and good, Amanda, but I don't believe you. Who's to say you didn't like what you got last night so much you're trying to sign me up for an *extended* engagement?"

As her features churn, her Adam's apple—the one visible flaw in an otherwise perfect creation—begins to quiver.

"Don't give me that macho crap, Paul. Look at the date. I deposited the funds yesterday morning. After Scavela set fire to your house, I decided it wasn't right to burden you with our battles. That's why Vaughn came to see you last night, to give you the money and say goodbye for me. I couldn't bear to do it myself. As you can see, the transfer took place well before he met you at Kelso's."

She's bursting with self-righteous indignation. What she says is true—the money was transferred when she said it was—but that could have been the plan, and Vaughn the bait.

Don't weaken, I tell myself. Keep pushing. She'll crack and give herself away. They always do. You know what you're up against now. After all she's done to deceive you, leave her with something to remember you by. Tit for tat, you might as well say.

"Once you and Vaughn made love, everything changed," Amanda says, her tone softening somewhat as if she's trying hard to be reasonable. "We decided to wait until we'd gotten you off the island to explain ourselves and give you time to think. Get past the petty bullshit, Paul, and recognize what's at stake for all of us—nothing less than the difference between a life of little consequence and one well lived."

For a moment, I find the idea appealing, but I quickly realize she's just buying her own snake oil. That never gets you anywhere. I sit back, fold my arms, and wait for what's next on the bill. I don't have to wait long.

"Can't you see how it's all come together for us? That had to be for a reason. Please don't give up on us. I've been worried all along you'd take things exactly the way you have. Don't be small minded about the money."

Small minded, my ass.

"C'mon now, Amanda. Spare me the speeches. Just admit the truth. You pocketed the check until you could take me hostage and negotiate my services. I'm sure you've used that strategy several times in your worldwide quest for love."

Amanda still looks like a woman, but now she's displaying a man's temper. A man who has always gotten what he wants. Until now. I can't suppress a triumphant smirk. I've almost broken through. When I do, it will be some small consolation—a redemption of sorts—to force Vaughn to abandon this charade and see himself for who he truly is.

Much to my surprise, Amanda seems to soften further as her eyes search mine for some trace of hope. I feel another tug inside. What is it about her that sucks me in every time?

"Please understand, Paul. I know how it looks, but we had to act fast. We weren't trying to kidnap you, for goodness' sake! When Vaughn was ordered to leave, I couldn't risk staying, and neither of us could leave you behind to be beaten or worse."

I feign indifference, and Vaughn's temper resurfaces.

"What are you afraid of, anyway? You who stops at nothing—even taking the law into your own hands like some sort of Bahamian Dirty Harry."

Shit!

"Yes, I found out what happened to that drug runner, and I'm not crazy about your idea of justice, though, in this case, I certainly understand. Let me put it to you this way. If you were willing to take such an enormous risk as that, what can possibly frighten you about a man in a dress?"

This dame certainly does her homework. Even so, digging up an inconvenient fact doesn't make her trustworthy; it just makes her well informed—and dangerous.

I study her yet again, trying to get a jump on where she's headed with this information. For a moment I see Vaughn's virility and temper surface, then fade; Amanda's refinement slowly re-emerges. It's like some sort of bad acid trip where everything melts, then morphs into a different shape. I'm spellbound, until a little voice inside says, "See . . . they're one person after all." I don't even know where it comes from. I rub my aching forehead and wish we could take a break. I've never had an interrogation as intense as this one.

Amanda finally wins the internal battle of the temperaments. When she speaks at last, her tone is composed, though I sense more than a trace of frustration in it.

"The money is already yours, Paul. Please take it and don't raise such a fuss over something so paltry when compared to what's truly at stake."

She's not begging. It's more as if she's coaxing a recalcitrant child. Unfortunately for her, she sounded just as credible when she was lying her fake tits off over Vaughn's bogus disappearing act. I slip into standard procedure and review the facts: Amanda Mulher *is* a black widow, spinning a web and wrapping her man in a cocoon. She doesn't do her victim in; she emasculates him, using Vaughn as the honey trap. She even used Chaela to get one over on me. I'll never forgive the bitch for that.

The results are finally in. Amanda's a user, nothing more. Not only can she afford to *be* who she wants; she can afford to *buy* who she wants. And of course, much to my disappointment, so can Vaughn.

Option two it is. Damn it. This interrogation's over. It's way past time for the indictment.

"Sorry, Amanda, sweetie, but count me out. I'm on to your game at last, and I've had it with your bullshit, your self-serving goodness, and your lies. You've got no credibility left. Nada. Your tales of missing persons, compassionate drug runners, and split personalities add up to just one thing. You're a psychotic pathological liar."

"Paul . . . please . . ."

All at once, she's a mess. The glamour and poise have disappeared in a flash. Her face is creased with anguish, and her eyes overflow with hurt. I've broken her spell at last. I seize my opportunity and zero in.

"You may not realize it, but you're deceiving yourself even as you try to put one over on the world. Your whole life is a lie. You can't be a real man, so you pretend to be a woman. That's a lie, Amanda. You enter a country on a false passport. That's another lie. You make up stories about a missing person when you're that person. More lies. Even if you tried to tell the truth, it would come out a lie. You're so morally corrupt it's toxic."

I pound the table to drive my point home, then yell, "For Christ's sake stop fucking with my head and get me the hell out of here!"

Amanda seems to work through a range of emotions: fury, outrage, righteous indignation, and, after a bit, resignation, which slowly wins out. She's no longer a beautiful woman, more a hunted animal waiting for the final bullet.

I reload, take aim, and fire.

"Be honest with yourself for once. You're no better than everyone else out there, lying and cheating to get what you want. The only difference is you have money to throw around in half-assed gestures that make you feel superior. If you can't face up to that, at least have the decency not to try to buy *my* ass the way you bought your sleazy hustlers."

Bull's-eye. Amanda recoils as if I hit her. Then Vaughn—for that is who I suddenly see, looking absurd in a wig, makeup, and evening gown—stands up stricken. His manicured hands grip the table so hard an artificial nail comes unglued.

Smug satisfaction wells up inside. I've broken through at last. His shoulders sag, his cheeks sink. He seems to fold into himself, his face deflating to a lifeless mask. There's no more self-assurance, no poise, no flair—just a messed-up, middle-aged fag in a dress who looks as if I just popped him one.

The transformation is as astounding as if a different actor has taken the place of the gracious, confident woman who came to the table. But there's been no substitution; it's been right in front of me since day one. Why the hell did it take so long for me to see it?

Incredibly, he tries one more time.

"I'm not trying to buy your services, Paul," he says, his voice cracking. "The truth is I'm hopelessly in love with you. You've just got to believe me."

There's no doubt he's terribly upset. Even as part of me wants desperately to back down, I decide to call the game.

"Don't talk to me about truth, Vaughn. You wouldn't know it if you tripped over it—it's the one thing you can't buy. If you're so eager to find the truth, start by looking in the mirror."

I stand up, push in the chair, and tear up the statement. I know it's a meaningless gesture and overly dramatic, but it feels right to do something physical in the midst of this mind-fuck. I slide open the doors, bumping right into William. The drink I desperately need spills against his jacket, then crashes to the floor. I reach up and grasp his shoulders.

"Keep whatever that thing is in there away from me, goddamn it!"

William stares at me for a moment, raises an enormous fist, then, after a sharp glance from Vaughn, slowly lowers it. Sliding both doors closed, William stands in front of them, arms crossed, biceps flexed, his fists clenching and unclenching. I get the message, race up the companionway, and start pacing the deck in a towering rage.

No one hands out that kind of cash as if it were pocket change, no matter how much they've got stashed away. There'll be strings attached—lots of them—of that, I'm certain. Once on that island, I'd be nothing but a walker on the arm of some mess in a dress, summoned to bed with a finger snap, like a two-bit whore. First chance I get, I'm on that fucking helicopter.

Thinking yet again of last night, I let out a groan. Here I was, sure I'd finally found the real thing, and it turns out I got hustled by a freak. As I breathe deep and try to keep from vomiting, other, gentler thoughts slowly intrude.

I went too far; I should have found a better way out than throwing Vaughn's lies in his face. After all, he saved my ass from Scavela, and he's done so much for Chaela. I could have shown a bit more class. What harm would that have done?

After an hour or so of self-destructive shit that goes absolutely nowhere, I go below to apologize and request the helicopter. When I reach the salon, I hear sobbing from Amanda's stateroom. A wave of regret overwhelms me until I push remorse back down with everything else. No emotional engagement. Period. Once a detective, always a dick.

I knock on the stateroom door and mumble a terse apology. There's no answer. Not that I expect one. I wait in the salon until William finally comes out. There's no question where his loyalties lie. He warns me off with a dark look that promises a severe beating if I so much as say a word. I retreat to my stateroom filled with disgust and, to my surprise, a touch of self-loathing.

William doesn't let an opportunity go to waste, does he, I think, downing a scotch in a single gulp.

The voice in my head doesn't hesitate.

"But you sure as hell do, every time, you fool."

The weather turns nasty overnight. About four in the morning, we hove to and stay that way for the better part of the day. In the eerie tranquility of our fixed position amidst churning waves, I resign myself to being in it for the long haul. No 'copter will fly out to us in this.

Next morning, neither Vaughn nor Amanda makes an appearance. I stick close to my stateroom, reading and watching videos. When he's not hovering outside Amanda's cabin like an abandoned lapdog, William sleepwalks through the motions of looking after me but says little. He's certainly doing an excellent job of keeping her away from me. I couldn't get to her even if I had a complete change of heart. Which I haven't. And won't. You can count on that.

The rest of the crew is pleasant enough, but it's made quite clear I'm on my own. Their flawless courtesy makes me feel like an outsider and a heel. I can't tell whether I'm loathed, thought a fool, or considered a matter of complete indifference. It was easier with the cops. I knew where I stood. They hated me for who I was. Perhaps they were right.

After two days, the storm passes. The one outside—the one on board is still raging, with no calm in sight. William tells me we'll stop for refueling in the morning. He's not fooling either of us; we've sailed the entire distance. The stop is so I can jump ship.

We reach Grand Turk at sunrise. Customs will open in a couple of hours. Then my nightmare ends. Alone on deck, contemplating the next empty chapter of my life, I review, for the hundredth time, the reasons I must leave all this behind. People know more of your shit on islands than anywhere else; gossip and sex are the only cure for unrelenting boredom. I was on the DL back in Grand Bahama because they'd have killed me for who I was. It doesn't take a PhD to figure out there's no DL when the man of your dreams wears Max Factor and a Double D Cup; you're out to the world. After the recent assaults on my home and career, I'm well acquainted as to where *that* leads. I don't have the fight left in me to choose that path again, even if it *is* made of moonlight.

Finally, we're cleared from quarantine. Without my having asked, my bags are loaded onto a small tender. I'm about to step on board when strong hands hold me back.

"I'll take you in, Mr. Paul. That there's for luggage and supplies."

It's William. This is the most he's said to me since Amanda and I had it out. He towers over me, his muscles rippling under a tight black polo shirt. His voice is subdued. I hear the contempt in it. To starboard, a rigid-hull inflatable is being towed toward us. William draws my attention to it.

"Miss Amanda, she lose the Zodiac on the trip to Grand Bahama," he says, as if anxious to prove a point. "It be swept off the davits in a storm. They jam. She couldn't pull it back on board. She cut it loose with the knife, which drop in the sea when the ropes part. We ordered this new dinghy to pick up here."

We get in. William starts the inboard. *Last Chance* lies at anchor, tranquil and magnificent. I'm choked up to be leaving her. She's the one lady I have no problems with. I watch intently as we head for shore and feel the same old wrench in my gut. I'm an outsider again.

We're about halfway from the wharf when William cuts the engine. I turn to see what's wrong.

"'Scuse me for sayin' so, Mr. Paul, but you an ass."

He says it so gently I can't help but smile, though my stomach flips at what could happen to me way out here without witnesses. He could snap my neck as easily as opening a twist-off cap and toss me overboard in two seconds, with no one the wiser. This is neither the time nor place to disagree.

"Yes, William, you're probably right."

"I know I is right. You an ass. You be leavin' the most wonderful person in the world, jes 'cause you can't accept their nature. You needs someone to tell you that, lest you make a mistake you'll regret the rest of your days.

"Miss Amanda, she do nuthin' but give, when she ain't got no need to bother. She a beautiful woman—a beautiful person—strong, full of courage, and damn good to her friends. She give me and Victor the freedom to be who we is. She offer you all that, and so much more. She offer you her love . . ."

I hunch forward, stunned he's privy to such intimate details.

"Yes, I hear what she say to you, and I'm not 'fraid to say so. I watch out for her. She and Mr. Vaughn—they *my* family now. And you? What you do? You refuse what she give with an open heart, 'cause she put on a dress now an' then.

"What's wrong wit you? You no better than the bastards that burn your house and turn you out."

What right does he have to say these things to me?

I quickly realize that out here, he can do whatever he damn well pleases.

"You be goin' nowhere fast all you life, then you turns down the world when a good person like Miss Amanda offer it to you on the silver platter. Why's that? I knows why. You make excuses saying you don't trust people, but I knows what you's really 'fraid of. You 'fraid of life, and you 'fraid of love—leastways you act all high and mighty when somebody like Ms. Amanda offer hers to you."

William is reading me like a book. He's the better detective by far if he's doped all this out just by studying me from the sidelines.

"What you gonna do when you land on that island there?" he asks, pointing toward the ominously named Cockburn Town. "Find you another twink to fuck and play at bein' in love wit? Never mind Mr. Vaughn, *Miss Amanda* be more man than you can ever handle, and still you go lookin' for somethin' bettah?

"You an ass. That be all I has to say to you, sir. You an ass."

Feeling emotionally drained, helpless, and effeminate, I can only shrug.

Nice work, William.

He starts the engine. We race toward the wharf, where my bags are being offloaded. I survey the island, yet another lonely island, and see my life returning to what it was—what it will be for as long as I live—standing on the sidelines in a cocoon of yearning, cynicism, and self-loathing.

William watches me intently. The boat is ten feet from the dock when he cuts the engine a second time. The tilt of his head, his dark eyes, and raised eyebrows ask the question.

I take a deep breath and nod.

William stands and yells, his voice reverberating across the water, its timbre more joyous than anything I've ever heard.

"Take it back. Take it all back! We's got us a *major* change of plans."

He places a hand on my shoulder. The simple gesture speaks volumes: safety, security, friendship—no, family—

and it summons tears from deep inside. I can only smile through them, thinking how lame I must seem to this giant of a man. All at once, I realize it doesn't matter. He's genuinely happy for Amanda—and for me. As he pulls me to him, I feel safe, protected, and loved. Everything I've yearned for all my life. William sure got things right; my bullshit about truth was just an excuse. Amanda lied when she had to; then, for my sake, she shared the deepest, most troubling recesses of her soul. We all lie when we're cornered. It's what we do when given the opportunity to make good that truly matters.

The irony isn't lost on me. While I made a career out of uncovering the truth in others, I've never faced my own. I've never been willing to risk loving someone in their entirety—with all their warts and blemishes, you might as well say. Until now.

We race back to *Last Chance* at full throttle. My eyes sting as the breeze quickly dries them. Before I climb on board, a plan comes in a flash of brilliance—if I do say so myself.

"William, we should get Miss Amanda's tray ready, don't you think?"

He understands immediately. Signaling Victor and the crew to retrieve my bags from the tender, William quietly beckons me below. He places a bottle of Dom Pérignon and two champagne flutes on an ornate silver tray. Given his words earlier about Amada's offer of love, we share a smile at the irony of this moment.

When we reach Amanda's stateroom, William taps on the door.

"Miss Amanda," he says in a gentle whisper, "time for your breakfast. Open the door."

"Is he gone?" she asks, in a voice so pain-filled I want to shout then and there that everything will be alright.

Amanda asks again, "William? Did you hear me? Is he gone?"

He hands me the tray and vanishes. I silently vow to make up for the grief I've caused by standing by Vaughn for the rest of our days. I feel certain, confident, and grateful as I hold my breath, not wanting to give myself away.

"*William!* Answer me this instant!"

I knock again. Louder this time. Finally, the stateroom door flies open. There, at last, stands Vaughn, in a white pantsuit. He's unshaven with no wig. His eyes are red, his face mottled. What's left of his makeup is smudged and grotesque. He's sort of half Vaughn and half Amanda. Couldn't be better.

"Girlfriend, you are one hot mess," I say, thrilled with the line that's come just when I need it most. "Don't you know a real lady never, ever, *ever* answers her door without checking her makeup first?"

Vaughn stares at me in disbelief, and slowly that broad, sexy smile I love so much transforms his tortured features. I don't need more of a welcome than that. I push my man back into the stateroom and kick the door closed. I kiss his lips and lower him to the bed. A wake hits just as I open the champagne, which sprays both of us. Knowing applause echoes through the salon. William, Victor, and the crew have assembled outside the door. Their catcalls, off-color comments, and cheers sound just like a benediction. I pull Vaughn close. We're crying and laughing at the same time. I'm drenched in champagne, with lipstick on my lips and smudged rouge on my face—and I could give a shit. I hear more footsteps outside the stateroom door. A second cork pops to the sound of applause and stomping feet.

Last Chance certainly is a Noah's Ark for gay men. These guys are true romantics. But then, I guess, so am I. Who knew?

I hold Vaughn tight, and, in my best imitation of Amanda that day at the police station, whisper, "You simply *must* understand, it was never about the money. I agree to sail away with you because I love you—and *finally* trust you love me."

The smile I receive is far more eloquent than anything mere words could convey. In an all-knowing instant, I understand all I'll ever need to know about Amanda Mulher. Much as she did for Vaughn, she's led me to a new life on my own terms. He and I owe her for that, and we'll be sure to take damn good care of her from now on.

Suddenly William's voice booms out, "All hands on deck. We's got us a *sweeeeet* twenty-five knots downwind to Barbados, and a whole new life jes sittin' there waitin' for us. What you sittin' on you asses fo? Hoist the mizzen and main, set the spinnaker, and let's see what this little lady can *do!*"

The crew cheers wildly, then race to man their stations. The engine fires, followed by the clank of the anchor chain, the whirr of the electric winches, and the sound of flapping sails. I lie beside Vaughn, holding him close, hardly believing it's not all just a dream. He smiles as if he understands. His fingers travel lightly across my chest; then they glide lower . . .

The engine stops. There's silence for an instant, followed by a slight jolt when the sails set, then *Last Chance* leaps forward like a thoroughbred.

William's exultant voice rings out once more. "Set course, 124 degrees, for Barbados. Ladies and Gentlemen, we be headin' home!"

THE
MIDNIGHT
SUITOR

"The houses on our street were identical. Their columned white porches, gray siding, flat roofs, even the diminutive tract of land between them, recapitulated the same utilitarian design, marching down to the harbor in smug, pragmatic lockstep."

"*N*o one expected it. No one. Ben Motta left for the war in '17 a regular Joe, and when he returned with that hussy, wasn't he actin' like the Lord Carew!

"Fancy ascot, tweed jackets, and all the highfalutin' language under the sun: don't cha know, my word, I say. Blather such as that. Why anyone would take up such Limey airs is well beyond me, but *he* certainly was above it all once he came back, that I'll be tellin' you for certain!"

At this juncture, a question was necessary, or Great-Aunt Kathleen's fragmented thoughts would shift to the crimes of the British, an inexhaustible—though not nearly so entertaining—topic.

"Where'd he find her, Aunt Kat?" I'd ask with as much feigned interest as I could muster for a story I knew by heart.

I'd grown up with the tale. My family lived on the first floor of her tenement, or triple-decker, as we call them in South Boston. The houses on our street were identical. Their columned white porches, gray siding, flat roofs, even the diminutive tract of land between them, recapitulated the same utilitarian design, marching down to the harbor in smug, pragmatic lockstep.

The neighborhood had once been an Irish bastion. Now, all that remained of those days were Aunt Kat's memories. At ninety-three, she seldom recalled recent events, but her remembrances of "back when" were carved in granite, and she readily shared them at the slightest sign of interest.

As an all-knowing teenager, I had a perverse fascination with her dour, maiden-lady prejudices and sanctimonious admonitions. She had a trove of warnings for me about what she called "the female of the species," which, as things turned out, I would never need.

Even so, Aunt Kat seemed determined to call the woman Ben Motta brought home from the First World War every name in the book. I reveled in the pejoratives she hurled at the villainess of the tale: hussy, floozy, tart, tramp, cat, jade (my personal favorite), minx, monster, and devil. Each epithet had its inviolate placement, which I awaited with ill-concealed delight.

Once back on course, Aunt Kat always told her tale as if for the very first time.

"No one knows where they met, me boy, but since you ask, I'd say just this side of hell. She was a beauty; I'll give her that, with dark, catlike eyes and long black hair. Black as midnight, that hair. She had little English, and he even less Portuguese, though I suspect what it was he wanted from her needed no translation to either party. I'd arrived from the Old Country eight years before, so I knew what for by then, and she was no blushing bride. Of that I'm certain.

"When Ben Motta didn't come home with the rest of his outfit, we gave him up for dead. Then doesn't he show up months later, bold as brass, the last doughboy to return to Southie alive. And with a floozy on his arm!

"One look, and Beatrice Motta, Ben's mother, wouldn't let his so-called wife in the house. She was convinced the tart wasn't Portuguese, but Cape Verdean, and no doubt suspected a bit of the tar brush. Old Mrs. Motta was a good Catholic, may God rest her tortured soul.

"Years later, when the tramp wanted Ben declared dead for the insurance, she insisted there had indeed been a shipboard marriage. Even with that, Mrs. Motta wouldn't budge. She went to her grave certain there'd been no such thing—at least not in God's eyes.

"There's a lesson to be had from that; I'll be tellin' you. Young men such as yourself would do well to listen to your betters. They've lived their lives and know their way in the world!"

With this admonition, I'd insist I was most anxious to listen and learn. Mollified, Aunt Kat would forge ahead, sitting upright in her chair, her watery blue eyes alight with scandal from more than seven decades before, her veined right hand worrying the small gold locket she always wore.

"Moved next door to this very house, they did, after Mrs. Motta barred her doors. To a tiny room with only two windows, and those not even facing the street. If they'd had a honeymoon, the spark went out on the crossin', for things were in a sorry state from the day they arrived.

"Me bedroom back then was across the alley from their room. On the third floor, where the storeroom is now. With naught but ten feet between us, I heard so much I was mortified for the both of them.

"Holy Mother, what fights! Your great-grandfather went over several times. She'd be screamin' so loud he was afeared for her safety. Never had so much as a bruise did she, though. I'll give Ben that. He never raised a hand to her, despite all she did to provoke him. She'd a temper like a cornered cat—all hissin' and scratchin'. After some of their rows, Ben would be bloody for days.

"It didn't pass long before I'd see him comin' home later and later. Spendin' his time and money down at Clancy's, just 'postponin' the inevitable,' was what he'd say. I have that from a reliable source. Elsie McGowan's brother was the barkeep. He told her, and she told me. The rest, I saw with me own eyes.

"So doesn't himself return one midnight full to the brim—and without his latchkey. Most of the boarders were workin' third shift, so the hussy could lock him out without a care, and hadn't she done just that!

"After poundin' on the door for a spell, he staggered to the side of the house nearest me and yelled up to the open window.

"'My sweet, the door is locked. Please descend and allow my entry.'

"His voice was all la-di-da, but you could hear the drink in it. He caterwauled outside that window for ten minutes or so, but the house stayed quiet as the grave. There was nothin' to be heard from her—no yellin', nothin'.

"Then I heard a draggin' sound. 'Twas like noon in the light of the streetlamp as I watched Ben adjustin' a wooden ladder aside the house. They'd been shinglin' the roof and left it overnight. It was a long one, capable of reachin' well above the third floor, and up it he went in his fancy britches, jacket, and waistcoat. The way was steep, the ladder bein' set on the far side of our grape arbor next to the boardin' house. He climbed slowly, stoppin' when his shiny shoes slipped on the rungs, then startin' up again when his courage returned. Once or twice the ladder shifted. Then he'd hold close to the house until the motion settled. 'Twas somethin' to see, I'll say that much.

"Soon he was above the arbor. In time, he reached the third-floor window. He raised it so as to get inside, and all of a sudden there was a sharp cracking sound, followed by a twanging noise like a piano explodin' to bits!

"Well, the good Lord be me judge, hadn't the jade gone and hit him over the head with his very own guitar. Quite proud of that guitar he was. Brought it back from Spain, or so he said. Well, Spain or the five-and-dime, it shattered like crockery and came to rest draped over his shoulders like a wet Chinese noodle.

"At first, me heart was in me mouth, fearin' he'd fall. But even though pretty well oiled, Ben had instincts enough to hold on for dear life. For a while, he must have been nigh to unconscious 'tween the drink and the knock on the head, for he didn't speak, just moaned and lay flat against the ladder, clutchin' one rung with his hands and another with his feet.

"I stood at me window, transfixed. I'll never forget the look on her face as she held the broken neck of the guitar like a dagger. Her eyes blazed with a hatred I'd never seen before, nor since, for that matter.

"Then she saw me and waved like a film actress with a big phony smile on her face. The Lord strike me dead if I lie. There I stood in me nightgown with himself draped over the ladder, and herself vampin' as if she were playin' Tosca at the Abbey Theatah.

"After a moment, she tilted her head. 'Should I?' was the question I read in her dark eyes. I knew without even hearin' it from her lips. I shook me head, no! I couldn't speak a single word, come face to face with the devil incarnate as it was, so I signaled frantic to let him be.

"She stopped for a moment as if to consider, even puttin' her hand to her chin like Theda Bara in the silent pictures. Then didn't the monster give me a grin, lean forward, and place both hands atop the ladder.

"It's all as clear in me mind's eye as if 'twas this mornin'. She was wearin' a long white nightgown trimmed with ostrich feathers. Shameless and revealin' it was, but all pure and white nonetheless. Didn't she look like the Angel of the Lord in that window, so beautiful and radiant? But the devil in disguise was she, as she leaned out and began to push, never takin' her evil eyes from mine.

"Now, 'twas strange how she did it. Not all at once, like someone in a fit of rage. She was more deliberate like. As if savorin' every moment.

"At first, nothin' happened, but then, ever so slowly, the ladder commenced to move. That's when Ben came to a bit. 'I say, my sweet,' says he, 'certainly there has been some dreadful misunderstanding, don't cha know? Help me in, dearest, and I'm quite sure we can lay to rest whatever might be troublin' you.'

"She said nothin', just pushed harder. Ben seized her arm as the balance shifted, but she broke free. He tried to grab hold of the windowsill, but it slipped from his fingers. Slowly at first, and then increasin' in speed, the ladder toppled backwards like a fallin' oak, until there was a terrific crash when it hit this house.

"I didn't know what to do. There, in the light of the streetlamp, for all to see, was the ladder, with the drunken git hangin' from the underside, leanin' just above me bedroom window. I was afeard that Old Lady McGowan might be sittin' at her observation post, as she did some nights when her neuralgia flared up. In those days, a girl's reputation could be destroyed faster than rain can ruin a picnic—and if anyone favored rain, it was Old Lady McGowan.

"'Jesus, Mary, and Joseph, Ben, you can't stay here,' says I in a whisper.

"'With that statement, my dear, I cannot begin to find argument,' says he, lockin' his feet around the rungs.

"'Well, you must get down! And put that godforsaken ladder away when you do,' says I, not knowing for the life of me if he even knew he was danglin' in midair.

"'Most desirous of obligin', my sweet, but I'm not quite up to it at the moment. Sorry to disappoint and all that,' says he.

"'What will the neighbors think?' says I, near to panic. I was in me summer nightgown and no fit sight for a man. What's more, I thought I caught him starin' up at me front.

"'Ah, yes, the neighbors,' says Ben in a slurred voice. 'Always a concern, what? One might be inclined to wonder if they think at all 'round here, don't cha know.'"

I always choked back laughter at this point. The scene was so easy to picture. From Aunt Kat's bedroom, I could see the house next door, the third-floor window, and the overgrown grape arbor in the side yard she'd tended religiously until her ninetieth year. Aunt Kat never noticed my mirth. She was too anxious to continue her tale. Her eyes alight, she'd lean forward in her rocker, her voice rich with intrigue.

"'Now, I won't be havin' any more of this nonsense,' says I to him. 'You simply *must* get away from me window this instant! I'll not be takin' no for an answer.'

"'My sweet, my most fervent wish is but to serve,' says he, 'though I am desolate to say I lack the capacity to comply at the moment. As you can see, I am but a poor rose between two thorns.'

"As he said this, I heard a laugh. I looked over and saw *her*, the one who caused this godforsaken mess, watchin' from her window. She waved again and did a little dance, twistin' and swayin', with her arms held over her head like a prizefighter.

"I lost me temper at that, and God knows where I found the strength, but I gave that ladder a mighty push. It moved towards her, seemed to stand upright for an eternity, then, due to our house bein' downhill, fell back again. I looked across. She was laughin' and clappin' her hands in glee, pointin' at me as if sayin', 'You're stuck with him, now!'

"That frosted me somethin', I'll be tellin' you. I ran to the hall closet and found your great-grandfather's nine iron. Just the thing, I thought to meself, as I flew back to the window me heart in me mouth.

"'Now, Ben Motta, be gone before I'm forced to take drastic action,' says I, gently pushin' him with the golf club to get me point across.

"Ben must have believed me, because ever so slowly he began to descend that ladder, arm over arm, his feet danglin' below him. He got down about ten or twelve rungs and then, without so much as a cry, he fell.

"There was a bit of a shudder, the sound of twigs snappin'. Then nothin'. I grew afeard he might be dead. He'd been high up, after all, and a fall such as that might break a man's spine. Not that I was sure he had one anymore, mind you. Even so, I'd no desire to confess the guilt of murderin' a fellow creature to Father McIntyre. The old bugger had recently chastised me for bein' too 'forthright' in me attire. I'd given him what for and asked who was he to judge gifts the good Lord had given to another. But murder, well, that was a different kettle of fish, bein' a mortal sin and all. Father McIntyre would be certain to have the upper hand.

"Finally, I heard Ben's voice waftin' upwards, like Lionel Barrymore. 'Fear not,' says he. 'All's well that ends well. This accommodation, rustic though it may be, shall prove sufficient for the night. And so, my sweet, I wish you a heartfelt good evening. My most fervent apologies for any and all inconveniences you may have suffered.'

"With that, he went quiet again. Lord be me judge if the drunken lout hadn't had the good fortune to land midst the grape arbor. Those tough old vines broke his fall.

"The dark-haired devil had left the window, so I had only the ladder left to deal with. I summoned all me strength and gave it a mighty push. It moved to an upright position, then slowly fell back against the other house with nary a sound. It was at this moment Old Lady McGowan's light came on. She had missed the whole thing; may the good Lord be praised."

Here Aunt Kat would take a dramatic pause, as if to highlight how close to destruction her reputation had come. Then she would sigh deeply, shake her head, and spur her story to the finish.

"At breakfast, I sat in trepidation, not knowin' what your great-grandfather might have to say. His bedroom was on the far side of the house. Even so, I could not imagine how he had not heard the ruckus. Yet he seemed in an especially fine humor when he came in from retrievin' the morning paper.

"'Well, Kathleen, 'tis a beautiful day, is it not?' says he in a hale-and-hearty voice that might be heard clear 'cross County Clare. 'Sleep well, I trust? Nothing to disturb the slumber of the innocent, I'll be hopin'?'

"'No, Father. Everything is fine,' says I, me heart aflutter. 'Why might you be askin'?'

"'Perhaps you might do me the honor of comin' outside so I can show you,' says he.

"'Really, Da, is this necessary?' says I. 'Whatever might you be talkin' about?'

"With that, your great-grandfather signaled I should cease my commotion and accompany him. He was a gentle man, slow to anger, but I could always tell if I'd gone too far.

"Lookin' into the side yard, I was near to faintin'. There atop the arbor was Ben, still passed out to the world. I was prepared for that, but not the rest. The broken guitar, its parts reunited, rested on his chest as though he was about to commence a serenade. What's more, the ladder was back at me bedroom window! She'd been doin' the devil's work in the wee hours, she had. The minx!

"'Seems to me Romeo missed a step on his way to the balcony; wouldn't you be after agreeing, Juliet?' asked your great-grandfather, with ever the slightest twinkle in his eye. 'Twas then I realized he knew more than he was sayin', and that I was in the clear.

"'Might we be after cleanin' this up a bit before Lettie McGowan commences her patrols for the day?' says he with a wink.

"Then your great-grandfather took down the ladder and put it behind the roomin' house. When he returned, he stepped under the arbor and shook the vines to rouse Ben.

"'C'mon, Your Lordship, rise and shine. Time's a wastin' on a beautiful mornin'.'

"Ben rolled over, realized he was nigh eight feet in the air, and grabbed hold of the vines in a panic.

"'Now, now, Your Grace,' says your great-grandfather. 'Seein' these vines have held you this long, there's nothin' to fear so far as I can tell. Just put your feet through that open space and lower yourself the rest of the way.'

"I looked up at the devil's window. The curtain fluttered. She was watchin', all right.

"Ben shifted, lowered his legs, then fell like a stone. From the window above we heard a cold, shrill cackle.

"'Now, Ben,' said your great-grandfather, with ever such a gleam in his eye, 'might I be after offerin' you a wee bit of advice?'

"Ben just lay there starin' up at him without so much as a word, but your great-grandfather pressed on.

"'Give up on that harridan. Any woman who would go to such lengths to get back at a man for takin' a wee half will kill him in his bed soon as serve him breakfast. Best to salvage what you can, chalk it up to experience, and move on to greener pastures.'

"Then your great-grandfather turned to point at all Ben's worldly goods where they lay, torn and broken, strewn across the lawn.

"With that, Ben rolled from under the arbor, stood on rickety legs, and solemnly shook your great-grandfather's right hand. Then didn't he bow to me and kiss mine!"

That foppish kiss might well have been the high point of a lifetime of piety and filial duty, so I always waited patiently while, as if of its own accord, that very hand clutched the locket on her chest. After a deep sigh, Aunt Kat would end her tale with the same lengthy sentence, in the same doleful cadence.

"Seein' movement in the devil's window, Ben bowed low, stretched out his arms as if to say 'you win,' and then, with nary a word, proceeded to shuffle away, never to be seen again."

The day finally came when Aunt Kat's hand had to be pried from around her locket. Unyielding in her prejudices to the very end, she died in the house she'd called home for most of her ninety-eight years. I returned from college for the wake and funeral. Kneeling at the bier, I found grief in my heart and repose in her withered old face. She was finally at peace.

When the family gathered to say good-bye, the undertaker undid the locket from around her neck. Handing it to me with an arch expression, he informed me it was my aunt's wish for me to have it. It burnt a hole in my pocket throughout the funeral, interment, and "at home." When the last guest left, I snuck up to Aunt Kat's bedroom and sat in her rocker. The locket opened with the ease of daily use. Inside was a tiny key. I had no idea what it fit, and, after searching in vain, put it aside.

Aunt Kat's memories lived on. The story of her midnight suitor became a treasured part of our family gatherings. My mother, having stoically endured Aunt Kat for decades, found joy in recounting the tale with all the intonations and mannerisms of the original. Mother's performance was such a hit we made a video of it during her last year to ensure the story would live on. My father watched the tape frequently once she was gone. After Dad died, my husband, Jamie, and I moved into the old house, taking a chance that attitudes toward gay marriage would soften as people embraced the new laws and Southie grew more gentrified. Our plan was to renovate, and—if we survived the experience—make the old place home to a fourth generation.

Jamie loved the video as much as I did, laughing at all the same places. We watched it often, and the tale worked its magic. He often told me to stop the "blather" when he'd had enough of my opinions on any given subject, and issued dire, if gratuitous, warnings about "the female of the species" in the same foreboding tone Aunt Kat had perfected.

One morning when he'd nearly finished gutting the third floor, he came running down the stairs.

"Look at this," he said, holding a diary he'd found tucked behind the eaves in the storeroom. "Do you think it was Aunt Kat's?"

I found the locket and tried the key. It fit, and the rusty lock clicked open. Inside was a treasure trove of tales about the crossing from Ireland, adjusting to life in America, and the day-to-day activities of a young woman in the years before the First World War. There were hilarious accounts of her decades-long battle with Father MacIntyre.

Near the back of the book, a photograph of a doughboy slipped out from between blank pages. Across it, in faded handwriting, was an inscription dated August first, 1917. Beneath that were the words:

To My Dearest Kathleen,

Wait for me, my sweet rose.

Forever yours, Ben

"I knew it! I always knew it!" I said triumphantly. "I knew she loved him!"

To my surprise, Jamie had nothing to say, though he studied the picture in rapt concentration. I chalked this up to down-east taciturnity and thought nothing more of it.

Our third wedding anniversary was celebrated amidst wreckage and renovation. We threw a party for friends and family that lasted until the wee hours. Once everyone had departed, I walked into our bedroom to find Jamie standing quietly with a package in his hand.

"I've got one more present for you. I hope it won't weird you out too much," he said, handing it to me.

Inside were two photographs in old-fashioned, matching frames.

"Where'd you get these?" I asked, stunned. "This is the same picture of Ben Motta, and the other is of Aunt Kat! We have this photograph of her somewhere in an identical frame. I remember seeing it when I was a kid."

My husband stood very still, studying me intently, his eyes alight with love and a wistfulness I'd never seen before. Finally, he spoke in hushed tones.

"I was named for my great-grandfather, Benjamin Morris. In my family, all that's known of him is that he was a down-to-earth, righteous man who moved north to start a new life when he encountered unknown difficulties in Boston."

I stared at Jamie, slack-jawed. He took a deep breath and continued.

"I recognized Ben Motta's photograph the moment it fell from your aunt's diary. I grew up with it. It was on my grandmother's mantelpiece in a place of honor, beside this picture of what was to us an unknown woman. When Gram died, my mother inherited both pictures, along with instructions they always be displayed together.

"I asked Mom about them at Christmas. It turns out they were all Benjamin Morris brought with him when he moved to Portland. According to what she was told, he insisted both pictures stay on his nightstand all his life. All he'd ever say was the woman was a fiancé 'irrevocably lost to me through my own stupidity.'

"My great-grandmother must have been quite understanding, for it's been passed down through the years that he died with your aunt's portrait in his hand. No one in my family ever knew her name. I never made the connection until I found the diary. I'd only seen photographs of Aunt Kat when she was old, or so I thought."

Jamie paused, his eyes searching mine.

"You see what this means, don't you?"

As I nodded, a flurry of warmth and affection swept over me. And, I swear, for the first time in my life, I heard Aunt Kat laugh.

EVEN IN
DEATH

"*Despite its dated, exaggerated style, the costume managed to accentuate Berta's supersized sensuality. I found her appearance unnerving, yet fascinating: the way Frederick Fleet must have felt when, from the crow's nest of the Titanic, he first saw the pale peaks of the iceberg dead ahead.*"

"*T*im. It's Berta. Wake up."

Her rasping voice promised delicious gossip and delectable scandal. At any other hour, she'd have had my full attention.

"Whaddya want? And why the hell are you calling so early?"

"I simply *had* to be the one to tell you, Tim. It's on the news. You won't believe it!"

Berta sounded amazingly like Tallulah Bankhead, though with breathless urgency instead of well-worn languor. Though intrigued, I was unwilling to seem too eager—as if I had no life. This was actually the case, but even at six on a Sunday morning, I was sensitive to appearances.

"What is it, Berta? Has Clinton finally admitted to giving Monica more than a hat pin?"

I'd had a running gag with my dear friend and neighbor ever since the earliest days of the Lewinsky scandal. Monica's famous kneepad comment had launched a volley of caustic exchanges that propelled my friendship with Berta to that place of ease where we could, and usually did, say anything and everything to each other. What's more, we knew when to leave something unsaid: the mark of genuine regard.

Aside from our shared sense of the absurd, Berta and I could not have been more dissimilar. I was an IT director at a Boston insurance conglomerate, new to management after years of coding in the trenches. My life (it seems hyperbolic to even call it that) spanned two disparate worlds: Boston was where I worked so as to live in Provincetown, where I husbanded my dreams and aspirations for some better, yet-to-be-discovered, future.

That was the easy bit. The challenge lay in the chasm between the "real" world and the one to which I aspired. Hopelessly marooned in the former, I viewed life's institutions and inhabitants with trepidation. I considered myself a propeller-head: socially marginalized and painfully out of sync with the rest of humanity. My self-appraisal had never been refuted—and with good reason: while college roommates were out getting laid, I built a computer from scratch. When friends came out, I stayed in, seeking dubious satisfaction from database optimization algorithms. More recently, I'd found compelling grounds to fear that the insidious culture of insurance, with its dire predictions, conformity, and mind-numbing bureaucracy, had begun to infiltrate my world view, offering the security of dull routine as a compelling alternative to utter social failure.

I was excruciatingly aware all work and no play had made me a dull, horny boy. Yearning for meaning beyond technology, duty, and the confining opinions of others, I often promised myself I'd break free, engage with life, find new friends, and maybe even fall in love, if only once. I was up for the challenge. Beyond ready, as my implacable hormones incessantly reminded me, with only two questions left to resolve before mounting a self-directed makeover of prodigious proportion: How did this gay lifestyle thing actually work? And, by any slight chance, was there a manual?

Berta, by contrast, was one of a minority of straight, devotedly married, loving mothers in Provincetown. A force of nature whose confidence, charm, and head-on engagement with life routinely assailed the pathetic, self-imposed constraints of my sheltered existence. How I envied her. Whether by genetics or well-practiced intent, Berta possessed more guts and a better sense of camp than the most outrageous drag queen on Commercial Street. She jumped—no, dove full tilt—into life with a brash exuberance that would draw men and women, gay and straight, into her orbit within minutes. Enchanted, I often studied her from the sidelines, timorous, uncertain, bedazzled by her energy and joie de vivre, wishing some of it would rub off on me. So far, I'd remained immune. While Berta channeled Zaza from *La Cage aux Folles* on demand, my best was Agnes Gooch. And then only when alone and safely behind closed doors in Provincetown.

"It's Ken Porter," Berta brayed, causing me to sit bolt upright, all thoughts of the ungodly hour banished for good. "That suicide guy, Dr. Cronin, did him in the night before last. It's all over the news."

I dropped any pretense of indifference. Ken had lived next door until a little more than a year before. Cronin was the infamous "Doctor Death" who assisted suicides in an effort to advance the right to die with dignity.

"No way. There must be thousands of Ken Porters," I said, while secretly hoping she was right.

"Maybe, but the dead one lived at his address in Cambridge, and the picture they showed looks just like him.

"The wake is tomorrow afternoon and evening. Come with me. I want to interview his family. There might be a book in it."

"Jeez, Berta, you're something else. Why would you *ever* want to dig up all Ken's bullshit all over again?"

"I'll tell you on the ride tomorrow."

"Give me one good reason why I should go with you to pay respects to a passive-aggressive creep who drove me stark raving mad?"

"Well, smart-ass, since you ask, I can give you four: first, I need a ride; second, I need somewhere to change; third, you owe me big-time for watching your place when you're away; and fourth, you should feel guilty for driving him out of town. By taking me to Boston, you get the joy of giving—from numbers one and two; along with absolution—from numbers three and four, which significantly cuts your chances of going to hell."

Berta *was* wonderful about seeing to things when I was away. In a sense, she safeguarded my dreams, making sure my condo, which, as odd as it sounds, I considered my spiritual home, survived winter's desolation. What's more, she'd rapidly become my dearest, most genuine friend. I conceded against my better judgment, as was often the case with Berta's schemes.

"OK. How about this," I said, resigned but still somewhat chary. "I'll skip work Monday and drive you to Boston. You can stay at the apartment and take the boat back on Tuesday. I'll have more to say about number four later on."

"Sounds great. I'll catch you later. I've got tons to do to get ready."

I hung up and pondered, for a single anxious moment, what extraordinary efforts were required to prepare for a wake; then dismissed the thought, rolled over, and fell back to sleep.

Monday morning, Berta crossed our street with a small satchel and a homemade garment carrier crafted from plastic trash bags. Her skin was pale from too little sun. Her round face still showed traces of the youthful glamour I'd seen in photographs, though thirty pounds and ten years of motherhood had wrought considerable change. These days, she exuded a Rubenesque sensuality, just a trifle faded, blowsy, and overstated, like an exotic lily that had bloomed the day before: still recognizable, but clearly on the downward slope of its defining moment.

She flopped onto the seat beside me and pulled her long black hair into a ponytail.

"Onward, Caruthers, to Boston town, and *don't spare the horses.*"

My jaunts with Berta were fun. There was more to be learned from her about P'town in an hour than in a year of solitary exploration. She was easier to be with than anyone else, except for those extremely rare times when she wasn't. Then it was hell.

As we rounded the Sagamore Rotary to Route 3, I decided it was time to tackle what had vexed me since her Sunday morning wake-up call.

"Berta, why did you say I drove Ken out of town?"

"I didn't say it. He did. Though half the town believes it."

"What did he say about me? And how'd you find out?"

"Well, after you drove him out . . ."

"I didn't drive him out!"

"OK! OK! I'm just kidding. Knowing how you felt about him, I never wanted to bring it up, but he used to call me a lot after he left. He was pretty sick with tumors and some muscle disease whose name I can never remember. He was also very hung up on you. He told me he prayed for your soul every day."

This was a lot to digest. I'd long maintained that Ken had managed his public image to an extraordinary degree, while allowing his neuroses to declare open season on me. From her vantage point across the narrow street, Berta was confident he was a harmless, well-intentioned nerd whose mild idiosyncrasies invariably pushed my buttons. Neither of us would yield our point of view, so before long, we'd agreed to disagree on the subject of Ken Porter.

"I didn't know he had tumors," I snarled. "I *do* know he was agoraphobic, manipulative, and obsessed with attracting attention. But that's mental, not physical illness."

I just knew I was right.

As president of our four-unit association, it was my duty to acclimate new owners. As with all things in life, I took the job seriously. I'd had high hopes for Ken as the ideal neighbor. On the phone, he seemed unusually considerate and appreciative, which went a long way with me. He may have sounded a trifle obsessive, but I chalked that up to home-buying jitters and thought little more about it.

As his closing date approached, Ken's incessant phone calls began to test my patience. His requests, usually involving trivia most would fail to notice, were couched in such a way it felt a breach of faith to deny them. Described as "one last little thing," each demand soon had a successor.

I first saw Ken face-to-face the day he moved in. He seemed a quiet, unassuming man whose appearance reminded me of Wally Cox: stringy brown hair, pale, freckled skin and wire-rimmed glasses. Ken gave the impression of a vague, humorless, retiring soul whom most would not give a second glance. Considering the outrageous alternatives P'town frequently supplied, I thought these stellar qualities in a next-door neighbor.

Despite Ken's milquetoast appearance, and my naively optimistic expectations, something about him was disconcerting. I isolated an annoying nasal whine that seemed to feign weakness while serving a potent need for attention. He was also far too forthcoming with personal information. As Ken readily informed me, he'd moved to town as part of a plan to combat his growing agoraphobia. After his mother's death, he'd extensively renovated the family home in Revere, apparently transforming the place into an opulent shrine to her memory. When his therapist diagnosed the house as an incubator for the rapidly escalating illness, Ken had reluctantly agreed to move. Flush with proceeds from a sexual harassment lawsuit and the sale of the shrine, Ken had come to Provincetown to "take life more slowly, make new friends, and get out more often."

Oblivious to my boredom, he droned on about various improvements he had made to his former home, as well as those *we* might now make to *ours*, a newly built, classic Cape designed to fit unobtrusively into a neighborhood of venerable, though modest, houses. I silently gagged over his suggestions: aluminum siding (specifically, not vinyl), pink pavers, and bright red, faux-brick Masonite chimneys.

Midway through his litany, I realized Ken seemed to think he'd purchased a social outlet—and, just possibly, a brand-new life—along with the apartment. Though growing concerned I was considered part of the deal, I struggled to be supportive, reminding myself of the stress of moving to a new community. Surely Ken would settle in, calm down, and move on. After all, *I* had. Eventually, as strangers morph into neighbors, the rhythms of day-to-day interactions establish themselves.

In this case, the rhythm accelerated from a courtly minuet to a demented jitterbug. Ken's calls escalated to four or five a day, even when I was at work. His ingratiating manner was supplanted by a tense, querulous tone as if he knew he was jangling my last nerve but was unable to restrain himself. Within two weeks of his arrival, I was trapped in my own home—a vacation one at that—too beleaguered to answer the door, lest it was Ken with yet another complaint.

His frailty and self-absorption conjured up my greatest fears. If I stayed my current course, I, too, might shrivel up and wither away, losing my sense of humor and becoming equally self-absorbed and ineffectual. The very sight of Ken began to remind me of my own pathetic state, and I began to avoid him. Where he'd hoped for friendship and perhaps even pity from me, he'd become anathema. Well aware of the dangers of small-town gossip, I kept my own counsel for some time. At last, pushed to the brink after five torturous weeks of incessant demands, I sent Ken a registered letter declaring I'd no longer discuss his concerns outside our quarterly condo meetings.

This bought only a brief respite, for the first meeting Ken attended was a travesty. In the space of three excruciatingly awkward hours, he introduced twenty-three grievances. His final and most heinous involved the lobsterman who lived across the street. His freshly pulled lobster pots reeked for two days each fall until they dried, and Ken considered the smell a threat to his health.

Berta, who lived but ten feet away from them, referred to the end-of-season scent as "Cape Cod Cologne," and dismissed any discomfort as the price of living by the sea. Ken found the smell intolerable and insisted I report our neighbor to the Board of Health, dismissing any concerns as to the man's livelihood or his family's legacy in having pursued the same difficult profession for generations.

Envisioning myself being run out of town by a passel of bearded men in yellow mackintoshes, I called for a vote. Ken's motion was defeated three to one. Well prepared for this eventuality, he produced a letter from a local attorney threatening to sue me under the Americans with Disabilities Act for any failure to comply with requests relating to Ken's health. When it dawned on me I'd been set up, I ended the meeting.

Within the week, I accosted the attorney on Commercial Street and described the full breadth and absurdity of the demands. Hinting at Ken's significant emotional baggage, I suggested the suit was likely to reflect badly on the lawyer's reputation, particularly if the local press got wind of it. The next thing I knew, the lawyer was threatened with a suit for not suing me, which only confirmed my growing suspicion Ken would take someone to court as readily as to lunch.

Once his lawyer quit, Ken upped the ante, leaving handwritten complaints in my mailbox or slipping them under my door late at night. A copy of each missive also arrived by registered mail, making it clear my every action or inaction was being documented for some nefarious purpose. There was an upside to all this. The ladies of the post office, who stood watch every Saturday as I signed reams of return receipts, openly expressed their sympathy. Few newcomers to town could claim such a social triumph.

Despite my best efforts to avoid it, I was awash in "condo mania" and growing more exasperated with each passing week.

Two months after the meeting, Ken cornered me to complain about the color of our mailboxes. He felt lavender an "indiscreet choice." Despite the inanity of the discussion and my intentions not to engage with him, I lost my temper.

"Goddamn it, Ken, are you so pathetic you have nothing better to do with your miserable life than harass your neighbors?" I raged. "This is a topic for either a condo meeting or a therapy group!"

Punching him in the face—a sudden impulse so strong I could barely restrain myself—promised to be the most fulfilling experience of my life. As I struggled for control, a thin smile gradually spread across his face. I sensed no fear from him, rather a strange hint of innervation. An electric, quasi-erotic sensation flowed through me, and I knew intuitively he lusted for a beating. Aghast, I stormed off without another word.

The memory of Ken's sick smile ravaged my thoughts. Knowing myself well enough to realize the risk of further incidents, I asked another owner to take over as president. As an attorney, he was well equipped to respond in ways that avoided legal action, sadomasochism, or incarceration.

Once I was no longer fair game, Ken seldom left his apartment. Instead, he hired contractors to upgrade his place, paying them as much for their company as for their skill. As he turned inward, his missives slowed, then ceased altogether. He didn't forget me, though. He hired someone to paint the mailboxes black, but I refused to take the bait. After six more months of needless renovation, he sold and moved to Cambridge. I repainted the mailboxes myself as the moving van pulled away, and considered that the end of Ken Porter. And it was, until Berta's call.

"Tim, what are you thinking about? You've been quiet for a long time. It must be a record for one of our field trips," Berta said.

"I don't think I should go to the wake. I'm sure Ken has demonized me to his family. They'll all hate me and blame me for his death."

"Don't worry. I've got a plan to deal with that."

"What is it?"

"I'll tell you later," she answered, patting my knee.

Once in Boston, we had a leisurely lunch, then headed to my apartment to dress for the festivities. Berta retired to the den. When she returned, her face was heavily made up with blush, mascara, and long false eyelashes. Her hair was woven into an elaborate French braid. She wore a strapless black evening gown with a scalloped bodice that glistened with hundreds of jet-black bugle beads. A gossamer black shawl rested on her bare shoulders. She did a runway turn to show off the dress.

"Berta! What the hell are you wearing?" I croaked.

In a rare example of understatement, Berta had once described herself as "full figured." Constrained by built-in stays, her pale breasts crested over the top of the elegant décolletage like an impending avalanche. The back of the dress was cut in a straight line just below her shoulder blades, exposing a hapless layer of flab forced upward by the tapered waist. Below that ominous gathering, the sheer fabric stretched perilously over her ample derriere. Finally, it fanned out in a sweeping Edwardian train.

Despite its dated, exaggerated style, the costume managed to accentuate Berta's supersized sensuality. I found her appearance unnerving, yet fascinating: the way

Frederick Fleet must have felt when, from the crow's nest of the Titanic, he first saw the pale peaks of the iceberg dead ahead.

"It's all I could get on short notice. What's the matter? Don't you like it?"

Berta did another quick twirl. The train followed suit, though seconds behind the ample engine that drove it, dislodging tumbleweeds of dust from under my couch.

"Who's your couturier? Morticia Addams?"

"I borrowed it from Steven, you asshole. I wasn't going to waste a Sunday driving to Hyannis in all the traffic. Besides, I refuse to spend money on something I won't use again. Since having the kids, I never get to dress up. I figured we could go for dinner at the Oak Room after we pay our respects, then maybe dancing. Let's have some fun for once. I never get to the city anymore."

I made one feeble effort before remorse set in, as she'd clearly known it would.

"You're wearing a drag queen's costume to a wake?"

Steven—a garrulous New Yorker known professionally as Auntie Perspirant—headlined a review of female impersonators at the Crown and Anchor. He was known for an amazing Bette Davis imitation. Berta was wearing his send-up of Bette's fancy dress from *The Little Foxes*.

"Why not? He doesn't have a show on Mondays."

Berta grinned. Having consistently encouraged me to stop worrying about appearances, she was clearly relishing the impression she'd made.

"Berta, I'm not going anywhere with you dressed like that, certainly not to a wake. You can take my car and go on your own."

I tried to sound firm, while already anticipating defeat.

"Can't do it," she said, placing her hands on her tightly bound hips.

"What do you mean you can't do it?"

"I can't drive a standard shift, especially in this rig."

"OK . . . Take a cab, then."

"You have to come as a witness. Don't forget, you owe me."

I surveyed the vision before me.

Why the hell not? I wasn't wearing the damn thing, and I didn't know anyone . . .

Persistent memories of Ken's slander surfaced. If half the town believed I'd forced him to leave, his family was bound to hate me.

"Berta, you said Ken blamed me for everything."

"Yeah, but who cares? You're not going as you."

"What?"

"You're going as my husband. Here, put this on," she said, holding out a thick gold band identical to the one on her finger.

"You took your husband's wedding ring away from him for me to wear to a wake?"

"Sure, why not? What's wrong with that?"

"Sometimes I just can't believe you, Berta. OK, I give up. I know I can't win. Let's go."

As I put on the ring, she strutted toward me, pulled me close, and planted a wet kiss on my cheek.

"I knew you'd see reason, *daaahhhling*," she said, sounding like a freighter in a fog bank. "You're nowhere near as much of an asshole as Ken said. You're even almost fun sometimes."

"Don't push it, Tallulah. Let's get out of here before I think better of things."

The funeral home was an enormous stucco mansion with coffered ceilings and dark wood paneling. Sooty stained glass filtered the interior light, tinting the shadows with dreary, faintly luminous patterns. Canned organ music played softly in the background. I studied the grand staircase and imagined Berta slowly, eerily descending it in Steven's drag.

"All right, Mr. DeMille, I'm ready for my close-up . . ."

Enchanted with the foyer's ornate detail, Berta set off to explore the downstairs rooms. In one, three elderly mourners with stunned expressions struggled to their feet. Berta, ignoring their stares, pointed out architectural details with loud, appreciative comments while I cringed in embarrassment. At long last, we were outside the room reserved for Ken's calling hours.

"Tim, look! The guestbook is empty," Berta said in a voice audible throughout the first floor.

"Maybe we're just the first ones here, Nancy Drew. Don't read anything into it," I whispered, hoping my response might dampen her enthusiasm or, at least, diminish her volume.

We entered a huge, dimly-lit room. A slight woman sat beside an open casket, staring numbly at the parquet floor. She had the same pallor, nondescript features, and stringy hair as the body beside her. The resemblance was disconcerting. I suddenly felt anxious, even as I reminded myself Ken was dead.

Sepulchral bouquets of roses, lilies, and gladioli filled the room and another behind it. Their cloying scent made my eyes water. I tried valiantly to stifle a sneeze but failed, letting go with a resonant honk. The woman looked up. Her startled eyes widened as Berta led me to the casket. Once we'd knelt to pray, Berta retrieved a set of rosary beads from Steven's evening clutch, then ran them rapidly through her fingers. As her lips moved, I prayed her imprisoned breasts, now resting passively on the upper rail of the kneeler, wouldn't escape their glittery harness and prematurely launch Ken to glory.

Wrapping up a display of religious fervor worthy of the Stabat Mater, Berta stood and sashayed toward the alleged sister. This time, the train drew lint from an ancient oriental carpet as it swept the floor. The Ken-like woman, looking careworn and intimidated, stood as we approached.

"Hello. I'm Alberta Shipley. This is my husband, Ed. You *must* be Ken's sister," Berta said as she strode forward smiling, reminding me of Kitty Carlisle's grand entrances on *To Tell the Truth*.

"Yes. I am," the woman replied in a wooden voice, ignoring Berta's proffered hand.

Berta was undaunted.

"You look so much alike. I could tell immediately. Ken lived next door to us in Provincetown."

Sister seemed to tense.

"Thank you for coming all that way."

"We are so sorry for your loss. Is there anything we can do for you?"

"That's very kind, but thank you, I'm fine."

"Did you ever visit Ken in Provincetown?"

"No."

It didn't take a degree in psychology to realize Ken's sister was in no mood to talk. Berta, however, appeared unable or unwilling to take the hint.

"He had a lovely apartment there and did wonderful things to improve it."

"I'm sure he did."

I tugged Berta's arm in an effort to silence her. It failed.

"Ken and I were very close. I spoke with him almost every day, even after he left town," she added as if I didn't exist.

"I'm sure that meant a great deal to him."

Sister was not about to give anything away.

I grabbed Berta's wrist.

"Let's sit down, *dear*."

Berta placed her arm on the woman's shoulder, subtly and effectively blocking my efforts to quash the interrogation.

"What's your name? Ken never mentioned he had a sister."

"Virginia."

Sister's annoyance was palpable by now.

"Well, Virginia, I'm sorry we had to meet under such difficult circumstances."

I dug my fingernails into Berta's palm. She glared, but released Virginia.

"Thank you for coming," Virginia said, returning to her contemplation of the floor.

I escorted Berta toward the rear of the room. She broke loose, headed to the front row of chairs, and sat as close to the coffin as she could.

"Berta, why are you sitting there? Shouldn't we leave Virginia to her grief?" I whispered.

"I want to hear what people say when they talk to her."

Her voice dripped with exasperation, as if I were a total idiot.

"Berta, for God's sake!"

Virginia glanced toward us.

Berta leaned over and stage-whispered, "Hush . . . Remember where you are."

I groaned, sat back, and feigned interest in the nude cherubs dancing across the ornate plaster ceiling.

We sat by Ken's body for an eternity, during which no one else came to pay their respects. Each time I pressed Berta to leave, she'd brandish her rosary beads, gather the train of her dress, and head to the coffin to pray. As I silently wondered why I'd ever agreed to come along, Virginia reinforced my doubts by staring at us as if we were escaped lunatics.

After eons of discomfort, and enough prayers to bury a Pope, calling hours ended for the afternoon, forcing Berta to abandon her vigil.

"OK, Vampira, that was totally creepy," I said, struggling to shed my mortification as we stood on the sidewalk, our eyes slowly adjusting to the light. "Let's get back to the apartment."

"Hell no, sweetie. We've got lots more work to do."

"What *are* you talking about?"

"Ken's place is only two blocks away. I want to talk with one of his neighbors. He gave me her name as an emergency contact."

"You've got to be kidding. Dressed like that? You look like Elvira, Mistress of the Dark, for God's sake!"

Berta snorted and strode purposely down the street. I stood for a moment wrestling with a novel thought . . . if Berta didn't care about her appearance, why should I? I took a deep breath, then scampered after her.

Once at Ken's apartment building, Berta searched the intercom listing, then pressed a button. After a moment, an elderly female voice crackled through the tinny speaker.

"Mrs. Ames," Berta said, her voice echoing through the ornate lobby, "I'm a friend of Ken Porter's: the man who lived in apartment 2005. I'm hoping you can shed some light on what happened to him."

"Has something happened to Ken?"

The woman's voice seemed to quiver with anxiety.

"He committed suicide. We've just come from his wake."

Great work, Berta, I thought. You'll give the old bat a coronary. A perfect end to a perfect day: *Murder by Intercom*—like something out of Agatha Christie.

"Oh, my goodness. How sad. I'm hardly surprised, though. He was so very, very ill, the poor dear."

Whoever she was, the old thing seemed resilient enough.

"May we come up and talk to you for a moment, please? My husband and I are trying to learn what happened to our friend."

"Certainly. By all means. Ken spoke with me often. I may just be able to help. I'll buzz you in."

We passed a dumbstruck concierge and rode the elevator to the twentieth floor. The woman who let us in appeared to be in her late eighties. Her apartment exuded good taste, with a glorious view of the Charles and the Boston skyline. She seemed somewhat familiar.

"Please bear with me," she said. "Over the last few years, I've gone completely blind, and my hearing has diminished as well. I'm Evangeline, by the way."

Her voice was aristocratic but feeble. A tall woman with patrician features, exquisite clothing, and beautifully coiffed gray hair, she moved with an ease that seemed to refute her claim. I suddenly recalled seeing her regularly at Symphony, where she sat two rows in front of me on Thursday nights.

Lucky break for Berta, I thought. There's no way a woman with this much class would talk to her if she could actually see that getup. My turn to contribute, I guess. I've got the opening gambit. Might as well use it. Here goes nothing.

"I'm Ed Shipley. This is my wife, Berta. We've seen you at Symphony, Mrs. Ames. Our seats are just two rows behind yours. Did you enjoy the Mahler last week?"

Berta blew me a kiss. I telegraphed a stern warning to behave. She stuck out her tongue.

"Oh yes, very much," Mrs. Ames replied. "Wasn't Kurt Masur simply magnificent? My daughter and I had *such* a lovely time. Please, *do* sit down."

The old woman gestured toward a vintage empire sofa, then sat on a Windsor chair. Berta surveyed the room, rolling her eyes in a "get a load of this joint" sort of way. I shot her another warning glance. I was the one who had gained acceptance from the old girl; we'd do this my way, or not at all. Berta got my point immediately and began her interrogation in a surprisingly gentle, almost cultured voice.

"Mrs. Ames . . ."

"Please call me Evangeline, dear."

"Thank you, Evangeline. How long did you know Ken Porter?" Berta asked, furtively removing a miniature recorder from Steven's clutch and silently placing it on the coffee table.

"He introduced himself when he moved here about a year ago. He was such a charming young man."

I stared at Berta in disbelief. Ken was forty-five, if a day. She wasted little time getting to the crux of the matter.

"Did he ever speak of his illnesses?"

"Oh yes. He had these horrible tumors on his spine and brain. The doctors told him nothing more could be done. He lived only for his work and to make things better for others. And then, if that wasn't more than a body could bear, there was the myasthenia gravis."

"He had myasthenia gravis?" I asked as Berta slid the recorder even closer to Evangeline.

"That was the diagnosis. Ken told me his motor skills were deteriorating rapidly. That's why he moved back to Boston, to get the best possible care so he could continue his charitable work for as long as he had left."

I shifted awkwardly in my seat. I'd had no idea the little prick was that ill. I'd been sure he was faking it. As far as I was concerned, he was a simple nutcase—if any nutcase could be considered simple.

"Did he discuss his work?" I asked, finding it hard to believe Ken had rejoined the rat race after months of hosting contractors and sending registered threats in Provincetown.

"Oh yes, all the time. He ran a charitable foundation for myasthenia gravis victims. It's a large, active organization and does a tremendous amount of good by providing funds to those in need."

I had an even harder time picturing the Ken Porter I knew as a philanthropist.

"What sort of things did he do?"

"He managed the website, identified health resources, helped with finances, and kept an online journal of his own experiences with the disease. Many wrote to say he was an inspiration and often asked his advice. He read me their notes whenever he came for tea."

It simply wasn't possible. Or was it?

Our conversation with Evangeline lasted nearly a half hour. To her, Ken was a saint; she had nothing but praise for him and his good works. Finally, there was no real reason to extend our stay.

Berta stood and said, "Thank you for telling us about poor Ken."

She seemed close to tears. I have to admit I felt pretty miserable, too. We said our goodbyes and headed down the hall toward the elevator. Before Berta and I could compare notes, an attractive man with close-cropped black hair came out of an adjacent apartment. I recognized him as a summer resident of our P'town neighborhood.

"André!" Berta shrieked, throwing her arms around him.

Instead of showing fear she might crush him to death, he seemed delighted. What was it so many people saw in her?

"Berta, honey, what *are* you doing here?" André asked, putting his free arm around as much of her as he could and guiding her back to his apartment.

He didn't seem to notice me, so I just followed them inside.

"It's a long story," Berta simpered.

I'd never seen her like this. She seemed flustered by André's attention. I could relate. He *was* extraordinarily handsome, dressed in a pair of tight-fitting black jeans that augmented his height, and a black T-shirt that accentuated his well-sculpted chest. Eyes of a startling deep cornflower-blue offset his mocha skin. Given Berta's agitation, I tried hard to play it cool, but could just manage an awkward smile.

A fine thing. Here are the two of us having the vapors over the same hot guy right after leaving a wake. Talk about a grim social life: the only thing missing was a bowl of Ovaltine. All kidding aside, André was way out of my league.

"C'mon in, babe, and give me the dirt," he said to Berta as we followed him into a room with spectacular views of Boston Harbor. "I wasn't going anywhere, really, just out to buy some food for Delia, here. She'll be willing to wait a bit for an old friend like Berta, won't you, girl?"

At the sound of her name, a stunning golden retriever strode into the room, her tail wagging. Recognizing a total pushover, she came right to me. As I pet her, I couldn't help but think: beautiful dog, gorgeous apartment, and a hot man. All three together. Do some lucky bastards actually get to find boyfriends like this?

At long last, Berta introduced me, using my real name, thank God. This was not the time to play her husband, no matter how slim my chances might be with this gorgeous man.

"I've seen you in P'town, André," I said, slipping the wedding ring into my pocket and making an effort to be somewhat less of a wallflower. "Have you been down lately?"

"No, not really," André replied with a sigh. "The place is Paul's, not mine. Now that we've split, I'm considered *de trop*."

"Sorry to hear about your breakup," I lied. "How long were you together?"

"Not all that long. It was doomed from the start. We had so little in common; we should never have tried. He's a circuit queen; I'm a *Masterpiece Theatre* buff. He likes Sarah Brightman; I love Sarah Vaughan. It was a classic case of MMQ—mismatched queens—and we knew enough to end it before things got nasty. To be honest with you, I'm cool with how things turned out, except for missing P'town. That place got to me in a big way."

"I'm sorry you haven't been able to . . ."

I could get no further before Berta barged in with all the finesse of a Roller Derby champion.

"Tim has a guest suite in his condo, André. I'm sure he wouldn't mind some company now and then."

"Um . . . yeah! You'd certainly be welcome . . .," I said, feeling the color rise to my cheeks.

"Thanks, Tim. I'll keep that in mind," André replied with a noncommittal tone that somehow managed to acknowledge Berta's pushy ways as well as my obvious discomfort. "I appreciate it. No doubt Berta knows how to find you."

"At all times, day and night," I said, savoring his gracious response while figuring the odds of a visit to be less than slight.

André offered drinks, which were readily accepted. After some gossip about mutual friends, Berta got down to business.

"I'm trying to figure out what went on with your next-door neighbor, Ken Porter; the one Dr. Cronin knocked off. I'm wondering if there's something in it I can write an article or a book about."

"It would be a short story, honey. The bitch was insane, a masochist, and a major-league pain in the ass. That's all she wrote."

Overjoyed that someone else got it, I couldn't resist joining in.

"Evangeline, the woman down the hall, thinks he's a saint."

"Yeah, but he treated her like some sort of mother figure and kept her unaware of all the bullshit he dumped on the rest of us," André said as he turned toward me, a man with a tale to tell. "She's clueless, the poor old thing. There'd be fights in Ken's apartment in the middle of the night. I'd hear yelling, screaming, and things breaking. There was some sort of ex-fireman fuck buddy who used to rough him up a lot."

"No kidding."

I caught myself leaning forward, fascinated. Whether by the story or the teller was becoming less certain with each passing moment. Something about this guy made me wish I were as poised, confident, and plain-old sexy as he was. Despite my minor-league status, André seemed to appreciate the attention, so I decided my motives were immaterial. He topped off my drink, then smiled at me before returning to his tale.

"One night, this skanky-assed hustler roused most of the floor by demanding more money from Ken. Apparently a good whipping costs extra. They fought in the hall until I called the police, who carted the guy away when Ken claimed he was being threatened by a stranger. Evangeline didn't hear a thing, thank God, and I wasn't about to clue her in. She's a grand old lady and doesn't need to be troubled by such things.

"Ken was always suing or finding ways to annoy people. Most of us are thrilled he's gone. I know I am. If Cronin actually put the bitch down, I'll donate to his defense fund. Ken infuriated me beyond all reason."

The fury of "infuriated" was stretched beyond its breaking point.

"I can relate," I said. "I had a similar experience with him in P'town. There was a time it took all I could muster not to punch his lights out."

"*Now* I know where I've heard your name before," André said, pointing a well-manicured finger at me as if I were the only person in the world. "At his first condo meeting, Ken told everyone in the building what a bastard you were. He said you drove him out of town, and we all felt sorry for him. Then, after four months of his insanity, I decided you showed incredible restraint in running him out of town instead of just murdering his tired-ass self."

I sat back in my chair, triumphant, though I still didn't think I'd run the jerk out of town.

"Look, André, I'd like to clarify a couple of things," I said, stunned to be speaking my thoughts before internally editing them. "No matter how it was represented, or what certain people think . . .," I stared at Berta just long enough to make my point, "I didn't drive him out. I simply stopped playing his game, and he up and left. Nothing more, nothing less."

"Well, you're a better man than I," André said. "I was about to go ghetto on his ass. If Cronin hadn't put the son of a bitch on ice, I'd have done it for him. That child had a way of bringing out the worst in everyone."

"Except Berta," I said, driving my point home with all the subtlety of a stake through a vampire's heart. "Sister Bertrille, here, thought he was one step away from beatification."

André laughed appreciatively before wagging a finger in her direction.

"Berta, honey, you're way off the mark, which is rare for you. That fool could have turned Mother Theresa into Lucrezia Borgia over a quick lunch."

Berta squirmed in her chair. It had to be obvious that André and I were ganging up on her, but for some reason, she didn't fight back. I'd been expecting a fusillade in return, but not a single shot was fired. Maybe she didn't dare tackle both of us at the same time.

After a pause, in which he, too, seemed to be waiting for a response, André turned back to me.

"Well, Tim, all I can say is that you showed a lot of patience and forbearance in dealing with that fool."

I felt nonplussed by Andre's attention, as if we were starring in our own movie with a first kiss in the next scene. At a loss what to do, I did nothing.

Berta regained her composure and teased out a few more details as if the prior exchange had never happened, then looked at her watch.

"Oh shit, we've got to run. Calling hours will already have started by the time we get there!"

"Berta, we're not going back?" I asked, unable to bear the thought of intruding on Virginia's grief yet again.

André smiled in commiseration. Apparently, he and Berta had shared a few escapades of their own. Their regard for each other spoke volumes. That, and our shared experience of the "neighbor from hell," endeared him to me even more.

"We have to," Berta said, annihilating my daydream by marching to the door. "What if somebody shows up?"

"André, thanks a million for the information and the drink. I really appreciate both!"

I was appalled at how effusive I sounded.

"No problem," he replied, with a winsome grin that made my knees shake. "Very pleased to meet you, Tim. Maybe I *will* take you up on that offer. I miss P'town," he said, putting his hand over his heart, "right here."

He felt the same way about the crazy place as I did.

As he handed me a business card, our eyes met. Seeing all too much in them, I looked away. André quickly turned his attention to Berta, who, most uncharacteristically, seemed to have missed the entire exchange.

"By the way, honey . . . love the dress! You *go*, girl!"

Berta beamed and sailed into the hallway. André winked at me, took my hand, and mouthed *good luck* in a way that left no doubt he knew her very well indeed.

Berta raced back to the funeral home, clutching the long black train in her right hand as passersby stopped in their tracks to stare. I struggled to keep pace while breathlessly pleading for her to reconsider troubling Virginia any further. At six fifteen, we raced breathlessly into the room where Ken's body lay. Virginia sat alone by the coffin, exactly where we'd left her. She jumped from her seat, clearly furious at our return.

"Who are you two? Harold and Maude? Showing up here again like this . . ."

Berta didn't miss a beat.

"Virginia, I want to know what actually happened. It's time for the truth. Out with it."

Suddenly, Berta no longer looked ridiculous, but compelling and trustworthy, despite her absurd attire.

"Why is it so important to you?" Virginia asked, cowering under the intensity of Berta's questioning gaze.

"Because I need to understand. At first, I thought I wanted to write about Ken, but now I realize I just have to know for myself. I've heard so many different stories about him. I listened to him, supported him, and spent sleepless nights worrying about him. If he was using me, I have to make my peace with that."

A cloud of sorrow seemed to pass over Virginia's face. It was the first trace of genuine sadness I'd witnessed.

"Well, you *already* know more than *I* do. We hadn't spoken since shortly after Mother died. Ken refused to let me have my share of her estate even though he had no need for the money. When I persisted, he sued me for harassment, claiming she intentionally left me out of her will. I just *knew* that will was forged, but I had to give up eventually to save my sanity. I took care of Mother for five years before she passed. She would *never* have treated me like that. As for *him,* he was abusive, vindictive, and amazingly petty once he got ahold of that house. He'd always been a bit of a pill, but when she died, it was as if he came unglued. I would like to know more, myself. I've gotten all these cards and flowers sent to me from people with mya . . ."

"Myasthenia gravis?" I ventured, feeling genuine pity for her and a surge of anger at Ken—even if he was dead.

"Yes, that's it. They want to know what happened in his last days. I don't know what to tell them. He hasn't spoken to me for years. I've been reading these sympathy cards, and things just don't make any sense. He's been such a shit, but they," she pointed to a decorative box overflowing with mail, "think he's a saint. Most of them say they are too sick or far away to pay their respects in person, but they all seem devastated and want me to support them the way he did."

Ken lay sedately in his coffin. Even there, he looked smug and self-satisfied. Surreptitiously, I slipped him the finger as Virginia wiped her eyes.

"Ken made all his funeral arrangements before he died. Everything was prepared in advance: the wake, the funeral, cremation—everything. Flowers have poured in, but no one has showed up except you two. It's been torture. I feel I have to be here, but I'm going mad just sitting beside his body reading all these cards. These people want so much from me, and I don't even know why."

She began to sob uncontrollably, her tiny body shaking in violent spasms. Clearly, she was in no condition to be left alone. I stood there embarrassed, not knowing what to do. Berta did. She put her hefty arms around Virginia and pulled her close.

"Enough is enough, Virginia. This is Ken's party, not yours. He's not going anywhere until tomorrow, and you don't have to stay here. Get your things. I'll drive you home. Tim will follow us in his car. I'll make you a nice cup of tea when we get there."

"Who's Tim?"

Virginia, poor thing, looked up at me, confused and more than a trifle wary.

"Oh, this is Tim. He's a friend," Berta said with a broad smile. "He was only pretending to be my husband."

"Why, for God's sake?"

Virginia hesitated, as if wondering whether to scream for help.

"We'll tell you everything when we get you home," Berta said, holding out her hand. "Give me your keys. I'll drive. You don't need to stay in this awful place one more minute."

Berta took Virginia's arm and maneuvered her toward the door.

"Can you drive standard shift?" Virginia asked, picking up the box of cards.

"Oh, sure. I learned to drive on one. No problem . . . No problem at all."

Berta scrunched her face and smirked at me. Once again, I'd been duped. Berta *could* drive a standard shift, but then, what couldn't she do?

We got Virginia home and explained what we knew. She seemed to take it all in, but in a sullen, uncommunicative silence that revealed a deep-seated hurt. Even Berta was unwilling to press her for further details. It was clearly the wrong time. As we prepared to leave, Virginia seemed to wake from her lethargy; she asked Berta to go with her to the funeral at ten the next morning, and Berta readily agreed. We said good night and walked silently to the car. There would be no Oak Room and no dancing tonight. Instead, we grabbed a light dinner at a local diner. Once home, I went straight to my room, leaving Berta seated at the kitchen table, deep in thought.

The next morning, I gave Berta cab fare, and we agreed to meet at the funeral home on my lunch hour. From there, I'd drive her to Long Wharf in time for the Provincetown ferry.

When I picked her up, she jumped in the car, bursting with excitement.

"Tim, you won't believe it. The only people there were Virginia, Evangeline, her daughter, and me. But there had to be at least two hundred bouquets of flowers."

"How's Virginia?"

"She's confused and extremely worried. She told me Ken left all his money to some ex-fireman in Worcester, including her share of their mother's estate. We have to do something to help her."

"This *may* come in handy," I said, showing Berta an article from that morning's *Globe* entitled "Autopsy Shows No Trace of Illness for Latest Victim of 'Doctor Death.'"

As she read, I drove quickly to Long Wharf. We rumbled over the cobblestones and pulled to a stop at the ramp for the P'town ferry. The final passengers were boarding, and the crew was preparing to cast off. Berta got out of the car, grabbed her satchel, and kissed me through the open window. It was high tide, and the boarding ramp rose at an incredibly sharp angle from the stone wharf to the boat. There'd been no time to change out of the black dress, so Berta had to improvise. She clutched the train and her luggage in one hand, and hauled herself up the gangplank with the other. It was something to see.

Suddenly I heard cheers from the horde of men on deck. Berta stood at the top of the ramp, grinding her hips and tugging the shawl back and forth across her shoulders as if she were starting a strip-tease.

"Hi, boys," she vamped, in a credible imitation of Mae West. "Are those guns in your pockets or are you just glad to see me?"

The crowd and crew responded with laughter, hoots, and applause. I smiled to myself. Berta always managed to pull it off. No matter where, no matter what.

I'd used up my lunch hour and was late for a meeting. Even so, I watched the ferry head out into the harbor. I couldn't bear to leave until it vanished from sight. As I hastened back to the office, I imagined the boat crossing the sunlit bay toward home with Berta standing at the bow, laughing and carefree, her train billowing in the warm breeze, surrounded by good-natured admirers and newfound friends.

Back at my desk, staring blankly at my monitor, I felt lonely, insignificant, and adrift.

The week passed at a snail's pace. Cronin assisted yet another suicide, then turned himself in to the authorities, as was his practice. This time, there was talk of denying bail. Coverage of Ken's story subsided quickly. The thought that Doctor Death's reign might be ending in a prison sentence was far bigger news than the suicide of an insignificant bachelor. Yet again, it seemed Ken would miss out on his fifteen minutes of fame. When I arrived in P'town Friday night, I found Berta waiting at my kitchen table.

"Tim, we've got to do something, right away," she said. "Virginia's frantic. She got this in one of the sympathy cards and faxed it to me. Read it."

Someone named Ray had written to say he'd decided to follow Ken's example and surrender to myasthenia gravis. Stating he'd turned his investments over to Ken some time ago, Ray instructed Virginia to take whatever money she needed to arrange things with Cronin before he could be prevented from assisting any more suicides. Citing instructions on Ken's website, Ray seemed confident Virginia routinely handled such gruesome chores. He'd provided his e-mail address to "expedite things," and urged her to move as quickly as she could.

"Goddamn Ken," I said, sitting back, stunned. "That son of a bitch! Ray can't be the only one. There's a high probability these so-called "instructions" will trigger copycat suicides. We've got to shut down that website and get to Ray before it's too late."

Berta sat down beside me as I fired up my computer. After a couple of searches, I found Ken's site. Dancing angels pirouetted around an airbrushed picture of his face, whose smile was that of a television evangelist. There was a message below the photo, written in black script framed by a thick border:

Dear Friends,

If you are reading this, I have gone to a better place. While my decision has not been an easy one, I want you to know I have exhausted all other options. Your friendship, support, and kindness often made my burden light, but as you know better than anyone, our suffering eventually grows too heavy for even the strongest of us to bear.

I leave the foundation and your generous donations in the capable hands of my sister Virginia, who has been instrumental in negotiations with Dr. Cronin, and whose unflagging support has made it possible for me bear the burden of this dreadful disease for as long as I have. Rest assured, when life becomes too painful for you, as it has for me, she'll be there for you as well.

Think kindly of me and be kind to yourselves. Until we meet again in a much better place, my sincere affection and best wishes go out to each and every one of you.

With love and hope,

Ken

"He must have arranged for this to be put on the website after his suicide," I said. "That's why Virginia got all those cards. He provided her contact information to lend credibility and, no doubt, incriminate her. I'll bet he's arranged for even more postings, and *those* will have Virginia's name all over them, too."

Ken's indictment of his only sibling was as appalling as his morbid enticements from beyond the grave. Even in death, his need for attention lived on.

"That bastard!"

I'd never seen Berta so angry. She was clearly on the brink of tears. I reached across the table and clasped her hand.

"That was his plan all along," I said gently. "What better way to leave your mark and get back at a world that has passed you by. He's the Jim Jones of the Internet."

As I scanned the posted tributes and responses on the page, my pent-up rage channeled itself into a frenzied search for something—anything—to subvert Ken's plot before it claimed its first victim. At last, I found it.

"Here we go. Look at this one, Berta. Listen."

I began to read aloud. Someone named Dan had read the *Globe* article. He expressed surprise the autopsy had revealed no signs of illness, and delicately questioned Ken's motives.

"This is how we'll get the word out. We'll use someone in the community to give us a toehold and lend us legitimacy," I said, feeling a rush of adrenalin and a bracing surge of confidence. "First, we need to get the *Globe* article posted on the website. While I'm scanning it, you find the webmaster's e-mail address."

Berta had the address by the time I'd finished. Typing as fast as I could, I pointed out that the webmaster would be an accessory to murder unless he immediately defused the deception he'd helped put in place. I insisted he post the *Globe* article immediately and stand by for further instructions.

"Berta. Get Virginia on the phone. We need a statement."

I explained to Virginia why, as Ken's designated successor, her involvement was essential, not only to help others but also to extricate herself from the trap her brother had set. Then I read what I had written so far. She was silent for a moment, but the instant I heard her calm, surprisingly forceful tone, I knew she'd go the distance.

"Damn him to hell. Go ahead and say whatever you want. Just let those poor people know what a sick bastard he was. Tell them his own sister says he was a pathological liar, a manipulator, and a thief."

I handed the phone to Berta and typed a quick e-mail to Dan, including all I'd written to the webmaster. I copied Ray with a plea to get in touch, then instructed the webmaster to post Virginia's statement. As I hit the send button, it felt as though I'd launched a guided missile right into the heart of Ken's global deception.

"Goddamn you, Ken," I yelled. "You always wanted me to whip your ass. Well, get ready, sucker. The time has come!"

Berta spoke with Virginia for a few minutes more, then hung up, shook her head, pursed her lips, and walked into my open arms. I rocked her slowly, offering reassurance. When she felt better, I refreshed Ken's website and found our statement prominently displayed beside the *Globe* article. The webmaster had also apologized for his unwitting complicity and implored Ken's followers to avoid rash decisions and carefully consider all we had to say. No sooner had I shown Berta his posting than e-mails and chat requests began to trickle in. I mixed drinks and ordered take-out for the long night ahead. We agreed to three-hour shifts to get us through to morning.

We heard from dozens of people whose responses ran the gamut of emotion. A few said our warning had saved their lives. Many told us they'd donated to Ken's cause for years. A handful had suspected him all along, and a few had already notified the authorities. Others expressed shock and confusion. We gently dealt with each person and asked them to alert everyone they knew in their online community.

Dan's expression of gratitude arrived at one in the morning, moistening my bleary eyes. I woke Berta and read it to her. He'd been working for hours, reaching out to all he knew, and enlisting others to do the same. He was confident word was getting out in time.

We finally heard from Ray at three. He, too, had been feverishly conveying our message since the moment he'd received it. He vowed never to surrender, and to trust his instincts in future. His promise brought tears of exhaustion and relief.

For the next two days, we did little else but answer e-mails and chat online. By Sunday morning, there were many signs our plan had worked. The chat rooms were bursting with incredulity and outrage. Ken's site roiled with hundreds of comments filled with anger and dismay. As the word spread exponentially, the number of e-mails dropped to a couple an hour, then one every few. By Sunday night, there were none.

The following Thursday afternoon, I sat daydreaming at my desk, counting each second of the twenty-six hours until the ferry would take me home to Provincetown, when my administrative assistant appeared at my office door.

"There are two women out front saying they have to see you. Apparently it's urgent. They certainly won't take no for an answer."

"Who are they, Joan?"

"The tall, loud one won't say, but if it's worth anything, she looks like Fortress Europa in a dress. She's the most insistent person I've ever met and in dire need of fashion help. The quiet one seems sane enough, though."

Joan's expression shifted from annoyance to mild amusement.

"Oh, and by the way, they seem to want to party."

"It's OK. I know them," I said, while simultaneously attempting to appear long-suffering, mildly annoyed, and grateful for her efforts at running interference. "You can send them in."

Sure enough, I looked up and there was Berta, wearing Steven's dress and holding a bottle of champagne in her hand. Virginia walked hesitantly beside her, cradling three champagne flutes. Before I could say a word, Berta removed the wire hood from the bottle and released the cork with a disquieting pop. It flew across the room, ricocheted loudly off my wall, and landed in my lap.

"Bull's-eye!" she chortled lewdly, then directed Virginia to place the flutes on my desk.

The ruckus brought a group of inquisitive colleagues to my door. Berta's back was to them, and she seemed not to realize they were there. She explained that the webmaster had surrendered Ken's incriminating instructions to the attorney general's office, which had confirmed an already ongoing fraud investigation. When Ken had first learned of the inquiry, he'd tried to hide out in Provincetown. As more facts were uncovered, he'd moved back to Boston, arranged his date with Doctor Death, and set Virginia up to take the fall.

Detailed donor records had been discovered just the day before. Ken was disbursing only twenty-five percent of what he took in. There had never been a settlement from any lawsuit, as he'd told me when he came to Provincetown; he'd been bilking the sick and dying for years and living off the proceeds.

"The AG is sending a forensic accountant to examine Ken's books and try to return as much of the money as he can," Berta said, glowing with pride. "By the way; we're a featured story in tomorrow's *Globe*. The attorney general told a reporter how you figured things out and got the message out just in time. That guy and his photographer are on their way here to interview the three of us. I figured your office was the best place to meet."

Berta poured the champagne, its bubbling effervescence as disconcertingly out of place in my office as her outfit. My thoughts darted from one emotion to another: pleasure at seeing her, tremendous pride in our accomplishment, smug satisfaction at having bested Ken, and a thunderhead of fear as to what my colleagues would make of all this.

"Congratulations, Virginia, I'm thrilled for you. That's fantastic," I said, in a trance-like tone. "But Berta, Steven's got a show tonight. What's he going to do for a dress?"

I stopped short, horrified and perplexed. Given the crowd at the door, I'd just set my carefully segregated worlds on a collision course, like some disaster scene from *Star Trek*.

"Oh, don't worry about it," Berta said, waving her hand in dismissal. "A friend from New York bought a fifties Balenciaga number at an estate auction and sent it to him. It's an original, and Steven adores it so much I don't think you could get him to take the thing off if you pointed a gun at him. He's doing Bette's scenes from *All About Eve* for a few days while his seamstress whips up a new version of this dress. He says it's too loose for him now . . . but I'm pretty sure that's just an excuse to get one with more beads and a *much* longer train. You know how you gay boys are—no matter how much you say to the contrary, size *does* matter. Anyways, when I told him how much you admired this one, he told me to give it to you with his compliments. So I decided to *give it to you* personally."

Berta leaned over my desk with an evil grin and jiggled her breasts in my face, eliciting raucous laughter and a couple of cat-calls. Finally realizing she had an audience, she turned and raised her glass. Her stentorian voice filled the room.

"Hi, folks. I'm Tim's friend, Berta Shipley. I was in the neighborhood, so I thought I'd stop by and let you in on a secret before the rest of the world finds out. Most of you know Tim as a workaholic boss, but I'll bet you've never gotten a glimpse of the real man underneath. The gentle, caring, saver of lives; the faithful, long-suffering friend; the man I adore almost as much as my husband. Ladies and Gentlemen—toilers in the salt mines of corporate America! I give you the protector of the ill and the abused. The hero of the hour! My dear friend, Tim! Read all about him in tomorrow's *Globe*!"

She drained her glass to loud applause, leaned over, and whispered, "Don't get your tits in a knot, sweetie; I brought a change of clothes for the interview. They're in the hall. I just wore this to freak you out."

Then she kissed me smack on the lips. As my face reddened, my colleagues, already well under her spell, laughed uproariously. Virginia cracked a toothy smile, blew me a kiss, raised her glass, and downed her champagne in a single gulp. The world had gone mad.

My colleagues rushed Berta, who further enchanted them with details of our adventure while I sat grinning sheepishly, imagining a torrent of gossip inundating my floor, the company—then the entire city—as my disparate worlds collapsed. None of the self-imposed compartments of my life could withstand such an onslaught. There simply was no stopping Berta; yet deep in my heart, I no longer cared. Whatever this insanity might be, it was life. And damn it, I was finally living. I reached for my champagne, drank deeply, then dialed my assistant.

"Joan," I said brusquely, causing my colleagues, and, much to my surprise, Berta, to grow ominously quiet, "a table for four at the Oak Room this evening at eight, if you would, please? Thanks! Oh, the folks from the *Globe* are downstairs? Send them up in five minutes."

I turned toward my friend and savior, who stared at me oddly, no doubt speculating on the fourth member of our party.

"Berta, before we start the interview, I have a quick call to make. No, you don't have to leave. Stay right there. I have no secrets from you. Well . . . almost none."

I dialed the number I'd committed to memory without ever having used it.

"André? Tim; Berta's friend . . . Great . . . And you? . . . Excellent. Hey, look, we've got something wonderful to celebrate tonight, and I was hoping you'd be able to join us . . . You can? Fabulous! . . . We're going to the Oak Room. My treat. It's a very special occasion. Can you manage black tie on such short notice? Fantastic. I just knew you could. I'll pick you up at seven thirty. We'll meet Berta and Virginia there."

Berta gaped at me, her arched eyebrow more eloquent than any sarcasm she might have deployed. I swiveled my chair, stifled a laugh, and lowered my voice.

"No, André, you don't know Virginia. It's a long story. I'll explain everything when I see you . . . Hey. While I've got you, I'm wondering if you're free this weekend. It seemed to me you could do with a P'town fix . . . You would? . . . Great. Let's take the 4:30 ferry. We should be in town in time for sunset. How 'bout dinner at The Mews afterward? Wonderful. I'll make a reservation. See you soon."

I placed the phone in its cradle, expecting an avalanche of inquisition. Instead, there was an atypical silence. Berta's mouth was still frozen in the same stunned expression. Sensing my advantage, I mustered my most charming smile.

"Berta, darling, one last thing," I said in an assertive tone—that of a man fully in charge of his life. "Don't bother to change for the interview . . . You look simply divine *just as you are.*"

THE END

ACKNOWLEDGMENTS

These disparate impressions, fantasies, and infatuations would never have coalesced into a book without support from so many kind and giving people. To my agent, Malaga Baldi, I offer continued gratitude for your unerring counsel. To the talented cover and interior designer, Adrian Nicholas, you make magic happen. To my editor par excellence, Cheri Johnson, you turn straw into gold. I'm proud of having inspired your favorite comment of all time. To my friend and mentor, Heidi Jon Schmidt, your class at the Fine Arts Work Center planted the seeds for this book, so yes, it's your fault, too. To my colleagues at HomePort Press, thanks for your support.

To my early readers: Liz, Jean, Tim, Bill, Marge, Elaine, Jeff, Bob, Kerry, Tony, Roger, Maggie, and most notably, James, many thanks for your patience and constructive feedback. To Ed and Colin—the heroic "Nepenthe crew"— your encouragement makes everything possible. To Vee, however did we survive to become what we are today—and wouldn't it be a dull world had we not? To Jayne and Janice, I honor your nuptials with this book. Your love for your friends and each other sets a standard to which we should all aspire. #FreeMomma.

And last—but oh, so very far from least—my heartfelt gratitude to my illustrator, Madeline Sorel, a goddess whose indescribable capacity to translate words into fitting images made writing this book more fun than its humble author had any right to expect.

A.C. Burch, 2016

CPSIA information can be obtained at www.ICGtesting.com
Printed in the USA
BVOW05s2249130616

451893BV00002B/3/P